# His strength, even when he was so obviously ill, was alarming,

and too late Kate remembered the subtle aura of danger that clung to him.

"Oh!" she cried as she felt Wroth's fingers tangle in her curls. She pushed her palms against the damp hair that covered his broad muscles, but she was trapped, held tightly against him. Heat surrounded her, along with the heady scent of clean sheets, male sweat and...Wroth.

Kate felt dizzy, disoriented, as she hovered only inches from his face. Then his lashes lifted, and the eyes that met hers were bright from fever, but surprisingly lucid. Was he awake? So stunned was she that Kate could only stare into the gray pools, her breath caught, her wits flown.

She felt his fingers slowly tighten in her curls. "Are you trying to kill me again, pup?" he asked, as clear as day.

Dear Reader,

Author Deborah Simmons is back this month with *Tempting Kate*, a Regency romp complete with a mistaken identity, an accidental shooting—by the heroine—and a touch of mystery. Don't miss this charming story of a noblewoman in desperate financial straits and the haughty marquis who unwillingly comes to her rescue. And be sure to watch for her short story in our medieval Christmas collection, *The Knights of Christmas,* coming in October.

*The Merry Widows—Mary,* is the first in award-winning author Theresa Michaels's terrific new Western series about three widows who form their own close-knit family on a farm in New Mexico.

*The Bride Thief* by Susan Paul, writing as Susan Spencer Paul, is the third book of her medieval BRIDE TRILOGY, featuring the youngest Baldwin brother, Justin, a delightful rogue whom his brothers have decided needs a wife to save him from his wayward ways. And the fourth book of the month, *Wildwood,* is a Western from 1996 March Madness author Lynna Banning about a young woman determined to involve herself in the investigation of her father's murder, despite opposition from the local sheriff.

Whatever your tastes in reading, we hope you'll keep a lookout for all four of this month's titles, wherever Harlequin Historicals are sold.

Sincerely,

Tracy Farrell
Senior Editor

Please address questions and book requests to:
Harlequin Reader Service
U.S.: 3010 Walden Ave., P.O. Box 1325, Buffalo, NY 14269
Canadian: P.O. Box 609, Fort Erie, Ont. L2A 5X3

# TEMPTING KATE

## DEBORAH SIMMONS

**Harlequin Books**

TORONTO • NEW YORK • LONDON
AMSTERDAM • PARIS • SYDNEY • HAMBURG
STOCKHOLM • ATHENS • TOKYO • MILAN
MADRID • WARSAW • BUDAPEST • AUCKLAND

ISBN 0-373-28971-5

TEMPTING KATE

**Books by Deborah Simmons**

Harlequin Historicals

*The Fortune Hunter* #132
*Silent Heart* #185
*The Squire's Daughter* #208
*The Devil's Lady* #241
*The Vicar's Daughter* #258
*Taming the Wolf* #284
*The Devil Earl* #317
*Maiden Bride* #332
*Tempting Kate* #371

---

## *DEBORAH SIMMONS*

Deborah Simmons began her writing career as a newspaper reporter. She turned to fiction after the birth of her first child when a longtime love of historical romance prompted her to pen her own work, published in 1989. She lives in rural Ohio with her husband, two children, two cats and a stray dog that never left. She enjoys hearing from readers at the address below. For a reply, an SASE is appreciated.

Deborah Simmons
P.O. Box 274
Ontario, Ohio 44862-0274

For my editor, Margaret O'Neill Marbury

# Chapter One

The marquis of Wroth was restless.

Waving away his driver, he decided to walk the few blocks to his London town house. It was nearly midnight, but the fashionable neighborhood still rang with the sound of coaches ferrying their glittering passengers from one ball to another, and Grayson Ashford Ryland Wescott, the fourth marquis, welcomed the chance to stretch his legs after a tedious hour spent among society's elite.

Unfortunately, the exercise did little to curb the odd sensation that had been plaguing him for months now, escalating today, on the occasion of his thirty-second birthday. He saw no reason for the unfamiliar ennui. In the years since he came into his title, at the tender age of fifteen, he had achieved everything he set out to do, attaining a position of wealth, power and prestige that was the envy of his peers. What more could a man want?

At first, he had put the vague discontent down to a lack of challenges in his life. He had gone as far as he wanted to politically, exerting enormous influence behind the scenes rather than in the House itself. Although his various businesses were thriving, he could easily hand over their management to one of his many capable employees. The pursuits of hunting, boxing and racing his curricle had palled as he grew older, and even gambling seemed little risk these days.

When the unnamed malaise persisted, Grayson had given some serious thought to settling down and establishing his nursery. It was high time he got an heir, and he found the notion of retiring to the country strangely appealing, if he could find a suitable wife.

His friends would have laughed at that, for his wealth and title had assured him a steady stream of women since adolescence, and despite his rather unsavory reputation as a breaker of hearts, mamas still threw their daughters at him. He did little enough to encourage them. His liaisons were more often with married women, attracted to his looks or his position, or members of the demimonde, who had no care for their reputations. Whatever their backgrounds, the ladies never held his interest for long, and he had never considered marrying...until recently.

Her name was Charlotte, and she had burst upon the London season like a breath of fresh air. Beautiful, innocent, intelligent and engaging, she was a vicar's daughter, and Grayson had found himself drawn to her unique brand of honesty. It had soon become plain, however, that Charlotte was enamored of her sponsor of sorts, the stuffy earl of Wycliffe.

Once he discovered where her affections lay,

Grayson had played his own small part in ensuring her happiness, and she had married the earl. What a waste, Grayson thought, and yet there was no denying that the two shared something special. Grayson stretched his legs, struck by an odd pang, before continuing on. Damn, but he was not jealous of that clock-minding Wycliffe! It was what the two had between them that he coveted.

Not that he believed in love or any of that nonsense, but the earl and his countess obviously shared a friendship based on common interests, companionship and simple affection that was rare among ton marriages. Wroth slowed his stride. That was what he wanted, but where to find it?

It seemed that all the women in London either were greedy and jaded or hadn't a thought in their heads, while most of the country gentry he viewed as slow-witted, and homely, besides. His own vicar's daughter was as plain as a rock, and just as exciting. A woman like Charlotte did not appear to exist, and Grayson wondered if he had somehow missed his opportunity and now was doomed to either go childless or settle for one of the grasping females of his acquaintance.

He was not accustomed to settling for anything.

Grayson's pensive mood clung as he approached his darkened town house. He had given the staff an evening off after the impromptu birthday celebration they contrived this afternoon, but he had no qualms about putting himself to bed without the services of the butler, valet and footmen who normally swarmed the halls. In fact, he rather enjoyed the solitude that met him.

It was not the first time he had walked through the shadowed rooms alone, and he certainly felt no threat as he drew off his gloves and tossed them on an elegant satinwood table. His reputation as a ruthless opponent extended from political circles right down to the streets, and was such that even the pickpockets usually left him alone.

Still, he had not earned his hard-won renown by relaxing his guard, and when he stepped into his study, his senses were roused to alertness. A subtle presence tickled the back of his neck and made him move casually toward the desk drawer that held his pistol.

"Hold there, gent!" a voice barked, confirming his suspicions, and a figure stepped out of the shadows of the thick draperies. Grayson would have laughed at the sight of the begrimed urchin, except that there was nothing funny about the weapon trained upon him. The young man was either very brave or very stupid, to dare the marquis of Wroth's own home.

Grayson found himself intrigued. Lifting one brow disdainfully, he eyed the ill-kept youth. "Do you think to hold me up?" he asked, incredulous.

His words seem to disconcert the boy, whose poorly fitting clothes and matted hair looked as if they could use a good wash. "I ain't no criminal. It's you who must answer for your foul deeds!"

Foul deeds? Grayson momentarily ignored the pistol, held in a surprisingly small but steady hand, and inclined his head in interest. "And to what, exactly, do you refer, young man? My opposition to the bill that—"

"I ain't talking about your politics. I'm talking about your morals, or lack thereof!"

Lack thereof? The youngster's speech held enough surprises to make Grayson study him closer. Despite his bedraggled appearance, the boy held himself straight, his feet spread in a ready stance for shooting. Yet there was something distinctly odd about him that Grayson couldn't quite put a finger on.

"No one threatens me, pup," he said. Although he did not raise his voice or change its tone, he conveyed a silky menace that had been known to make grown men shudder.

The urchin didn't even blink.

"I'm here to avenge my sister, whom you seduced and got with child," the young man said. Grayson could not mistake the accent this time, or the cool delivery. This was no ordinary guttersnipe. Who the devil was he? And what was this business about a sister?

"I can assure you, pup, that I do not consort with females of your family's ilk," Grayson answered smoothly.

"Don't take that high-stepping tone with me! You liked her well enough when you ruined her. Now it's time to pay the piper."

"And that is you, I assume?" Grayson said, inclining his head in a contemptuous fashion that made the boy flush. Strange little fellow. Grayson couldn't help admiring his heroics, however misplaced, but he had no desire to take a bullet for the sake of them. "Look here, I have no idea what you have heard about me, but I do not prey upon virgins of any stamp. Perhaps your sister is simply trying to protect herself—''

"My sister is not a liar!" the boy said, stepping forward angrily. It was the move Grayson had been waiting for, and he lunged, taking the boy to the floor with the speed that had made him an excellent boxer. He wrested the gun away, but the youth fought like a hellion, knocking it from his hand, and it skidded away. Nor could Grayson easily retrieve it. He had his hands full trying to subdue the body beneath him, which was kicking and flailing like a wild thing.

It was only when his groin came up against that of his opponent that Grayson began to suspect the truth. Startled, he looked down at the face below him. It was contorted in fear and rage and marked with dirt, but beneath the grime was a clear complexion, gently curved cheeks, thick, dark lashes and eyes the color of amethysts. What the devil? Thrusting a hand beneath the youth's baggy coat, Grayson found his answer when his fingers closed over a small but perfectly formed breast. A female!

The stunning discovery distracted him just as the girl, obviously taking exception to his groping, settled her teeth into his arm. She bit down hard enough that he released her with a curse, and then Grayson was not quite sure what happened. He saw her reach for the pistol, but before she could even lift the weapon, it discharged.

Grayson felt the sharp, searing heat of metal ripping through his flesh, but he managed to surge shakily to a standing position and lurch toward the desk that held his own pistol. Having no intention of dying at the hands of this dangerous female, he knew he must not give her a chance to reload.

He needn't have made the effort, for she leapt up and dropped the weapon as if it were suddenly distasteful. Facing him with an expression of horror on her delicate features, she cried, "Gad! You've been shot!"

It seemed that the pup had quite a grasp of the obvious. "Yes," Grayson agreed, before crumpling to the floor at her feet.

Kate Courtland stared numbly at the prone body of the marquis. She had come here to scare him, maybe even to get some badly needed funds to support the child that her sister was carrying, but, angry as she was with the man, she had never intended to harm him.

Her first inclination was to flee from the terrible scene, but how could she leave him here like this, his tall, graceful form prostrate, his dark vitality quenched? Kneeling down beside him, Kate saw the telltale red stain upon his coat and bit down on her knuckles to stifle a gasp. What if he bled to death? The house was silent as a tomb, and she had no idea when the servants would return.

His tanned skin had gone pale, and Kate leaned over him, noting the lock of dark hair that had fallen over his forehead. His eyes were closed now, but she had seen them. Clear and gray they were, and fringed with dark lashes under elegant brows. His was a man's face, with sharp planes and a strong jaw, but he was also beautiful, like an archangel fallen to earth.

Gad! Kate leaned back on her heels and swore more forcefully under her breath. The man was injured, and she was admiring his looks! Yes, he was handsome and polished, yet every inch a male, with an underlying strength that spoke of steely determination, but these very attributes were presumably what had plunged Lucy into disgrace. Kate shook her head. She had never thought to agree with her younger sister, but, apparently, they concurred on one thing. The marquis of Wroth was as appealing as he was dangerous.

He presented no threat now, Kate thought, although the realization gave her no satisfaction. Whatever his sins, she could not leave the man to die. Bending over, she tried to lift his shoulders, but he was heavy. All muscle, she remembered with a blush, for she had felt the press of his body weighing her down during their struggle.

Pushing such thoughts aside, Kate continued her efforts. She had just managed to get him into a sitting position when she heard a low sound at the window. Whistling softly in answer, she soon saw the grizzled head of her coachman poking over the sill.

"I thought I heard a shot," Tom said, and then his dark eyes grew wide. "Cor, Katie, what have you done now?"

"I put a bullet in him."

Letting loose a stream of foul curses, Tom climbed

through the opening. "Damn it, girl, now you've done it! The likes of him ain't worth a murder charge, or do you fancy a rope around your lovely little neck?"

Tom's words froze Kate in the act of trying to get the marquis to his feet. She had never considered the repercussions should her carefully laid plans go awry, but they had, and the consequences were more serious than she could ever have imagined. She cringed to think what would happen to them all if she was caught here, dressed as she was, with the wounded marquis.

It was an accident. Kate knew she had never even touched the trigger, but who would believe her? She had snuck into the marquis's home and threatened him. From the way Tom was glaring at her, it seemed even he had judged her guilty.

"Damn it, girl, I should never have agreed to this fool errand," the coachman muttered. "Breaking in was bad enough, but did you have to kill him, too?"

Kate stilled the panic that threatened to cloud her thinking and shot a stern look at Tom. "He's not dead, yet. Now, help me get him to his feet."

"What for? Are you going to bury him in the garden?"

Kate ignored her coachman's sarcasm. "No. We're taking him with us."

"*What?*" Tom's gravelly voice rang out loudly, and the marquis stirred in her arms.

"You heard me," Kate said, pushing her small frame under one of Wroth's wide shoulders. "Now help me, Tom, before we're both arrested."

*"And you think that kidnapping the gent's going to help?"*

"Lower your voice! I'm not going to kidnap him, just make sure that he doesn't pop off. Now hurry!" Kate urged, firmly eyeing the man who had become much more than a servant in the past few years. Their gazes locked and held until Tom's skidded away in resignation. Blowing out a disgruntled sigh, he heaved the marquis up and moved across the room.

"He ain't no lightweight, this one," he muttered as Kate slipped away to retrieve the errant pistol. She could see no blood upon the carpet, thankfully, and went swiftly to the window to help Tom lift Wroth through the opening.

"He's got the looks of the devil himself, and muscles, besides," Tom said, gasping for breath as he dragged the body out into the night. "You're borrowing trouble with this one, Katie. Make no mistake about it!"

"You just get him to the coach," she answered sharply. "I can handle the marquis."

Kate's confidence flagged when Tom draped Wroth over the cushioned seat and climbed out onto the box, leaving her alone with the injured man. He was still unconscious, and the front of his coat was soaked with blood, making Kate wonder whether he would survive the trip to Hargate. She leaned across the space between them to get a good look at his wound in the dim light of the interior lantern.

Probing the spot as gently as she could, Kate was relieved to find no sign of the bullet. He was lucky, for it appeared to have gone straight through his shoulder, but she still needed to stop the bleeding with something. She was shrugging out of her coat when a jolt sent Wroth sliding precariously near the cushioned edge.

Muttering one of Tom's favorite oaths, Kate swiftly slid into the opposite seat and laid the marquis's head on her lap. His dark lashes lifted, and he groaned before closing them again. "Hang on, Wroth," she said softly. Her lips trembled over his name, and she pursed them tightly together, angry at her own reaction. Turning her grimy coat inside out, Kate pressed the clean lining to the wound while she tried to recapture the outrage that had driven her to his town house.

"Conniving bastard! If you had kept your breeches on, you wouldn't be in this predicament," she whispered, but her soft tone robbed the accusation of some of its sharpness, and the shadowy confines of the coach seemed to close in on the two of them. Wroth stirred, turning his face toward her, and the movement heightened Kate's awareness of him, resting upon her thighs, his head cradled so intimately.

Her knowledge of males was limited to Tom and memories of her father, a rather distant but kindly figure. Vaguely she recollected the presence of stable boys and footmen, but they were nameless and faceless, long gone now. She had never been this close to a man in her life.

It was disturbing. Her breath grew ragged, and her fingers faltered as they held the cloth tightly to his shoulder. Under her palm, Kate could feel the mus-

cles that spread from his broad chest, and she knew
that this was no idle-rich dandy, but a strong, virile
man. She shifted, dismayed, yet she could not escape
the weight of him—or the feel of him.

Her cheeks flaming, Kate tried to concentrate on
his sins, but, in all honesty, the marquis of Wroth
had surprised her. She had never expected her sister's
lover to be so mature, so confident. So...dangerous.
He had caught her off guard with his dark good looks
and the disdainful lift of his brow. Unfazed by her
threats, he had stared, cool as you please, at the pistol
she pointed at his heart. Apparently he had just been
waiting for his opportunity to strike.

Her color rose higher as Kate remembered the ease
with which he had knocked her down and the way
his body had covered hers. Hot and heavy and...
something indescribable. Then his face had hovered
over hers, shadowy with intent, and his hand had...
Gad! Kate flinched, startled by the vivid recollection
off his fingers closing upon her breast. A strangled
noise escaped from her throat.

Bloody hell, it was easy enough to see how Lucy
had been seduced! Indeed, Kate felt as if she owed
her sister an apology. Although she had never
blamed Lucy aloud, she had silently accused her
many times. All those uncharitable thoughts about
her sister's lack of common sense and weakness of
will returned to mock her.

For if this man, with his cool, confident air and
his warm, competent hands, had been Lucy's temptation, then Kate could well understand her sister's
submission. Indeed, she found herself wondering just

what it would be like to succumb to the shadowy promise in his clear gray eyes, to fall from grace with this dark angel.

Sometime during the trip home, Kate checked Wroth's wound again. She had managed to stop the bleeding, and judging from the sound of his even breathing, she could abandon her immediate worry that he might die in the coach. However, his improved condition brought a new concern. Increasingly, Kate feared that he would wake up.

Several times she had seen his eyes flutter open, and once she could have sworn that he studied her with detached interest. Her nervous fingers had faltered then, pressing too hard against his ragged flesh, and he had gone off again with a groan.

Kate had felt guilty, but relieved. After all, what would she say if he was suddenly alive, awake and coherent? *Sorry I shot you, my lord, but now I plan to undo my mistake as best I can, if you'll just come along quietly?*

Somehow, as she studied his handsome face in the dimness of the coach, Kate could not imagine this man coming along quietly. Ever. For the first time since entering the town house, she began to wonder if Tom was right. Perhaps she was borrowing trouble by taking on someone who looked to be as dangerous as the marquis. But what else could she do?

Kate was never more eager to see the soft light in her own window, welcoming her home, as she was this night. Her relief at reaching her destination lasted until Tom pulled open the door of the coach, took one look at the marquis cradled in her lap and swore in disgust. "Mind that you don't find yourself in the same fix as your sister, Katie, girl," he muttered.

Kate gave him a cold glance that conveyed just what she thought of his warning. "I've stopped the bleeding, but I'll need to clean and dress the wound thoroughly, if he's not to pop off from a fever. You can put him in Papa's old room."

With a grunt of disapproval, Tom grabbed the marquis and heaved him half onto his back. "Careful, now!" Kate couldn't help admonishing Tom, although the glare she received from him made her want to call back the words.

Ignoring the coachman's attitude, Kate jumped down and hurried toward the door. If they could get the marquis to bed without Lucy hearing, she could tend to his injury, find her own rest and deal with her sister in the morning.

Unfortunately, her streak of bad luck was holding firm, for as soon as she opened the door, she heard Lucy's voice from the landing. "Katie, is that you?" her sister called, in a wavering whisper that made Kate feel guilty for having left her alone.

"Yes, it's me. Go on back to bed, dear."

"What are you doing at this hour? Is that Tom with you? What on earth has he got?" Groaning, Kate looked up to see Lucy descending the stairs with a candle while Tom started up, the marquis at his side.

"Go back to bed, Lucy," Kate ordered, knowing she was wasting her breath. Lucy had as strong a will as the rest of the Courtlands, when she chose to exercise it.

"What have you got there, Tom? My God, is that a man? What happened? Who is he?"

Tom, who was faltering under the strain of the marquis' weight, heaved himself up the last few steps and said, "It's your fellow, Miss Lucy."

"Mine—? Katie, what have you done?" Lucy rounded upon her sister just as Kate reached the top of the stairs.

"There was an accident. I didn't shoot him on purpose, I can tell you that much," Kate said, brushing past her outraged sister to open the bedroom door for Tom. She followed the grunting coachman into the room and watched him dump the marquis upon the bed with a groan, just as a bloodcurdling shriek erupted behind them.

Lucy stood in the doorway, clutching the frame as if to hold herself upright. "You shot him! Katie, how could you?"

"Never mind that. Tom, help me get this coat off of him," Kate instructed, bending over to remove the blood-soaked material.

"Don't you dare touch him!" Lucy wailed. Before Kate could respond, Lucy rushed to the side of the bed and pushed her away. "Wroth! What have they done to you?" she cried dramatically as she threw herself at the prone body of the marquis.

Kate watched dispassionately as Lucy, ever mindful of her limited wardrobe, stopped short of the wet coat. Her lashes fluttered as if she might swoon for a moment, but then they flew open and she stared at the marquis with a horrified expression on her lovely face. Jerking back from the bed, Lucy settled her hands on her hips, arms akimbo.

"That is not Wroth," she announced, lifting a finger to point it accusingly at the man in the bed.

"It most certainly is," Kate said.

"I ought to know better than you, and that is not him!" Lucy protested. "Why, Wroth is young and handsome, not old and cruel-looking."

The strain of the evening's events made Kate raise her voice in exasperation. "This man is certainly not old! Nor is he cruel-looking." She paused to eye the marquis. He was definitely not soft, but it was power and determination that hardened his features—not a mean streak, she would swear upon it. And handsome? Kate had never seen a man more beautiful in her life.

"I don't care what you say, he is not Wroth!"

"Who is he, then?" Kate asked.

"I don't know, nor do I care!"

"Girls! Girls!" Tom's admonitions rose above the squabbling, drawing Kate's attention. She swiveled toward him, just as Lucy did, with the same question on her lips.

"What?" Lucy fairly shrieked.

The coachman heaved a great sigh. "You had better quit arguing and do something, before the fellow bleeds to death all over the best bed linens."

## Chapter Two

Grayson drifted in and out of the nightmare. Just when his head began to clear, he would feel a jolt, followed by a sharp rush of pain that sent him back into oblivion. He was not willing to surrender, but each time he thought to struggle, he heard a deep, soothing woman's voice, lulling him into the darkness once more.

She stroked his forehead. It was not a sexual touch, but rather a gentle, maternal motion. His mother? No, she had been dead for years. And this woman was whispering something about temptation. Had he fallen asleep in a brothel? That was not his style. He had been either drugged or attacked by some ruffians, who had obviously left him the worse for the encounter. And the woman?

With great effort, Grayson managed to lift his lashes. At first he couldn't focus, but then he saw a shadowy face take shape, and in it, eyes the color of amethyst. Her eyes. Who was she? He opened his mouth to speak, but then his whole body lurched and rough hands grabbed at him, lifting him and... nothing.

She was touching him again. Grayson felt the intriguing brush of fingertips across his shoulder, gentle, but capable. She was wrapping something around him. Had he been injured? He could not remember.

"I refuse to stand here while you...handle a strange man's chest!" A different woman's voice, high and grating, sounded, followed by footsteps.

A snort, but a female one. *His* female. "Seems to me that's what got us in this mess, Lucy," she muttered. "You and some stranger's chest."

"Cor, Katie, it weren't the chest what caused the problem!" A man. A rough baritone. Chuckling coarsely. How many people were here? Grayson tried to clear his head, but the woman rested a hand on his forehead, distracting him with her smooth palm. He remembered it. Soft and soothing.

"Better dose him up with laudanum," the man said, and Grayson fought to rouse himself.

"He isn't conscious," his female protested. *Good girl,* Grayson thought, relaxing once more.

"He'll be awake soon enough," the man muttered. "And then I promise you that there'll be hell to pay."

*How right you are,* Grayson thought grimly.

When his mind finally cleared, Grayson had the good sense to keep it to himself. He had enemies, and though he had thought himself untouchable, there was always a chance that one of them had gotten reckless. Unfortunately, the dull ache in his head and his shoulder assured him quickly enough that he had been hurt, and badly.

It all came back to him then. The begrimed urchin who was not a boy. The gunshot. And then what? All he had was a hazy memory of the young pup and flashes of conversation. Had he passed out? Damn, it was hard to believe that he could go a round with Gentleman Jackson himself, yet a bullet had rendered him helpless as a babe.

He was not accustomed to feeling helpless.

And no longer would he, Grayson decided. It was time to wrest control of the situation from whoever was behind it. And he was fairly certain that someone had to be paying the pistol-wielding pup who had attacked him, for he had ruined no one's sister. With the possible exception of Charlotte Trowbridge, innocent virgins held no allure for him, and he certainly had never gotten one with child. His father had lectured him early on about a man's responsibilities, and he had sired no bastards.

Keeping his breathing low and even, Grayson listened for any sound that would indicate he had company. Vaguely he remembered the presence of a man and a woman, along with the girl with the gentle touch and pleasing voice.

Nothing. Grayson heard only the call of birds outside his window. Deliberately he fluttered his lashes, while snatching a quick look at his surroundings. He was alone. Opening his eyes, Grayson first inspected his shoulder, where he found a clean dressing covering the wound. Moving his arm experimentally, he sucked in a breath. Although it hurt like hell, he was grateful that the bullet had not struck him any lower.

Glancing downward, he realized that he was naked from the waist up, and the discovery brought back memories of the girl's light caresses. Fool, he told himself immediately. The chit was probably some street thief who would do anything for money, including shooting an unarmed man.

But he was in no grimy prison. With increasing amazement, Grayson studied the room. Spacious and open, it glowed with the morning sun that shone through the open draperies. The walls were white panels with touches of gilt, and the ceiling was elaborately carved. Although few, the pieces of furniture, including the large bed in which he lay, were fine examples of Louis XIV.

With some effort, Grayson managed to ease himself to his feet. He swayed and righted himself with a swift grab at the bedpost. Blood loss, he thought, willing away the trace of dizziness. Slowly he put one foot in front of the other until he reached the window. Keeping to the wall, he peeked out through the draperies and drew in a long, slow breath at the sight that met him. Instead of the sooty skies of London, he was met with green lawns and the unmistakable outbuildings of a country home.

Where the devil was he?

Neatly arranging the toast and jam and tea upon the tray, along with the last of the ham, Katie headed toward the stairs. It was a peace offering for their guest, as she had come to think of him. She had no idea who he really was, but she was responsible for shooting him in Wroth's study and dragging him here, and now she was going to make her apologies.

Although Kate sincerely hoped he was the understanding sort, from the looks of him, she doubted it. Perhaps a nice breakfast would make him more amenable to explanations. Drawing a deep breath, she started up the steps, cursing the skirts that got in her way. Out of deference to their visitor, she had forgone her usual breeches for one of her old gowns, but even at a size too small, it was cumbersome. Snatching at the material with one hand, she balanced her burden in the other as she hurried toward Hargate's largest bedroom.

Pushing open the door with her hip, Kate peeked in, relieved to see that the man was still abed. Although she was sorry for his injury, she suspected that the mysterious stranger would be much easier to handle prone than upright. Well she remembered his cool confidence in the study, and it made her wary.

Apparently not wary enough, for she crossed the threshold only to be halted abruptly by a hand that clamped down hard over mouth and an arm that snaked around her from behind. As she watched in dismay, the tray toppled to the floor, spilling its contents on the Aubusson carpet. A sound of horror was caught in her throat when she saw the last of the ham topple from its plate. Angry now, Kate tried to get a leg around to fell her attacker, but her fiendish skirts kept her imprisoned, and then she was pulled back against a body that she knew in an instant was that of their guest.

"Wroth!" she cried against his fingers, but it came out as nothing more than a muffled gasp. No matter, for this man was not the marquis, anyway. Perhaps he was a criminal who had been intent upon burglarizing Wroth's town house, Kate thought wildly, before her good sense denied it. She tried to think clearly, but he leaned over her, his breath tickling her ear, and her immediate fears for her person receded in the face of a new threat. She flushed, suddenly aware of the length of him, pressed to her, touching...

"Are you alone?" he asked, in a voice that evinced no strain whatsoever. Apparently a bullet wound did little to ruffle this man's composure! Kate nodded quickly in answer, then eyed him in amazement as he pivoted swiftly and silently closed the door behind them.

Her relief at no longer being held to his muscular form was short-lived, for he turned her toward him, and Kate found herself confronting his bare chest, only inches from her face. She had viewed it last night, of course, but in the light of day, it took on a new vitality, its muscles rippling beneath its dusting of dark hair. Remembering the feel of that expanse, Kate sucked in a sharp breath. She tried to focus her attention elsewhere, but it was caught by the sight of his exposed nipple, brown and hard, and she felt blood surge to her cheeks.

"Who's behind this?" he asked roughly, and Kate jerked her gaze back to his face. Confident and intent, he seemed oblivious of his state of undress— and her inappropriate reaction. She swallowed hard, seeking her usual calm demeanor, but she kept being distracted by his closeness. His height. His heat. Despite her efforts to deny it, warmth stole through Kate's limbs and pooled in the lower half of her body, leaving her brain devoid of reason. Unable to form an answer to his question, she simply stared up at his dark angel's visage.

Despite his threatening stance, she felt no menace emanating from him. His eyes were not cold and bleak, but a clear gray that spoke of difficulties overcome, achievements won, and a solitary life that touched something deep within herself. She could admire this man, Kate suspected, slightly awed by the prospect. Then her gaze slid lower to full lips, so very near and poised to speak, and she stared, fascinated.

"You're the one," he whispered. "You bit me."

"Did I?" Kate murmured. She tried to concentrate, but his fingertips slid across her mouth in a slow, exotic glide that made her breath go ragged beneath them. Her lips trembled and parted as his face moved closer, and her lashes drifted shut just as his open mouth came down upon hers, hot and firm and intense.

She was melting. Slowly, irrevocably, sinking into a netherworld of dark sensation. A heavy, delicious languor surrounded her, robbing her wits and making her arms snake up around his neck. This man was the source of it all, with his naked chest and his wonderful kiss, and she leaned into his muscular body, seeking...

When his tongue touched hers, Kate gasped, astonished. One of his hands closed around the back of her neck, holding her steady, and then the dance began. His tongue swirled and delved and stroked, coaxing hers to do the same. Hesitantly she assented, and knew another dizzying drag on her senses, for he tasted like nothing she had ever known—like warmth and shadows and forbidden longings. Her fingers slid down to his shoulders, seeking purchase on that hard flesh.

Then, suddenly, he was gone, swaying away from her, and Kate blinked up at a face devoid of color. Alarm cleared her head quickly as she saw a red stain that had not been there before mark his bandage. She had reopened his wound!

"Sit down!" she cried, urging him backward to the bed. He seemed bemused by her concern, but willingly took a seat on the edge. Tossing aside the pillows that had disguised his exit, Kate pushed him down against the blankets just as the door swung open.

"Here now, what's this?" Tom asked, in a voice rife with suspicion and warning. Obviously, the sight of her straddling the covers with a half-naked man did not please her old coachman.

"He's bleeding again!" Kate answered. Although she slid to the side of the bed, she refused to turn around, unwilling to let Tom see her crimson face. She had no desire to explain that the damage had been done by her own questing fingers! Nor did she wish to describe what had gone before. Busying herself with changing the dressing, Kate schooled her face to show nothing to either the curious coachman or the man who had so shattered her composure.

What had she been thinking? All this time she had chastised Lucy for being seduced, while she had just let herself be kissed by a total stranger. Not only that, but she had returned his attentions willingly. Eagerly! Just the thought of that hot, dark place to which he had taken her made Kate's hands fumble with the wrapping.

"Still, you should not have come in here alone, Katie girl," Tom scolded, walking toward her. He stopped nearby to study the man, who lay quiet under her ministrations. "This gent might be dangerous. What's that mark on his arm?"

"That's where I bit him," Kate answered, her face flaming anew. "Last night," she felt compelled to add. A muscle jerked beneath her touch, as if the stranger were amused by that small admission, and she yanked on the linen angrily.

"Ahem…" Tom mumbled. "Well, if you're done coddling him now, move away from the fellow. I've a mind to get some answers."

Far from appearing concerned about the upcoming interrogation, their guest only leaned back on the pillows in a more comfortable position, his muscles flexing as if to taunt her. Hurriedly Kate finished her task, jerking her hands away from the warmth of his skin and shifting her attention to his face.

Her eyes caught his, and without speaking, he lifted one dark brow in the arrogant manner she remembered from the confrontation in the study. She had known then that this man would always be in complete control of any situation in which he found himself. It had annoyed her yesterday; now it alarmed her. Who was he? And how would he treat those who had done him ill? Kate shivered at the thought.

"Comfy now?" Tom jeered. Apparently he was oblivious of the threat posed by this man, but Tom had never been particularly perceptive. It fell to Kate to read the more complex nuances of those few people with whom they came in contact.

"Actually, no," the stranger answered evenly. "I would be a lot more at ease if you would tell me just who the hell you are and who you are working for."

Tom's mouth dropped open, and Kate felt a shudder of admiration for the wounded man's composure. Despite his prone position, stretched full length on the bed, he was cool as you please, and subtly menacing, besides.

Recovering himself, Tom grunted rudely. "Don't tell him anything, Kate," he advised. His face had taken on that stubborn cast that made her want to groan. So much for her peace offering! So much for trying to make the man feel like a guest. The breakfast! Biting back one of Tom's oaths, Kate ran to where the tray had fallen and tried to clean up the mess. Perhaps if she washed off the precious piece of ham...

"I'll be asking the questions, gent," she heard Tom say in a belligerent tone. "Just who the hell are you, and what were you doing in the marquis of Wroth's study last night?"

"As puzzling as it may seem to one of your intellect, I am Grayson Wescott—"

"Aha!" Tom said, turning triumphantly toward Kate.

She scrubbed at the carpet with a linen napkin, trying vainly to remove the jam stain. "I believe Wescott is the marquis's family name."

"Eh?" Tom looked puzzled. "Some relative, are you? Were you staying with Wroth? He's not saying he is Wroth, is he, Katie?"

"He is *not* Wroth! I told you last night that he does not resemble Wroth in the slightest," a haughty voice declared.

Kate glanced over to see Lucy standing in the doorway, looking fetching in one of her best gowns. Her condition barely showed. Still, the sight of it was enough to make Kate swallow hard. How could she possibly have let the stranger kiss her, even if he was the most handsome, confident and powerful of men? Was that how Lucy had begun, melting in a warm embrace, only to end up carrying a child?

"I assure you, Miss—?"

"Don't tell him who you are, Lucy!" Tom warned. It was the wrong thing to say to Lucy, of course. She immediately lifted her head and tossed her auburn curls in rebellion.

"And why not? I am proud of my family name! I, for one, have nothing to hide from this…this ruffian! When he finds out whom he is dealing with, he will take himself off soon enough."

Kate eyed Lucy with some alarm, dismayed by her efforts to sustain their position. Although the stranger did not look like a gossip, what if he carried the tale of his imprisonment here back to London? Their ruination would be complete. "Lucy, be a dear, and return the tray to the kitchen, will you? I'll take care of this," Kate said, her casual tone belied by the look she sent her sister.

Although Lucy obviously wanted to refuse the request and remain right where she was, she contented herself with glaring at their guest. "I shall leave it to you to put him in his proper place!" she declared, before turning on her heel and regally exiting the room.

"Now, Mr. Wescott, or whoever you may be—" Tom began.

"Is that the sister you spoke of, the one with child?" the stranger asked, inclining his head toward the door through which Lucy had departed.

Kate felt her cheeks bloom again, but she held her head high. "Yes," she answered honestly.

"Well, it seems that we have quite a coil to unravel," he said, gazing at her from under heavy-lidded eyes. Bedroom eyes, Kate reflected, annoyed at the turn of her thoughts. He had propped one knee up, and appeared thoroughly at home in her father's bed, his dark hair tousled, his chest bare. Suddenly, Kate wished he would cover himself, if only so her eyes would not continually drift to that beautiful, dark expanse.

"What coil? What are you talking about, man?" Tom asked.

Her mouth thinning determinedly, Kate walked to a dresser and pulled open a drawer, rummaging for one of her father's old nightshirts. Most of his clothes had been commandeered for their own wardrobes, but such intimate wear remained intact. Grabbing one, she turned and tossed it to her guest. "There. You can put that on," she instructed.

"He won't be needing your Papa's underthings! He ain't staying long enough." Tom protested. "I'll take him back to London today, whoever he is."

"No, you won't, Tom. He's still shaky from loss of blood," Kate argued, trying not to remember just how solid he had seemed a few minutes ago, when she was pressed up against his muscular form. "And what if he gets a fever?" she asked. Although it had not been her intention, she had shot this man, and being responsible for his injury, she felt obliged to nurse him back to health—or at least until he could get up and around without bleeding anew.

"I am not going anywhere," the man announced, in the kind of voice that demanded attention. Both she and Tom turned to stare at him. His expression was polite, but Kate sensed an indomitable will behind it. Even reclining amid the pillows, he held himself just a little aloof, as if born to command, and she felt a growing unease at the enormity of her mistake. She could no more handle this man than she could a charging beast.

"And why not?" Tom demanded angrily.

"Because I intend to find out just who has been using my name to seduce young women."

"What? What the devil do you mean? What's he talking about, Katie?" Tom asked.

Kate's dismay escalated as the truth dawned.

"I have never seen your sister before in my life," the stranger explained dryly. "And the last time I checked, I was the only marquis of Wroth."

Grayson eyed the duo calmly, while they stared as if he had sprouted two heads. Although his name was not always a welcome one, still, he could never recall receiving quite this sort of reception before. It was interesting, to say the least.

Apparently unconvinced of his parentage, the old man, called Tom, was still inclined to argue. "Here, now, Lucy says—"

Grayson halted him with his most damning look. "I am sure that the lady, Miss Lucy, is speaking the truth as she knows it, but since I am Wroth and I have not seduced her, it stands to reason that someone has been using my name, although I am at a loss as to who would be so imprudent."

Tom gaped, scratching his bristly chin in confusion, but the dark-haired girl, obviously more intelligent, nodded. It was easy to see that she was in charge, for both Lucy and Tom took orders from her in the manner of those of long habit. Intrigued, Grayson found himself watching her closely. She did not look old enough to run a household, but she had a serious, capable air that told him she could manage very well. As if to prove his thoughts, she proceeded to draw herself up to her full height—she stood not much above five feet—and unflinchingly apologize for shooting him.

"I must tell you that I regret very much your injury, my lord, and will do my best to remedy any inconvenience that this…*misunderstanding* may have caused you." Despite the pain in his shoulder, Grayson found himself admiring her pluck. He could not wait to hear exactly what she had planned for him, should he have been her sister's seducer. A wedding ceremony at gunpoint had most likely been the plan, and he could not help but be relieved at Lucy's imperious rejection. The auburn-haired chit with the grating voice did not appeal to him in the slightest, while this Kate…

"Naturally, you are welcome to stay here until you are sufficiently recovered," she said, as politely as if they were discussing the weather, and not the attack upon his person and his subsequent abduction. Really, she was most intriguing.

A low growl from the corner made him glance toward Tom, who apparently took exception to the offer of such hospitality. He hitched up his trousers and glared at Grayson in a decidedly menacing fashion. "He looks to be well enough right now. I can take him back to London soon as I ready the horses."

"Nonsense," Kate responded in that take-charge tone of hers. "He needs food and rest. Now let us leave him to it." Turning to Grayson, she said, "I shall send Tom up with another tray, since the other was spilled." For the first time, her amazing composure seemed to desert her. She cast her eyes downward, and as Wroth watched the slow bloom of color in her cheeks, he felt an answering stirring in his loins.

Then, with a nod, she took her leave, dragging a reluctant Tom along with her, and Grayson felt oddly bereft at her absence. Damn, but she was an extraordinary creature! He found it difficult to reconcile all his images of her: the filthy boy; the gentle healer; the competent woman who took charge of an awkward situation without blinking an eye; and the innocent who had returned his kiss with tentative passion.

Grayson frowned grimly. He did not care to examine that small lapse in his judgment. He had waited for one of his jailers to arrive, not expecting to see the begrimed urchin again until she had walked through the doorway. Although it took Grayson a moment to recognize the demure young girl as the pistol-wielding pup of the night before, he had had no doubts once he looked into those eyes. Luminous eyes, they were like none he had ever seen, serious and clear. Guileless. Lovely.

Enthralled, Grayson had made a feeble attempt to question her before giving in to the lust that seized him in a grip that was truly remarkable, considering his recent injury. But all thoughts of his shoulder had been forgotten when he took her mouth. She tasted of mint and sweetness and delight, with an underlying passion that took him by surprise. He shuddered to remember the first bold forays of her tongue. She had ignited him effortlessly, and he had wanted nothing more than to feel her breast beneath his palm again, without a layer of boy's clothing to cover it. More than that, he had wanted her naked beneath him, small and slender and...

Hearing the rapid rise of his breathing, Grayson pushed such images forcefully from his mind. It must be his condition, he decided. Never before had he let himself be carried away by the thought of fondling a female. He was a skilled lover, but he never lost his head. Nothing disgusted him more than a supposedly intelligent man who made a cake of himself over the latest fashionable female.

But Kate was neither, and Grayson knew he had been extremely careless to let himself be so distracted from his situation. He was lucky to find himself a victim of mistaken identity, rather than at the hands of someone truly dangerous—though he had an odd suspicion that the inimitable Kate could be dangerous enough, in her own way.

Who was she? Although her speech and bearing proclaimed her a woman of quality, her gown was faded and ill-fitting. And despite her eventual response to his kiss, it was obvious that she was an innocent. As beautiful as she was, Grayson thought she must have lived a protected existence to remain so pure and unaffected, but what sheltered female would dress up as a boy, break into a nobleman's study and shoot him? He knew a few women who could handle a pistol, but none who could have succeeded in besting him.

And how had she become the leader of this odd trio? If her sister truly had been ruined, why was a male relative not seeing to her welfare? Instinctively Grayson knew that the rough-looking Tom was not a part of the family. Yet why was he treated as an equal, rather than as a servant?

And what of the sister's alleged seducer? Had the man truly claimed to be Wroth, or had the girl concocted the story to placate her sister? She would not have been the first to claim that a nobleman, and not the traveling tinker, had sired her child. And, if so, she would not be happy to have her ruse exposed.

Really, the whole business was more entertaining than the theater. From the identity of the players to the country home that formed the backdrop, it was a fascinating puzzle, and Grayson could not wait to begin putting all the pieces together. Not surprisingly, he no longer felt the suffocating press of ennui that had plagued him for months, and the realization made him release a sigh of relief.

Hell, if it were not for the bullet hole in his shoulder, he would be enjoying himself thoroughly.

## Chapter Three

Grayson lifted a brow in contempt when Tom came barging in with his breakfast tray. The old man was the worst excuse for a servant Grayson had ever seen, plopping down his burden with total disregard for the tea that sloshed over the rim of the cup. Obviously, Tom was not accustomed to waiting at table.

Eyeing the spill askance, Grayson wondered if Kate and her cohorts were hiding him from the rest of the household, for he had yet to see a maid or serving girl. He was determined to investigate later, but right now he was hungry. He watched, amused, when Tom pushed the food at him, as if begrudging every bite, then stepped back and hitched his trousers in an irritating manner.

Situating the tray neatly on his lap, Grayson glanced at the man, who was glowering at him. "Is there something else, Tom?" he asked.

"That there is, my lord," Tom answered, drawling the address as if he did not believe Wroth to be himself. "Kate's a bit kindhearted, but I won't have her suffering for it.'' His thick, peppery brows drew together. ''Fair warning. I've got my eye on you.''

''Do you now?'' Grayson asked, undisturbed.

''That I do,'' Tom growled, as if taking exception to Grayson's attitude. ''And I'm thinking that maybe you're Wroth and maybe you ain't.''

''And maybe you're an extremely incompetent servant or simply a kidnapper who botched my murder,'' Wroth said, calmly spreading thick country jam upon his toast.

When he glanced up, Tom had paled significantly. Frowning at the reminder of his criminal activities, the old man slunk out of the room with a disgruntled expression that entertained Grayson enormously. He settled down to eat with a slight smile.

When he had finished, Grayson set the tray neatly on the floor, annoyed at himself for missing his phalanx of servants and the French cook he kept at his country seat. Although edible, the meal had been small and simple, certainly not the elaborate fare he was used to in homes such as this. Which brought him back to one of the myriad puzzles that he had yet to solve.

Slowly easing his way out of bed, Grayson winced at the pain in his shoulder. The meager breakfast lurched in his stomach, and he was thankful it had been small. Obviously he was not up to his old self, as yet, but he gritted his teeth and rose to his feet. He did not care to be bedbound.

More importantly, he needed to do some investigating, not only to satisfy his curiosity, but to protect himself, as well. Although his hostess was both intriguing and appealing, Grayson had nothing except her assurances that these people did not mean him harm. He intended to make sure they were as innocent as they pretended before closing his eyes again.

Pushing the bed pillows into the shape of a body once more, Grayson slipped to the door and silently turned the handle. Outside, the hallway stretched before him, the carpeting elegant, if a little worn, and the silence palpable. The quiet spoke for itself, for he had never been to a country home where servants were not bustling to and fro and guests were not idling in their rooms or gathering for cards and entertainment.

Not here. Grayson did not meet a soul as he prowled the upper rooms. Indeed, the first few he entered appeared as though they had been empty for some time, a thin layer of dust making him wonder again about the mettle of the staff. When he finally came upon some signs of occupation, Grayson lifted a brow in surprise, for clothing and hats and gloves littered a crowded collection of furniture that looked to have been taken from other suites. Surely, no self-respecting servant could endure this mess.

Lifting a silk gown of bishop's blue to his nose, Grayson drew in the cloying scent of gardenias. Not Kate's. He let the dress fall to its place, draped over a chair-backed settee, and glanced around. A large mirror rested on a vanity where a number of perfume bottles and a quantity of other female paraphernalia could be found. Lucy's, he suspected, remembering the auburn-haired chit with the grating voice. Al-

though it was cluttered, there was nothing really unusual about the place. He went on.

A connecting door led to another room that was
obviously Kate's. Grayson knew its owner at once,
because it reflected the somber, clear-eyed girl. Neat
and spotless, without the romantic trappings and
lace-trimmed pillows of her sister's boudoir, it
housed little more than a bed, a dresser and cupboard, a chair and an inlaid writing desk. The mirror
that lay atop the pristine dresser top was small, part
of an ivory-handled set of brush and comb that spoke
of necessity, not vanity. No perfume. The mysterious
Kate had smelled faintly of mint—or had she simply
tasted that fresh and inviting?

Grayson frowned. He pulled open drawers and
cupboards, but could find nothing except a rather
pitiful wardrobe that included some boy's clothing,
like that she had worn into his study. Incredibly, he
was seized by an odd agitation at the possibility that
a husband or other male might be in residence here
with Kate.

He shook his head in denial, and the room itself
seemed to spin. Reaching out for the bedpost, Grayson steadied himself and took several deep breaths.
No, he would swear that the girl had never even been
kissed before. And there were no signs of male hab-
itation, except for a few shirts and trousers, which
made him wonder where Tom slept.

Grayson realized that puzzle would have to wait.
Although the dizziness seemed to have passed, he
did not care to test his endurance and come up want-

ing. Regaining his feet, he moved silently back to his own room.

As it was the largest and most comfortable, Grayson wondered why neither of the girls used it. Perhaps they were poor relations who had no choice of housing, or mayhap the occupant of this particular bedroom was away. Many people spent more time in London than in the country. He had noted several blank spots on the walls where paintings might have hung. Had the owner of the home fallen on hard times? That would explain the dearth of servants, but how, and why, were the girls living here?

Grayson felt an ache in his head to match the one in his shoulder, and he pushed the pillows aside to lie full length upon the bed. He needed to get his strength back—and soon. Scowling at his own weakness, he closed his eyes. At least he had found nothing suspicious in the upper rooms. It confirmed his gut instinct that Kate, her sister and their grizzled companion were as harmless as they professed to be. And common sense told him that the obnoxious Tom wouldn't be so anxious to send him packing if there was a reason for keeping him imprisoned.

Yes, they were an innocuous group, two young girls and an old man, and none of them truly dangerous, if he ignored the fact that they had broken into his town house and put a bullet hole in him. The abduction, he suspected, had been Kate's way of making amends.

Grayson woke to a persistent pounding. It seemed to be a part of him, throbbing through his head, his shoulder, his dry throat and his eardrums, deafening him. He opened his eyes and stared at the figure of an old man. One of his grooms? No. He shook his head and swallowed as he recognized those thick, peppery brows, drawn down in disapproval.

"If you think to cozen them into letting you stay by keeping to your bed, I'm here to tell you it won't work," Tom said, in an excessively loud and unpleasant voice. "And I'm not waiting on you anymore, either, *my lord* or not. Here's your shirt," he said, tossing something at him. It lay on Grayson's chest like a lump of rags. "It's been washed and mended as best it could be, so you can dress for supper. We keep early hours, so see that you're down by seven o'clock." With a scowl, he hitched up his trousers and marched to the door.

Grayson blinked. Even his eyelids hurt. Damn, but he could not recall ever feeling this bad. With a groan, he sat up and grabbed his discarded garment. Once the finest money could buy, it now sported a new seam along the shoulder. He shuddered, aware of just how close he had come to taking his last breath.

The effort it cost him to get the damn thing over his head and properly situated at his wrists had him dizzy and gasping. What the devil was the matter with him? Leaning over, he managed to put his boots on without the aid of a valet, but he was panting from the exertion.

He looked around for his waistcoat and coat, to no avail. Obviously his other clothing had not yet dried, and though he was not accustomed to dining in his shirtsleeves, it was an improvement over eating in bed, wasn't it? Grayson was not sure, His shoulder and head were aching so much that his stomach was forgotten.

Courtesy, if not curiosity, required that he make an appearance, so he opened the door and moved along the hallway. The main stairway curved down to a tiled entranceway, but no butler or footman met him when he reached the bottom. Pausing to catch his erratic breath, he stood blinking up at the painted ceiling and was seized by a sense of familiarity. Had he been here before, staring at the historic scenes, or was this a hazy memory from the night before, when he had faded in and out of consciousness?

With no attendant to lead him, Grayson was forced to follow the sound of voices along a columned gallery. His steps faltered, as he again wondered if he had walked this way before, even though he knew he could not have done so last night. The strange feeling persisted, however, and, coupled with the need to find his way without help, created an eerie sense of unreality.

It continued when he reached the large dining hall, where his motley band of abductors waited: Kate, as lovely and untouched as an angel; her sister, scowling shrewishly; and the ubiquitous Tom, who looked as if he'd be more comfortable in the stables than surrounded by fine china and crystal.

"My lord," Kate said. "You look a bit pale. Should you be up and about?"

Grayson watched her move toward him, as if in a dream, her face gentle with concern, her fingers reaching for him. Perhaps she would stroke his brow again, he thought dazedly. She came to a stop before him, her dark curls shining gloriously in the candle-light. He wanted to touch them.

"Are you all right?" she asked.

Grayson tried to execute a bow, but dizziness overcame him. "No," he managed to answer her formally, before everything went black.

For the second time in two days, Kate watched in horror as the marquis of Wroth collapsed onto the floor. She knelt beside him and put her hand to his forehead, her worst fears confirmed.

"He's burning up! Tom, carry him upstairs again!"

"Really, Kate!" Lucy exclaimed, obviously disgusted. "You should never have brought him here. Now look at him."

Kate did, and her heart ached to see him brought low again, his handsome face pale and wan, his eyes closed, his tall body felled by fever. She swallowed painfully. "I'll see to him," she whispered.

"Oh, very well. I'll keep supper for you," Lucy promised, "but I might as well eat his portion. No sense letting it go to waste, after all."

"No, of course not," Kate replied, in response to her sister's cold-blooded behavior. It was a defect of her character that Lucy rarely considered anything more important than her own wishes, but she had suffered much in recent years, and could be forgiven for selfishly wanting an extra helping for herself and her child.

"I would have left him upstairs, if I'd known I'd have to drag him back up again," the coachman grumbled as he hefted the marquis's prone body.

"Then you should not have let him come down," Kate said, without sympathy. "I should have checked on him, as I planned, rather than let you talk me out of it."

"I tell you, it ain't proper for you to be tending a gentleman!"

Kate gave an inelegant snort as she followed the coachman through the gallery and up the stairs. "As if that matters now!" Was she the only one with any sense in this household? The marquis of Wroth was injured and sick, suffering by her own hand, and no one seemed the slightest bit concerned. Indeed, the others appeared put out. "How *inconvenient* of the man to fall ill from the bullet I sent through him!" she said, tossing the biting sarcasm at Tom's head.

He ducked and hurried forward, dumping the marquis unceremoniously on the bed that had once been her father's. "Guess I'll have to get his boots off of him again."

"Yes, and the shirt, as well." Kate spoke calmly enough, but she felt panic beating at the back of her mind, and pushed it away. She had to think clearly now, if she was going to save him. And there could be no "if" about it. Although they had been buried here in the country for a long time, she had heard Wroth mentioned before. *Rich, powerful, dangerous.* Those were words that were used to describe him, and although Kate had not heeded them when she was bent upon revenge, now they returned to taunt her.

For one fleeting moment, she pictured herself dangling at the end of a rope while an eager crowd chanted, "Murderess!" Then she rolled up her sleeves and got to work. "Fetch Mother's recipe book, please," she told Tom as she sat down beside the marquis to check his dressing. "And see if there are any spirits in the house. There might be some brandy in the cellar. And bring up a bowl of water, straight from the spring, so it is especially cold."

Tom hesitated, and she shot him a look that questioned his delay. "It's not proper," he protested, with a mulish expression.

Kate nearly gave in to the hysterical laughter that bubbled in her chest. "Proper? *Proper?* How could that possibly matter now? Lucy is already with child by a man who pretended to be someone he isn't!"

"Well, that doesn't—"

Kate cut him off with a sharp glance. "We must fend for ourselves, Tom. You know that."

The two shared a poignant look until Tom dropped his eyes and mumbled one of his oaths. "Well, it ain't right." He gazed at her again, suddenly apologetic. "I'll take care of him."

"No," Kate replied firmly. She had entrusted Wroth to Tom today, and he had failed her, whether by accident or by design. It had only reinforced the lesson she had learned a long time ago: The only way to ensure that anything was done was to do it herself.

Waving Tom away, she waited until she heard his

footsteps leave the room before she checked her charge. Beneath the unnatural flush that stained his cheeks, she could see the strength and beauty of his face. He had kissed her, this elegant, assured noble-man, Kate thought, still amazed by the memory.

She had no notion why he had done it. Perhaps he thought her a housemaid, eager for a tumble, or maybe he thought any girl who would dress as a boy fair game. Whatever his motivation, Kate was se-cretly thrilled by his fleeting interest. In the quiet struggle her life had become, she had never thought to visit the dark, sensuous world she had known in his arms. Now she would have that small wonder to carry with her always.

Snorting at the strange, sentimental turn of her thoughts, Kate leaned forward, turning her attention toward the sick man. He was her responsibility, and if she had other reasons for saving him besides self-preservation, she did not care to examine them.

Kate opened bleary eyes and turned them toward the bed, lit by a brace of low-burning candles. Wroth had thrown off all the covers and was tossing rest-lessly, and the only thing she knew to do was bathe him with cool water. Originally, she had just wiped his face, but as the evening wore on and his body warmed, she had boldly pressed the wet cloth to his arms and his chest. It had gained him some respite, but now he was thrashing again, hotter than ever. Kate's eyes darted down to the breeches that still covered him.

Tom would never approve.

Lucy would have an apoplexy.

To the devil with them, Kate thought, determination firming the line of her lips. She would do whatever was necessary to save this man's life, and if she had to see him in his underclothes to do so, it was no one's concern but her own.

Pulling the covers down to the bottom of the bed, Kate moved toward his waist. She knew how to work the fall, for she often wore boy's trousers, but it was one thing to dress herself and quite another to undo the buttons that covered the front of the tall, virile marquis. Her fingers fumbled against the body beneath, but finally she had his breeches open. Grabbing a fistful of material at either side of his hips, she tugged hard, and nearly fell facefirst upon his thighs at the sight that met her eyes.

He wasn't wearing any drawers.

Sitting back on her heels, Kate drew in a deep breath and stared at the large male member that lay nestled in a thicket of dark brown hair. "Gad," she whispered to herself over the pounding of blood in her ears. Suddenly she felt as hot as the man on the bed. Feverish. Out of her head.

Swallowing hard, Kate forced herself to look away. There was something positively common about a woman who stared at a prone man's private parts, she decided. Perhaps all these years of struggle and solitude were taking their toll and her wits were fleeing her. God forbid. Her wits were the only thing that held them all together.

Drawing in a deep breath, Kate positioned herself over his hips again and tugged at his clothing while trying not to look at what she had uncovered. Unfortunately, the breeches would not give way easily. They fitted like a second skin and clung tenaciously to his sweat-soaked body, and Wroth did nothing to help. In fact, he abruptly turned over, nearly taking her with him.

Swaying on her knees, Kate righted herself once more and gripped the material, which was now twisted around his thighs. "Good," she muttered. "Now I no longer have to look at…that." Instead, she found herself staring at his narrow, tightly muscled behind. "Bloody hell," she whispered, flushing anew.

As if in reply, Wroth groaned, and, alarmed at the possibility that she might be caught admiring his nether regions, Kate gave the breeches a swift yank. Although she fell back upon the blankets, gasping from the effort, she had them at last. Scooting off the bed, she tossed the garment to the floor and refilled the bowl from the bucket of spring water Tom had reluctantly left with her.

It was a good thing her old coachman could not see her now, she thought, a bit giddily. Not only had she wrestled the clothes from a man, but she had enjoyed her view of the resulting naked form. A strained giggle bubbled in Kate's chest as she placed the cloth on Wroth's back, away from the dressing that covered the wound.

Her amusement fled when she touched the golden skin that covered his taut muscles. Languor, sweet and drugging, stole over her, gentling her hand, slowing the strokes that cooled his fever but stoked her own. The feeling was so foreign and compelling that Kate took her time, letting her fingers drift over smooth flesh and her gaze linger over ridges of hard male muscle. There was no harm in it, after all, she told herself, for he needed to be bathed, and he would remember none of this.

He was so beautiful, Kate mused, as she wiped down firm thighs dusted with dark hair. If only she could keep him... The thought startled her so that Kate dropped the cloth onto the sheet. Retrieving it from between his legs, she tossed it into the bowl, heedless of the splash.

This would not do at all. It was one thing to admire his body and treat his wounds, but Kate wanted no bond forming between her and this man. It was bad enough that she had shot him, making her feel responsible for him, and bad enough that he had kissed her, making her feel grateful to him, but she had no room for any other sentiment concerning the marquis of Wroth.

As Kate stared at him in dismay, the lethargy that had settled over him under her ministrations abruptly departed and he rolled onto his back, throwing out one long arm to reveal the dark shadow beneath. He groaned, as if protesting her decision, or at the very least the end of his bath, and his fist banged against the headboard.

"There, there," Kate said. "Stop thrashing about. Wroth!" What had he said his name was? Grayson Wescott. "Grayson. Sh, Grayson." She was leaning over him, dragging his arm back beside him, when suddenly she found herself pulled down on top of his chest. His strength, even when he was so obviously ill, was alarming, and too late Kate remembered the subtle aura of danger that clung to him.

"Oh!" she cried as she felt his fingers tangle in her curls. She pushed her palms against the damp hair that covered his broad muscles, but she was trapped, held tightly against him. Heat surrounded her, along with the heady scent of clean sheets, male sweat and…Wroth. Kate felt dizzy, disoriented, as she hovered only inches from his face. Then his lashes lifted, and the eyes that met hers were bright from fever, but surprisingly lucid. Was he awake? So stunned was she that Kate could only stare into the gray pools, her breath caught, her wits flown.

Slowly she felt his fingers tighten in her curls. "Are you trying to kill me again, pup?" he asked, as clear as day.

# Chapter Four

Grayson clutched the silky strands that clung to his fingers and wondered if he was dreaming. She had been stroking him again, but not just his brow, and there was nothing maternal about it. He had felt her unmistakable touch on his back, on his buttocks—hell, even between his legs! Yet the shocked look on her face spoke only of innocence and horror.

No dream, this was a nightmare. A nightmare of heat and sensual caresses that came to nothing but a throbbing groin, a thudding head, and the frightened face of a lovely young girl. Uttering a foul curse, Grayson fell back upon the pillows and heard her scramble away, only too eager to escape him.

She was back in a moment, trying to force some cold tea on him, when the only thing he wanted to taste was her. Pushing away the obnoxious stuff, he turned over and buried his face in a pillow that held her scent. The darkness drew him in, and he went, eager to lose himself in its depths.

Even the nightmare was preferable to a reality such as this.

* * *

Tom hitched his trousers and walked into the empty kitchen, his stomach growling at the lack of breakfast smells. Usually Kate was already up baking bread long before now. And there was always a little something ready for him. Where was she?

Abruptly he remembered where she had been when he left her last night, and he hurried toward the servant's stairway, taking the worn steps as fast as his aged legs could carry him. He didn't even stop at Kate's door, but went straight to her father's old room and walked in, without bothering to knock.

His fears, vague and formless, faded away as soon as he saw her. She was asleep in a chair beside the bed, curled up like a kitten, her dark curls tangled, her lovely face serene. The smile that formed at the sight of her disappeared when he glanced at the man stretched facefirst out on the bed. Barely covered by a pile of blankets, the fellow was a sprawling mass of hard muscle.

He didn't look like any marquis.

Tom's eyes narrowed at the broad expanse of naked male back while he contemplated a quick trip to London. If he couldn't take this gent with him, then maybe he could at least put his ear to the street and see what he could hear about the real Wroth. Yes, he thought, scratching the stubble on his chin, after breakfast he would do just that. But meanwhile, his belly was rumbling, and since he didn't want to disturb Kate, he backed out of the room, pulling the door shut silently behind him.

In a few minutes, he was down in the kitchen, lighting a blaze in the big fireplace and slicing some

of yesterday's bread for toast. Lucy liked hers just
so, with a dab of butter and jam. And if she didn't
get it, they would all suffer.

He had just poured the tea when she arrived, a
vision in one of her mama's dresses that she had
reworked into a new style. Not that he knew what
was what with ladies' gowns, but Lucy always
looked lovely, even if she spoiled the effect with her
manners sometimes. Like now.

"Where's Kate?" she asked in a petulant voice.

"Up tending His Lordship."

Lucy frowned. "Really, you would think that man
was more important to her than her own family. See
how she is neglecting us?"

Tom grinned at her inclusion of him among those
of her exalted heritage, but hid his amusement from
her. She would not like to be reminded that she had
just adopted a coachman. He placed her plate before
her, and was rewarded with one of her beautiful
smiles.

"Oh, bless you, Tom!"

He brushed off the careless compliment as he sat
down to join her. Although the eggs he had fetched
from the henhouse were cooked as well as he could
manage, they were not as tasty as any of Kate's
dishes, and his thoughts drifted back to the girl upstairs.

"She's got that wounded-pup look again," he
muttered between bites.

"Who?" Lucy asked, absently, as she reached for
her cup.

"Why, Katie, of course!"

Glancing over at him with some surprise, Lucy drew herself up regally. "Katie may not be a great beauty, but at no time has she ever resembled a canine."

"No! Katie don't look like a dog. She has that expression she gets whenever she brings home one of her injured curs, or a bird with a broken wing, or that one-eyed cat." Tom shuddered and looked around, half expecting the mention of the feline to conjure up the creature. The furry devil was well-known to steal your supper when you weren't looking.

Once convinced the cat was not lurking about, he turned his attention back to Lucy. "You know how she must take in every sorry creature that she comes across."

Lucy assumed a thoughtful expression, then frowned slightly, as if the effort had pained her. "Well, I suppose he is rather like all her pets, in that he is hurt, but she will nurse him back to health and then he shall be on his way." She lifted a pale hand and dismissed the stranger with a languid wave.

Tom paused over a mouthful of eggs. "I don't think it will be that easy, Miss Lucy."

"Whyever not?"

Tom laid down his fork. "Remember how she looked when that pigeon flew away? And that lamb with the bad leg disappeared?" At Lucy's reluctant nod, he continued. "Well, this fellow is a lot bigger than any of those dumb animals. What do you think she'll do when he takes off?"

"Rejoice, as I will!" Lucy said, not bothering to

hide her distaste for the gent. "Really, it is not at all the thing to have a strange man recuperating in Papa's room, and when he is sufficiently recovered, Kate will demand his departure!"

Tom shook his head. "No, I tell you, a man's a bit different from a dog or a bird. What if she gets attached to him? What happens then, when he up and leaves her?"

"I am sure I don't know what you are suggesting, Tom," Lucy said, obviously bored with a conversation that did not focus upon her. Having finished her breakfast, she pushed her plate aside and rose to her feet. "But I refuse to worry my head about Kate. She always knows what she is doing."

Tom let her leave the dishes to him without a protest, but he could not agree with her assessment of the situation. As usual, Lucy could not see farther than her nose; nor could she be bothered with any problems. But Tom could feel trouble brewing, could feel it in his bones. He had known it the moment he set eyes on the big fellow that Kate had shot.

"Whatever happens, it won't be pretty. I can tell you that," he muttered to himself. "Not pretty at all."

Kate bathed him again. Sliding her cool cloth along his hot skin, she tried to suppress the guilty warmth that spread through her at the feel of him beneath her fingers. It was a vain effort, as was her attempt to keep one eye on his face, just in case he suddenly roused to awareness, for her attention was ever diverted by the muscles bunching under her touch.

So engrossed was she in her task that when the door opened, she started, snatching up the cloth furtively as she turned to greet Tom, who stood frowning near the threshold. He took a few steps into the room to survey the scene and then scowled disapprovingly at the man in the bed. "Ye gods, Katie, let me put a nightshirt on the fellow, at least. It isn't seemly for him to be lying there half-naked, and you caring for him."

Glancing down swiftly, Kate was relieved to see that the covers were neatly pulled up to Grayson's waist. She had washed and hung out his breeches earlier, but obviously Tom had not seen them—or he would be complaining about more than the marquis's bare chest.

She pulled herself upright. "And just who is going to tend to him, if I do not?" she asked, unmoved by Tom's frown.

He glanced at Grayson's bronzed torso and mumbled something about the man not looking like a marquis. Then he turned back toward Kate. "I will," he offered glumly.

Kate snorted. "I can imagine that easily enough. You would have the man drowning and the mattress ruined in no time. No, Tom. He is my responsibility, and I will see to him." Realizing that her fingers had tightened possessively around the cloth in her hand, Kate purposely released them, dropping the soft material into the nearby bucket of springwater.

"Well, if you can tear yourself away from the lad

for a moment, I have something that needs discussing," Tom said, grudgingly giving way on the issue of Grayson's treatment.

Kate's relief at his capitulation was brief, for she recognized all too well the gruff tone in his voice that bespoke ill news. Her heart, already burdened by so much, sank anew. What more could she face? What more could they all manage? Drawing a deep breath, she forcibly shored up her flagging spirits and nodded slowly. And with one last look at the man in the bed, she followed Tom through the doorway.

Lucy was waiting in the drawing room. It was her habit to prepare tea for these little talks, just as though they were enjoying nothing more than a pleasant social visit. Of course, Kate had to admit that Lucy's contribution to the exchange was normally limited to the refreshments.

Once she had taken her seat, Kate received her cup and saucer and hid a smile at Tom's desperate attempt to balance the delicate china on his knee. Then she thanked Lucy for her preparations and, without delay, glanced toward Tom, who had called this session.

"I went to London this morning, after finishing my breakfast," he said grimly, and panic flared in Kate's breast at his words. Why had he gone without telling her? And what had he learned? Were the Bow Street runners after her even now? *Murderess!* Kate's fingers trembled as she sought to control herself. She would need her wits about her now, more than ever, and she drew a deep, steadying breath as she listened to the coachman.

"I sniffed around our man's neighborhood, and I can tell you one thing. He's Wroth all right." His disgruntled admission caught Kate by surprise. Of course the man was Wroth! She had had no doubt of it, really, since the moment she faced him in his study.

"He is not!" Lucy argued. Kate turned toward her sister, who was tossing her auburn curls indignantly. "I have told you before! That old, ugly fellow upstairs in not my Wroth!"

Poor Lucy. For once, Kate could see through the haughty surface to the wounded woman who refused to believe the truth. Although never the bloodthirsty type, Kate fervently wished that she had managed to shoot the real culprit—the man who had so cruelly deceived her sister—instead of the innocent marquis.

"The gent in your papa's bed is Wroth, Lucy, and you must accept it," Tom said, gently. "I asked around, and there is already some concern about his whereabouts. Although he's gone off for days before on a gambling streak, some of his staff are worried that he's sent no word after two nights, especially since he was last seen heading home from one of those fashionable balls."

"A coincidence, nothing more!" Lucy protested. "That proves nothing."

Tom silenced her with a look and continued. "He sent his driver on and walked, which has a few people fearing that he was attacked by footpads, but most scoff at the idea of anyone daring to take on Wroth. Apparently the man has quite a reputation for being able to handle himself," Tom said, pausing to eye Kate meaningfully.

She flushed. Of course Grayson was dangerous. Tom had no idea just how much. "Go on," she said evenly.

"Then there's the business about the gloves. A few of the servants think he actually was home, since his gloves were inside, but no one knows for sure if those were the pair he was wearing when he set out. Seems as if there's a bit of confusion, because the staff had been let off for the night after a little celebration. It was his birthday, you see."

His birthday. Kate wanted to squeeze her eyes shut against the news. Resolutely, she kept them open, but she refused to look at Tom. "How old is he?"

"Thirty-two," Tom answered in a surprised tone.

Kate watched as a light drizzle began to tap on the window pane. Thirty-two. He was exactly ten years older than she, and far more experienced with titles, power, life...and kisses. But he was not aged. No, not as ancient as Lucy would claim. "Well, at least there is no trail to us."

"No, not as I could gather," Tom said, and Kate nodded with relief at their reprieve.

"But I don't understand," Lucy protested. "I tell you the man is not Wroth! Why do you persist in pretending that he is?"

Tom turned to her, his grizzled face wearing a tender expression. "I saw his portrait, Lucy. He's Wroth, which means your fellow isn't."

"How can that be—?" she cried. Her voice rose, loud and high, before breaking in confusion, and

Kate flinched. As annoying as Lucy's petulance sometimes was, Kate did not like to see it stripped away, leaving her sister naked and vulnerable.

"I don't know, Lucy," she said, her throat suddenly thick with emotion. "We can only guess at his reasoning. Whether to hide his true identity or to play at being what he was not, your gentleman lied about his name."

"No!" Lucy stood, her hand at her throat. "No! He is rich and famous and powerful, and he is coming back for me. You'll see! You will both see!" she promised, before rushing from the room in tears.

Kate watched her leave, then glanced at Tom, who was shaking his head sadly. Although Kate knew he expected her to go after her sister, she did not have the heart for it. And right now, she had more pressing concerns than Lucy's disappointment. The real Wroth was gravely ill, and she must return to him.

The thought made her rise suddenly, and if Kate felt more connected to the man lying upstairs than she did to her own flesh and blood, she was reluctant to admit it.

Grayson tossed and turned for three more days, lost in the grip of a fever that Kate did not know how to ease. She neglected her duties, snapped at Lucy and Tom and rarely left the side of the bed where her victim thrashed and groaned. She forced him to drink, bathed him and soothed him as best she could, but now, as the evening set on the fifth day since she had boldly climbed through his study window, Kate felt exhausted, physically and emotionally.

It was the latter that dismayed her. Lucy was the sensitive one. She was the sister who was prone to vapors, who wore her feelings like a banner for all to see, soaring from the heights of excitement to the depths of despair so swiftly that Kate could only blink in amazement.

Kate, on the other hand, was the quiet one. Calm and capable Kate. Strong and sensible, she was the sister counted upon to think things through, to arrange and execute whatever needed to be done. The past few years had been a struggle, but she had managed—until now. Even her foolish confrontation with Grayson had seemed like a practical solution at the time. They needed money, and the father of Lucy's child, by rights, ought to help them. Perhaps she had taken some pleasure in intimidating the man into the bargain, but she had never intended to hurt him.

For once, her carefully laid plans had gone awry. Not only had she crossed the wrong man, but she had wounded him, besides. And now, unable to help him, she felt overwhelmed with despair at the loss. It was an emotion so deep and painful as to confuse her.

Kate told herself that her grief stemmed from her own culpability. After all, if not for her, he would not be here, suffering so. Yet she knew it was more than that. Despite the briefness of their encounters and the terseness of their few conversations, she felt something for the marquis of Wroth that went beyond her responsibility and his powerful effect on her senses. She felt as if she had been waiting all her life for him to arrive.

And it scared her to death.

Even if he survived, the elegant, powerful Grayson had no place in her existence, other than to destroy it. Kate shivered, as if she might break apart from the excess of sensibilities. *Overwrought.* How often had she used that word to describe Lucy? And now it fitted her—a witless, helpless mass of nerves.

Kate felt a hot pressure behind her eyes and blinked angrily. She had not cried since her mother's death so many years ago. Nothing, *nothing,* had made her give in since, and she was not about to start now. But when she looked at Grayson's handsome face, pale and drawn, his vivid strength sapped, she dropped her head and wept.

Kate cried for all the times in the past that she had not, for all the hopes and plans of the Courtlands that had come to naught, and for the man before her, who was so much more than anything she had ever known. She wept silently, the tears coursing down her cheeks and clogging her throat until she turned her face and snuffled. She might have remained there, spent, but for the soft tickle of hair that was not her own.

Gad, she had laid her cheek against his chest! Kate sniffed abruptly, both horrified and comforted by her strange berth, for even after days and nights in the throes of a fever, Grayson still emanated strength and power. The sensation of safety, of protection, was so strong that Kate let herself drift in it. How long was it since she had counted upon anyone but herself?

She smiled, imagining the great force of the marquis of Wroth behind her, surrounding her, keeping her close.

As if lost in a dream, Kate slowly rubbed her cheek against the fine dusting of dark hair that pressed against her. Dampened by her tears, it felt soft and slick, but did not disguise the hard muscles beneath. Drawing a deep breath, she took in his scent, underlying the smell of sweat and bed linens, and knew a heady longing such as she had never felt before.

"Is this some new torture?"

Kate jerked up her head so swiftly that her sight blurred. She blinked, not daring to move, as Grayson's face came into focus, his eyes clear and one dark brow gently cocked in question. Or was it amusement? Kate blushed scarlet and hopped back into her seat by the bed.

"I was...uh, listening for your heartbeat. You've been very ill."

"Well, I'm not dead yet," he said dryly. And Kate wondered just how a man who had been sick for days managed to keep his aplomb. Did nothing daunt him? Did he ever doubt himself, in the long, quiet hours of the night? "But perhaps you had better check again. It seems to have accelerated alarmingly."

Kate eyed him skeptically, noting the ever-so-slight curve of his lips. Was he laughing at her? She tried to look detached as she laid a palm against his forehead. It was cool. Blessedly cool, at last.

"Your fever's broken!"

"That one, at least," he whispered. He seemed to

lean into her hand, and Kate could not resist stroking a strand of dark hair from his forehead. For one long moment, her eyes locked with his, and she felt the drugging warmth that came with touching him. It seeped into her bones, threatening to steal her wits, as she stared, fascinated, into his gray eyes, eyes that were alive with a wealth of knowledge and experience. Thirty-two years of it, to be exact.

Kate sat back abruptly, pulling her fingers from his skin and tearing her gaze away. It lighted upon the teapot. "Here. Have some of the tea I brewed you. It is a restorative from my mother's recipe."

He lifted his brows at that, but obediently took a drink from the cup she held out to his mouth. Obedient? Grayson? Kate nearly laughed at her misjudgment. This man would do nothing but what pleased him, and Kate could not help envying that kind of enlightened selfishness. It was something she could never indulge in.

But she indulged in an altogether different luxury as she watched his lips close over the rim, reminding her of the way they had taken hers. She blinked, trying to force away the sweet, hot image, but then she found herself entranced by the muscles in his throat as he swallowed.

This was madness! She had never been one to prevaricate or hide herself. That was Lucy's venue. Hers was the direct gaze, the clear truth, and yet she found her eyes faltering, her hand trembling as it held the fragile china. Her attention dipped lower, but the hairy, muscled expanse of chest that was so close to her was just as disconcerting. Heat rose in her cheeks, swamping her limbs and clogging her throat, as she stared at one dark male nipple.

"That is all I can manage at present."

Startled to hear him speak, Kate glanced up at his face. He had leaned his head back against the pillows, his thick lashes hiding his eyes, but the slight smile that played upon his firm lips left her wondering if there was some hidden meaning to his words.

The subtle threat was there, destroying her pleasure at his well-being, for with his recovery came a host of problems, not the least of which was Grayson himself. One of the things she had heard about the great marquis was that one did not cross him. His revenge was always swift and sure and merciless. Ruthless, Kate had heard him called, and she shivered, imagining the strength that had drawn her so compellingly being used against her.

What would he do to someone who had had the temerity to shoot him, albeit accidentally? And how could she defend herself—and them all—when he was back on his feet?

# Chapter Five

Grayson closed his eyes, suddenly exhausted from the simple effort of drinking her obnoxious brew. He was tired, deathly tired, but he was not accustomed to sleeping in front of an audience. It smacked of a vulnerability that he did not care to embrace.

He had never been vulnerable.

Grayson drew in a long, slow breath, waiting for some sound of her departure. He fully expected her to go. There was no need for her to stay, because he obviously was not going to die. Not now, anyway. But she did not leave. Instead, he heard her sink back down into the chair by his bed, the sweet perfume of female warmth wafting over him, along with a gentle hint of mint.

He could order her from the room. He was used to commanding. Unlike some of his peers, he wore the mantle easily. He never drank to excess, never ate too much or let lust rule him. Sometimes he gambled a little recklessly, and he had been known as a daredevil in his youth, but his mind had never been fogged or his body weakened—until now.

It was a strange feeling, this loss of his own abilities. He did not like it, and yet, he did not feel as threatened as he might have expected because she was here.

The pup who had shot him.

That ought not to comfort him, he thought wryly, but he accepted her little tale of mistaken identity. More than that, he believed the stark regret apparent in those amazing eyes of hers. How could he distrust a woman who woke him by weeping all over his chest? And hers had not been the delicate tears of a lady feigning distress. Hers had been the deep, soulful cries of someone hurting, and he had wanted to heal her wounds, assuage that ache, solve every last one of her problems. But he could barely sit up.

Frustration roused his senses, and he lifted his lashes to study her, only to find that she was warily watching him, too. Was she afraid? No. He had a feeling that not much frightened her, yet there was a strange spark in her lovely eyes. If not fear, then what? Passion?

The notion brought back his dreams of her—half lucid, half crazed offerings of an eroticism like nothing he had known before. Cool caresses. Fevered desire. They all swirled together in hazy memory, but when he looked at her now, simple and prim in a worn sprigged-muslin gown, Grayson knew they could have no basis in reality.

And yet...the stirring in his lower anatomy reminded him that he was completely naked. Who had stripped him and cared for him? He knew it had been her, but he asked anyway. "You have been tending me?"

She nodded. A blush stole up her cheeks, bringing life and color to her pale face, but she met his gaze directly. This one would not refuse a challenge, he thought, vaguely excited by the notion. At least one part of his body seemed unaffected by his injury or his illness, and although the thought heartened him, it was a bit inconvenient. He slid one knee upward, hiding the evidence as best he could.

"Why?" he asked bluntly.

"There was no one else," she answered, just as plainly.

The mysteries that surrounded her loomed before him once more. Who was she? What was she, this girl with the serious demeanor and the courtesan's hands? Some figment of his imagination, perhaps? Had he conjured her out of his own restless ennui? She looked nothing like Charlotte, with her small frame and boyish body, but she shone with a purity that knifed into his soul. Strength. Honesty. Intelligence.

Grayson drew a ragged breath and closed his eyes against such fancies. Obviously he was not yet in his right mind. Rest. He needed rest, and although he had never even fallen asleep in the presence of anyone, not even any of his long line of mistresses, perhaps he would relax, just this once.

Kate heard a loud thump and, balancing the tray she held in one hand, she pushed open the door to her father's bedroom, her heart in her throat. To her relief, Grayson was not lying in a heap on the floor, as she had feared, but was sitting on the edge of the bed, obviously intending to rise.

"What are you doing?" she cried, rushing forward to place his breakfast on the nearby table.

"I cannot stay in this bed one moment longer," he replied, in an arrogant tone that dared her to refute him.

"Well, you certainly cannot leave it!" Kate said. "Just yesterday you were consumed by fever!"

"And today I am not," he said, his gray eyes boring into her.

Kate refused to let him intimidate her. "You must regain your strength. Look, I've brought you something to eat."

"More gruel?" he asked, cocking one dark brow disdainfully.

"No," she shot back. "Bread and milk, and a bit of stew."

*"Milk?"*

"Yes, milk," she said, putting her hands on her hips. "I suppose you would prefer brandy or champagne?"

"Well, I certainly will not drink milk. I am not some swaddling babe for you to nurse!"

Kate glanced down the length of him. He had put on one of her father's nightshirts, but it barely hung to his knees and she could see the muscled calves below and his bare feet, finely boned and arched. Suddenly, she was swamped by the memory of touching those feet, of running her fingers over those toes, and her cheeks blazed.

He need not prove his manhood to her; she was all too much aware of it. Forcibly Kate jerked her attention back to his face, certain that she would see a sardonic gleam in his eyes, but they held no amusement. Their cool gray color belied the fire that leapt in their depths, sending heat stealing through her limbs until she felt weak. Kate turned abruptly, physically breaking away from the gaze that so enthralled her, and busied herself with his tray.

"You cannot keep me here forever, you know." Kate's hands stilled, his words slicing through her like a knife, and she sucked in a sharp breath, glad her face was hidden from him. Naturally he wanted to leave. She had always known he would, but the impatience in his voice still hurt. After all, she had spent nearly a week caring for him, tending his every need and worrying that he might die. She blinked, annoyed at herself for feeling anything for the arrogant nobleman.

"I must get on my feet in order to take care of myself."

Kate heard his frustration, but said nothing. Disdainful, domineering ass! She stared at the milk, wishing she could force it down his ungrateful throat.

"Damn it, pup, I have to use the chamber pot!"

Kate whirled on him then. "And just who do you think managed that when you were sick?"

His features hardened into a harsh mask, while his eyes blazed fury, and Kate took a step back, suddenly aware of all the strength and power that was leashed, temporarily, by his recent illness. The dark stubble of unshaven beard on his face made him look less like a marquis and more like a very dangerous man. He would be a formidable foe, and she wished she could call back her hasty admission. He was not one to ask for help or appreciate it when given, no matter what the circumstances.

"I remember you touching me," he said, his voice as cutting as a blade. "Do you want to do the honors again…or do you only fondle unconscious men?"

Kate felt her face flame, and she pushed away from the table so violently that the breakfast tray rattled. Striding to the door as quickly as was possible without relinquishing her dignity, she damned the skirts that hindered her. She wished for her old trousers and her old life—before Grayson had appeared to complicate everything.

At the threshold, she turned. "Fall flat on your face, then," she said, managing to keep both her expression and her tone cool. "I've picked you up for the last time." The well-aimed taunt failed to prick him, however, for Grayson neither cursed nor scowled. He simply lifted those dark brows, and she wondered how he could look so damned smug wearing nothing but her papa's old nightshirt.

Kate did not slam the door, but went straight to her own room and tugged off the faded, tight gown, to replace it with a pair of old trousers, a shirt and a soft waistcoat. She was through playing the maid for that arrogant beast!

Marching down to the kitchens, she began to make some long-overdue bread, taking her anger out on the fat lumps of dough. If Grayson was well enough to get about, he was well enough to leave! He could go this afternoon, she told herself, denying the ache that formed in her chest. Instead, she pounded the dough more fiercely, startling Cyclops, the one-eyed cat, away from his spot by the fireplace.

Kate straightened then, astonished by her own heat. She was the quiet one. Calm, capable Kate. She never lost her temper! And as soon as she recognized that, her fury ebbed away. She was being foolish, undone by the irritating presence of Grayson and exhausted by her efforts to heal him.

Now he was well, and she had best be rid of him. Perhaps Tom could return him to London tonight, she mused. The darkness might keep him from divining their location, and he would never be able to connect the three of them to Hargate. Kate frowned. Although it sounded logical, she suspected that blindfolding the canny lord would not help. He could probably smell his way, if he wanted.

Kate felt the drag of discouragement and shoved it aside, along with her worries over her part in Grayson's illness. Obviously, the marquis wanted nothing more than to get away from them. If they were lucky, once gone he would not pursue the matter—especially with a magistrate.

Kate took his dinner up to him only because she knew Lucy would not do it, and Tom... Well, the way Tom had been acting—like a mongrel marking his territory—it would be just as easy to do it herself. She arranged the slices of fresh bread, meat pie and cherry tart on the plate. It had been good to bake, she thought with a firm nod. She felt better than she had in days, and she was determined not to let Grayson ruin her mood.

He was abed when she entered, but not asleep, for she quickly caught his gaze, clear and assessing. Those sharp gray eyes missed nothing, she realized, swallowing at the daunting knowledge.

"Here is your dinner," she said, putting the tray down on the bed. "After you've finished, I'm sure Tom would be happy to take you back to London." There. She had said it. Let him leap for joy now. She moved to the table, unwilling to see his relief.

"I'm not going anywhere."

Startled, Kate glanced over her shoulder to find him watching her with his usual composure. "I told you that I do not intend to leave until I ferret out the scoundrel who used my name."

So he had said, but that had been before... Kate looked down at the remains of the breakfast tray, stubbornly refusing to feel anything. "But you said you would not...be kept here forever."

"I meant confined to the bed, pup."

The richness of his voice seeped into Kate's bones, warming some part of her that she had not known was cold. Declining to melt, she straightened her spine determinedly. "Don't call me that."

"What? Pup? Poppet, then," he said, and she turned her head to look at him. His lips were curved into a hint of a smile, but she could see no trace of his infamous disdain. "I do not like being bound to the bed, or even to the room," he explained, gesturing to encompass his prison. "I have never been ill before, and I cannot say I care for it."

Kate felt her own mouth twitch in reply. This was all the apology she would get, but she would take it. Hiding her pleasure, she reached out for the breakfast glass and found it empty. She swiveled toward him. "What did you do with the milk?"

He lifted a brow. "What do you think?"

She put a hand on her hip. "I imagine you tossed it out the window."

His lips curled just enough to warm her insides. "What a poor opinion you hold of me! I drank it."

"You what?"

"I drank it. I grew thirsty, and suspected that you would not bring me anything else until it was gone."

"What a poor opinion you hold of me," she echoed. He grinned, and the effect was astounding. Surely even Lucy could not deny the beauty of the man when he revealed that expanse of straight white teeth. Staring numbly, Kate watched his gaze drop.

"What the devil are you wearing?" he asked.

Kate flushed, remembering her trousers. When she put them on, she had been angry and out of sorts. Now she found she did not want to face his contempt. "I have work to do," she said brusquely.

"What kind of work?"

"I keep busy," she said.

"That's no answer."

"It doesn't matter. These clothes make it easier to get about. I like them." She knew her cheeks were bright with color, but she kept her chin up, and her gaze level with his.

"I like them, too." His voice seemed to deepen, flowing over her like rich chocolate, and Kate felt the touch of his eyes everywhere. She swallowed. Apparently she had been wrong to suspect he would disapprove, for he never behaved as one would expect. "I'm surprised your father allows you to wear them," he added.

"My father is dead."

"Your brother, then."

"I have no brother."

"You must have a guardian."

Kate stiffened. "That I do, but he does not care what I wear." For all her uncle cared, they could be languishing in rags, but Kate had already said too much. She recognized the spark of interest that flared in Grayson's eyes, and purposefully relaxed her stance. The man was trying to pry information from her! "Eat your dinner," she said roughly.

"Only if you join me."

"I already ate."

"Stay with me, then. I'm infernally bored. Do you have a deck of cards? Perhaps we could play."

He looked so hopeful that Kate could not deny him. "All right. I'll fetch some."

"Books, too?"

Kate nodded. "What shall you have?"

"You choose for me." Although he spoke casually, Kate sensed that nothing about the man was casual. *Calculating* would be a far more accurate description, for behind the cool countenance was a keen mind that would rival anyone's. But what could he expect to gain from a few volumes out of her father's library?

Kate sucked in a sharp breath as she recognized

his game. She would have to make sure that there were no plates or personal notations in the books she brought him, or he would discover her identity all too easily. In spite of herself, Kate smiled at his cleverness. She would enjoy crossing swords with the marquis—as long as he did not draw blood.

She turned to go, and Grayson let his gaze slide over her slowly. She had a nice, slim figure that was not as boyish as he had first thought. He liked the way her dress had tightened across her breasts when she put her hands on her hips, and he missed the view, now that they were covered up by a shirt and a waistcoat. Still, he had to admit that the trousers were appealing, too, for they clung to her legs, not tight enough to be too wicked, but not loose enough to hide anything.

He watched her leave, his attention focused on the gentle curve of her buttocks encased in the soft material, and he wanted to haul her back into the room and onto the bed with him. "Damn," he murmured, surprised by the force of his reaction. Obviously it had been too long since he had enjoyed the charms of a female.

Leaning his head back, Grayson tried to remember, but he could not recall exactly when or with whom he had last been intimate. Clarice? Lady Ann? He had released his last mistress after the onset of his ennui, but had never replaced her, relying instead on the eager ladies of his acquaintance to satisfy his needs. Their faceless bodies melted together in his mind, not nearly as intriguing as the slender figure of the poppet.

She was a clever thing, too. Courageous and clever, but possessing none of the artifice of the bored London females. His body stirred, and Grayson lifted his knee, wondering if the unusual reaction was due to his prone position. Perhaps once he got back on his feet, Kate would no longer arouse him. Logic told him that would probably be the case, but, oddly enough, he hoped it was not.

She returned, carrying a stack of books that she placed beside the bed, and Grayson found himself staring at her hair as she knelt near him. A deep, rich brown, it gleamed. Fresh. Beckoning. Grayson's mouth curled at his own fancies. The sober Miss Kate would hardly welcome his advances...or would she? She had come to life in his arms when he pinned her against the door, only a few days ago.

Yes, he thought with a smile, there was passion in her, the kind that had made her stand before him, pistol raised, to avenge her sister, and the kind that had made her touch him when she thought he would not know. Grayson's body stiffened at the knowledge, and for the first time in his life, he faced the prospect of wanting something even he, the rich and powerful marquis of Wroth, could not have. It fired his determination to discover her identity, for that was the only way to be certain that she was unavailable.

She glanced up at him then, and Grayson let her see his desire. It shook her, although he suspected she had no idea what, exactly, he wanted of her. He might not know her name or her circumstances, but she was innocent, Grayson was sure of that. And despite her absurd costume, she was well-bred. Normally, such traits would put her out of his reach, for, as he had sworn to her before, he did not seduce young virgins.

And yet, if she was a poor relation, a governess or some other member of the house staff, he could press his suit without compunction. Kate would have security and comfort and money enough to aid her sister, while he would have a new mistress to rival any of those past. Heat shot through him at the notion, and the clear violet eyes that had held his faltered before it. Then she straightened abruptly and tossed the cards on the blanket, beside his hand.

Oh, she possessed passion, his little poppet, but she was smart enough to avoid it! Grayson's lips curled in amused appreciation as he reached for the deck. "Piquet?" he asked, shuffling the cards easily.

She blinked, as if dazed, and Grayson smiled, pleased by her reaction to him. Although she might not acknowledge it, the poppet was definitely attracted to him. She did not simper or flirt like most women, but flushed angrily when he caught her admiring him. A most intriguing reaction, Grayson thought, dealing out the cards as though she had consented to play. When he noticed her gaze on his hands, he paused to draw in a low breath. If she kept that up, it was going to be a very uncomfortable game—for him. Grayson shifted his knee, to better disguise the erection that strained at the blankets.

"Shall we play for guineas?" he asked, hoping to

divert her attention. Although he had never reached the limits of his legendary control, he had a feeling that Kate could test them mightily.

"No."

"Pennies?"

"No. I will not play for money," she said. She lifted her head to eye him with calm defiance. "I do not approve of gambling."

Grayson smiled at her pretense of propriety, for he had already found out what he wanted to know. She had no money, that much was obvious. But what of her background? "Should I worry that your guardian will take offense at our little game?" he asked, picking up his cards.

Innocent that she was, she missed the subtle nuance that a more experienced woman would have parlayed into a flirtation. Instead, she stared at him, her lips a firm line. "Tom thinks we would be ill-advised to tell you anything more."

Clever girl that she was, Kate had easily divined his intent. He felt both proud of her and challenged, as he had not been in years. "Tom?" he said contemptuously. "You trust his judgment?"

She wavered only for a moment before fixing him with the clear, direct gaze that so appealed to him. "Perhaps not, but how do I know you will not turn me over to the magistrate and cheer while I hang?"

The question startled him so much that Grayson barked out a laugh, but Kate's expression remained somber. "You cannot think that I would like to see you swing," he said, incredulous. She did not flinch, but held his eyes with her own, as if seeking the truth in them.

Grayson felt oddly shaken—and annoyed—by her distrust. "I assure you that I have no desire to snuff out your extraordinary existence," he said, lifting a brow disdainfully.

His words seemed to puzzle her. "I shot you."

"Quite accidentally, I recall," Grayson replied. "I was there, you might remember."

She flushed and nodded, but said nothing. Suddenly, Grayson wanted to shake her out of her calm, courageous pose. She did not trust him! Considering that she was the one who had put a bullet in him and dragged him here, Grayson found that a bit astonishing. And grating.

His eyes narrowing slightly, he studied her, wondering just how he could gain her confidence. Although her head was held high, he noticed the rapid rise and fall of her chest and recognized the wariness riding just below the surface. Damn! Grayson felt like grabbing her and dragging her down on top of him, dissolving her doubts in the heat that flared between them.

He did not. Without knowing who she was, he could not touch her, and she seemed determined not to tell him. Frustration surged through him. He was not accustomed to being denied, and he did not care for it.

"Very well," he said, feigning indifference. "Believe what you will, poppet, but you have been wrong before about me."

Grayson saw the flicker of surprise in her lovely

eyes and leaned back, watching her from under lowered lashes. He was used to getting what he wanted, and the little poppet would be no exception.

In political circles, he was known for both his thoroughness and his tenacity. Ruthless, some people called him, but he simply did not suffer fools or delays easily. And, although he was sometimes forced to compromise, he never gave way. Grayson's lips curved slightly as he contemplated his newest adversary. Poor Kate had no idea just how far she was out of her depth.

When he was through with her, Grayson would have not only her name, but the passion that raged inside her, as well. The little poppet would be his, body and soul.

# Chapter Six

Grayson slipped out of bed and tested his legs. Better. Stretching untried muscles, he walked to the window and looked out. The late-afternoon sun was glinting from behind the last of the rain clouds, creating an eerie brightness on the green lawn below. Taking a deep breath of the country air, summer-warm but refreshing, he was reminded of Kate.

He missed her.

Odd that, but Grayson put it down to his forced imprisonment. Even one's jailer looked good after a while, and Kate was not ugly or stupid. Rusty at first, she had soon given him several good hands at cards, while he regaled her with London gossip.

He had even coaxed a laugh from her, and had basked in its glow like a boy with a sweetmeat. Kate was too somber, too burdened by God knew what. Grayson rubbed his smooth chin thoughtfully. He would soon find out. After innumerable games of piquet, she had found him some shaving things and left him to his own resources, but he did not intend to linger here.

Stirring from the window, Grayson searched for his clothes, relieved to find them hanging neatly in the wardrobe. Obviously there were servants somewhere, for they had cleaned and returned his garments.

Grayson took his time dressing. There was no need to hurry, and he had no intention of pushing himself too hard. He wanted out of the damned room, not another sentence of bed rest. When he finally tugged on his boots, he looked down at himself with wry amusement. His valet would have a hemorrhage if he could see the mended and poorly ironed shirt that graced the famous marquis of Wroth. Although Grayson was by no means a dandy, he was accustomed to the finest of materials, superbly tailored to his frame, and he found that it irked him to look less than his best, especially for the poppet.

Grayson smiled wryly at his own vanity, for he doubted Kate would notice. She seemed to be more interested in him when he was wearing nothing at all. Drawing in a sharp breath at that observation, Grayson forced his thoughts back to his shabby attire. Once he found out more about Kate's situation, he would have to send for some fresh clothes.

The house was silent, as usual, when Grayson left the bedroom, and he slowly descended the staircase, without seeing a soul. Pausing at the bottom, he gazed up at the ceiling and knew again a strange sense of familiarity. He had been here before.

He wandered into a large receiving room and on into what were obviously the state rooms, each one teasing at the corners of his memory. Having visited many a country home in his thirty-two years, Grayson searched for something readily identifiable, but found nothing. And saw no one.

It was eerie, really, and if Grayson had not fully recovered his wits, he might have thought it all some bizarre dream. He had hoped to find a servant to question, but his footsteps echoed forlornly, as the only sounds of life. He paused in the dining hall, staring at the mural of a fox hunt for a long time, trying to place it, to no avail.

Whoever owned the place had fallen on hard times, Grayson noted as he again saw the telltale signs of slipping fortunes: an empty side table, and a blank spot on the wall that marked a missing painting. That explained the lack of a large staff, but surely there had to be someone managing the house. In exasperation, Grayson finally sought the ground floor.

Past a buttery that looked woefully understocked, he heard noises, and the distinct aroma of simmering chicken led him to the kitchen. At first, Grayson thought the vast room empty, as well, for instead of the usual cook, his staff and the scullery maids, there was one lone figure standing at the long wooden table.

Kate. Grayson recognized the short, dark curls that teased her nape, and stared, stunned. When she had gone off to ''see to'' supper, he had never imagined that she would prepare it herself. A home this size had to employ some servants. Hell, *everyone* had a cook, except the city's poorest inhabitants. Out here in the country, it was a given. And yet, there she was, her gloveless fingers wrapped around a common potato.

Although Grayson made no sound, she suddenly turned, as if aware of his scrutiny, and her lovely face registered shock at his presence. "Grayson!" she cried, and he wondered if she was ashamed to be discovered toiling over food. "I mean...my lord..." she stammered, his address coming uneasily to her lips. "You should not be taking the stairs yet. You are not well!"

Grayson remained where he was, firmly in control of his composure, and yet he felt as if something had shifted. Whether the floor, himself or the earth beneath him, he could not decide, but the movement rocked him right down to his soul. Although not given to premonitions, he knew that his life would change forever because of this woman who was not concerned about herself or the drudgery she had undertaken, but about him, his health, his recovery. Grayson realized then that he wanted her, no matter who or what she was, and he would have her. It was that simple, and yet so complex.

She was eyeing him with a peculiar expression that told Grayson he had let the silence drag on too long between them. Yet he, who was known for his eloquent speeches, had no idea what to say. He was not prepared to share his momentous discovery, and even if he had been, it would have sounded foolish, inane, the stuff of coxcombs like Raleigh and his set. The thought made Grayson lift a brow in chagrin, and when he finally spoke, it was of more mundane matters. "I believe our singular acquaintance has given you leave to call me by name. Gray,'' he added, prompting her.

Kate's gaze lifted to his, and he saw a slow, answering heat that made him wonder if he could take her right now, right here, atop the marred face of the old table. Although his mind rebelled at such an impulsive act, his body cried its assent.

"Gray," she whispered. His name had never been invested with such innocent yearning, and Gray strained at the limits of his control. In an effort to maintain it, he eyed the blade in her grip. "I hope you are not planning to carve me up, now that I have recovered from the bullet wound."

She stared at him, as if dazed, then glanced down at the large piece of cutlery and waved it in the air. "No, I was just—"

"Get back, you bastard nobleman!" At the shout, Gray looked up in time to see Tom charging into the kitchen as if Kate's virtue were threatened. As well it was, but Gray knew that he would not have to force himself on the passionate poppet. Whatever her proper demeanor, her eyes had told him as much.

Obviously, Tom cared nothing for such subtle distinctions, for he threw himself across the room at Gray like a wild man. Despite his recent illness, the day had not arrived when Gray could not move faster than a lackwit twice his age, and he neatly stepped out of the way, just as a cat, apparently startled by the noise, leapt down from a perch above the fireplace. Hissing and spitting, the beast pounced on Tom's chest, throwing the old man backward to sprawl upon the floor.

After felling Tom, the feline shot past Kate, knocking the potato out of her hand, just as the exterior door opened to admit her sister. The cat brushed Lucy's skirts as it made its escape, and she swayed on the threshold while the potato rolled to a stop in front of her feet. A hand at her throat, she gaped at it, then at Tom, who thrashed upon the tiles, clutching his scratches and releasing a string of foul curses that impressed even Gray. Kate, meanwhile, called scolds after the departed beast, brandishing her knife like a weapon.

"Katie!" Lucy cried, in the whine that Gray was beginning to recognize. "I tell you that my poor nerves cannot bear such common behavior, such foul language. Oh, it is dreadful!"

Gray had not made his way to the heights of political power without the ability to read people swiftly and correctly. The skill had told him Kate was harmless long before she had explained it herself, and now it told him that Lucy was a spoiled miss who was concerned neither with Tom's injuries nor with a possible threat to her sister. She was centered solely upon herself.

While Kate turned to look helplessly at the man on the floor, Gray stepped from his place in the shadows. "Why aren't you helping your sister with supper?" he asked, his tone silencing the entire room.

"I...I am too delicate to be slaving away in this hot, foul place!" Lucy replied, recovering herself quickly. "I become queasy around food."

"Then you won't eat any, will you?"

"Gray." He heard Kate's voice admonishing him, but he ignored it.

Lucy, obviously heartened by her sister's support, tossed her auburn curls. "I most certainly will."

"If you want to eat, then I suggest you assist, as will I," he said. Although Lucy appeared inclined to protest, he had held his title too long to brook disobedience from anyone in his orbit. She gave him a petulant glare, but kept quiet. Satisfied, he glanced down at Tom, who was staring up at him stupidly. "And you, Tom?"

"Of course I'll help Katie. I always do!" he said, scrambling to his feet, his scratches forgotten.

"Good. Then I suggest we begin." Although Gray had no notion what went on in this kitchen or any other, he had committed himself to a task. And he never turned back. "How can I help you?" he asked Kate.

She turned to him, and he saw again the yearning in her eyes, not sexual this time, but a stark, open longing that flashed briefly and was gone, replaced by her usual composure. Gray wanted to call it back, to discover every last one of her desires and fulfill them. "Really, there is no need for you—"

Tom cut in. "The devil there ain't! If I had known you weren't the lazy wretch I supposed, I would have set you to plucking the chicken."

Masking his distaste for chicken plucking with a lift of his brow, Gray met the old man's assessing gaze with his own. There were not many who could suffer his stare for long, and Tom soon faltered, muttering something unintelligible and looking to Kate.

She was obviously used to giving instructions, for she spoke quickly and firmly. "Tom, see if there are any apples left in the pantry. Lucy, you may set the table. Gray—" She paused, but continued resolutely. "Gray, you may slice the potatoes."

"Here now, don't be giving the man a weapon!" Tom protested. But Kate paid him no heed, and with a rude noise, the old man headed from the kitchen, while Lucy went about her business with an indignant frown. Gray knew the very second he was alone with Kate once more, for all his senses seemed to sharpen in her presence.

"Here," she said, holding out the knife and a fresh vegetable. Gray looked down at her hands, surprised that he had never noticed the signs of her labor. Hers was not the pale, soft flesh of the idle. Kate's palm was pink and work-roughened, and yet he craved her touch as he had no other. When the moment stretched out between them, too long, Gray silently took the potato and quickly cut through it. He went on to the next, but she stopped him.

"You have to peel them first," she said. Her mouth tugged upward at the corners, her lovely eyes laughing, and Gray smiled at his own faux pas.

"Rather demanding mistress, aren't you?" he asked.

She laughed, and the sound was so free and fresh that Gray reveled in it before turning back to his work. It sustained him during his efforts, for although he vaguely recalled whittling something at an old gardener's knee when he was a child, he had not wielded a knife since. And he had no desire to see any more of his own blood.

When he finally had finished, he found himself as proud of the mound of slices as he would be of a particularly taxing speech. He smiled smugly until Kate presented him with a pile of carrots and onions. The former had to be washed, and the latter peeled, a foul task if ever there was one. He decided to raise the wages of every member of his kitchen staff, in London and at his country seat.

Tom, who seemed to be excessively slow completing his own business, lounged against a wall, smirking, and Gray suspected that even the dreaded chicken plucking could not be worse than chopping the oily, foul-smelling onions. He had never held the vegetable in high esteem, but even his low opinion was rapidly sinking. His nostrils flared, his eyes began to burn, and he wondered what his political cronies would think to see the all-powerful Wroth reduced to such a dreadful chore.

Those who knew him would be shocked, he mused, and Gray was forced to admit that he was vaguely alarmed himself. Kate had already shot him and put him through a fever. Now she had him plying the meanest of trades befitting a lowly scullery wench.

Although his lips curved slightly in bemusement, Gray could not be blamed if he was a little leery over what else she had in store for him.

Kate finally let herself relax when they removed to the drawing room. She had been tense ever since

Gray appeared, on his feet and offering his services, in the kitchen. She still wasn't sure what to make of his strange behavior. Although isolated from society for a long time, Kate was not such a chawbacon as to suppose that the rich and pampered members of the ton had begun assisting their servants!

Yet the marquis had done his best. At first, Kate had worried that he might cut himself, for he was obviously unaccustomed to peeling potatoes and she wanted no further injuries laid at her door. However, he soon had been wielding the blade with a speed and precision that made her think he could do anything and everything well. Her suspicion was reaffirmed when he carried platters to the hall with an careless elegance that would have put even the most punctilious footman to shame. Apparently the man could excel at any task or enter any venue, from that of a dockworker to that of a duke, and reign supreme.

Still, Kate was not entirely comfortable with his help, and she was glad when they all took their seats at the long table, the hard-won, if simple, meal before them. She had even sent Tom to fetch a bottle from the cellar. Although the marquis undoubtedly was used to much fancier food and drink, Kate enjoyed the rare treat, and sipped her wine slowly.

Now it warmed her as they moved to the drawing room, easing the strain of a situation so bizarre that she felt like laughing. Lucy did not help matters, for she presided over the company as if they were members of a country house party, when for all her fine manners she wore a made-over gown that concealed her pregnancy!

And then there was Tom, a coachman who normally would have been in the kitchen doing the dishes, but had stayed to glare daggers at their guest. Even the marquis looked a bit tattered around the edges in his damaged clothing, though he held himself with a nobility that the rest of them lacked. And finally there was Kate herself, perhaps the strangest of all, dressed in boy's garments, just as if such a costume were ordinary attire for an evening's conversation.

Only there wasn't any conversation. Kate became acutely aware of the silence soon enough, and although her duties as hostess required that she do something about it, the very thought sent a hysterical bubble upward, to lodge in the back of her throat. She coughed. She did not know what Gray was used to, but she was sure that this was not it.

Hargate's amusements were limited at best. Lucy was a competent pianist, and sometimes Kate sang along, although she could barely carry a tune, yet she could not imagine Gray being impressed. More often, they read aloud to each other from their one resource, the vast library, but lately, Lucy had pled tiredness, and Kate rose at such an hour that they retired early.

Gray, who probably caroused in London until dawn, could hardly be expected to go straight to bed, she mused. The very thought sent a sweet lethargy drifting through her body as she remembered the way he had looked just this afternoon, all tousled and handsome in her papa's nightshirt, and before, when he wore nothing at all... Flushing, Kate jerked upright, struggling against the effect of the wine and memories of Gray in a state of undress, asleep and appealing.

"I have been here before." Gray's low declaration made her start, and Kate glanced over to see him eyeing the ceiling's elaborately carved moldings curiously. Each one held a scene from Hargate's original grounds, though the landscape had certainly changed since they were created.

"Impossible!" Tom snapped, and Kate was inclined to agree. The house had not seen guests in years. Besides, she would have remembered Gray. One did not forget such a personage as the marquis of Wroth. She shivered.

No, she was reasonably certain Gray had never visited Hargate. He was probably just trying some new tack to pry information from them. Weary of the game, Kate would have willingly told him all, but she had learned to trust no one. And what, really, had she to rely on, but the man's own word and the melting heat he seemed to conjure in her belly? Ha! She nearly snorted aloud. Undoubtedly it was that same dangerous blaze that had made Lucy an unmarried mother.

"You ain't never been here, and I'll swear to that!" Tom muttered threateningly.

"Oh? And have you always held such a unique position in the household?" Gray asked, one dark brow rising slightly.

Tom flushed. "That ain't any of your business, is it now?"

Kate felt a throbbing behind her temples and realized she should never had indulged herself with the wine. Now, instead of stepping between the two men, she felt like letting them kill each other right there in the drawing room.

As if echoing her sentiments, Lucy yawned, covering her lips with a dainty white hand, and for a moment, Kate wished she could be as carefree as her younger sister. Lucy never worried about other people's tempers, or money, or where their next meal was coming from. Lucy had felt free to sample the forbidden pleasures of a man's body, and knew no guilt about it. Instead, she would soon be rewarded with a baby, a precious infant to love, but she would never bother to concern herself with how the child would be clothed and fed.

Kate started, shocked by her wayward thoughts. It was the wine, she decided. Although she had consumed only two glasses, it had been a long time since spirits were served at Hargate. Her small sips had obviously made her giddy, grumpy, out of sorts. And somehow, it was all Gray's fault.

Rising to her feet, she sent him a cool glance. "We retire early here in the country, my lord. And since you are only now recovering from a fever, I suggest you do the same."

A lift of that infamous brow told Kate that he was surprised by her words, but he only nodded. His agreement disturbed her, perhaps more than a protest would have, for she knew how imperiously he treated all and sundry.

He would always be in control, overpowering, overwhelming, and yet the knowledge, instead of dismaying her, sent tendrils of heat snaking through her body until she colored and left the room, not caring whether he followed or not.

Although Lucy rose to accompany her sister, Kate was the one Gray watched, his eyes drawn by the gentle sway of her bottom, encased in the soft material of her trousers. She was not tall, but her legs were well proportioned to her height. Slender and shapely and strong. Desire coursed through him.

"You keep away from her, you hear?"

Tom's harsh voice cooled his ardor immediately.

"Excuse me. Did you speak?" Gray asked, fixing the older man with an arrogant stare. Obviously Tom had a reckless disregard for his own safety, because Gray was in no mood to be badgered. He had been shot, abducted, and bedridden for the first time in his life. On top of all that, his increasing sexual frustration made him unusually irritable.

"I got my eye on you, and that's a fact," Tom declared.

Although Gray knew a grudging admiration for the old man's protectiveness, he could not allow such insolence to continue. He rose to his feet with a deceptively lazy grace. "I fear you will have to take your *eye* off of me, because I'm going to have a bath, and I would like as much privacy as can be obtained in the kitchen." Distaste crept into Gray's voice at the thought of such accommodations, but he needed to wash, and he had been informed that the house lacked the proper plumbing or servants for anything else.

The old man stood and scowled up at him. "Well,

don't think I'm going to help you! You can fill those buckets yourself. Toughen you up a bit," he added, his tone taunting.

Before Tom could draw another breath, Gray grabbed hold of his shirtfront and slammed him up against the wall. The old man blinked and shook his head, as if to clear it, while Gray held him fast. "And are you so certain I need...toughening up?"

Staring in amazement, Tom mutely shook his head, and Gray quickly took advantage of his silence. "Now, let us get something straight, Tom," he said in a cool tone. "You will adopt an attitude of respect toward me, not because you like me, but because it is my due. I have no desire to disrupt your unusual household or to cause Kate any grief, but if you do not treat me in an appropriate manner, I will be forced to knock you senseless." He paused to make sure that the man understood. "What shall it be?"

Tom's dark eyes flickered with something akin to awe, and he licked his lips. "Well, there's no need for any of that, now that we know where we stand and all, my lord."

"Do we?" Gray asked, his brow lifting.

Tom nodded, then shot him a shrewd glance. "Of course, my lord—as long as you don't hurt my girls."

"I assure you that I have no intention of distressing the ladies," Gray answered, releasing his grip, and Tom's feet slid back to the floor.

The old man managed to look pensive for a moment as he eyed Gray, but he eased himself away silently. "I'll just leave you to your bath and wash the dishes in the morning, then."

"You do that," Gray said, as he watched the fellow back out of the room. He waited until Tom had disappeared into the gallery, then leaned against the wall himself and released a harsh breath. Damn! He had pushed his weak body too far, but it had been worth it to establish his authority. He was no bully, but neither would he allow some lackwit to run roughshod over him. *No one* ran roughshod over him.

Gradually his breathing slowed to normal, and Gray turned his attention to his long-delayed toilette. Stepping forward, he halted abruptly as he realized no servant would be in to clear the room. With a low oath, he retrieved his wineglass and blew out most of the candles. Taking up a candelabra, he walked through the darkened rooms and down to the kitchen.

Eyeing the facilities bleakly, Gray nonetheless stoked the dying fire, found the buckets, filled them and hung them on hooks over the growing blaze. Dragging a brass tub from its place in the buttery, he positioned it near the hearth, but when he reached for the hot water, he burned his fingers.

Swearing vehemently, Gray felt like abandoning the whole business and waiting until tomorrow, when, by God, he would get some staff here, but having gone this far, he refused to forgo the pleasure of a good soak. Although he was not a fastidious man, his hair needed washing, and he did not intend to let himself go to seed, like some of his peers.

This time he managed to fill the tub without further injury, and he was soon stripped and ensconced in the hot water, a sliver of soap in hand. Gray fingered it idly. From its texture, it appeared to be homemade, and he found himself angrily contemplating the image of Kate forced to toil over a steaming vat of lye. Cursing again, Gray lifted the sliver to his nose and breathed in the faint scent of mint. Kate's.

It smelled positively delicious. Gray wondered if he could find some fine French soap with just the same fragrance. Although he was not accustomed to buying such personal items for any woman, even one of his past mistresses, he did not pause to study this sudden change in his habits. He decided to have his secretary check into the matter.

After cleansing his hair, Gray leaned back and let out a low, ragged breath. He had pushed himself too hard today. Too much standing and walking had made his weak muscles ache and his shoulder hurt. Sinking deeper, he let the heat soothe his smaller pains, but when he closed his eyes, he had another cause for discomfort.

Erotic memories of his last bath, at Kate's hands, assailed him, making his breath catch and his body tighten. As he had been half out of his mind at the time, he could not be sure what had been real and what he had conjured from his fevered imaginings, but she had washed him, of that he was certain, and the thought effectively banished the simple pleasure of the tub.

Seized with the urge to repeat the exotic ritual when he was in possession of his wits and a fully functioning body, Gray could only grind his teeth in frustration. He had never been one to keep his desires leashed, but until he discovered his temptress's identity, circumstances forced him to do so. Letting loose a low breath, Gray tried to recapture his initial enjoyment of the relaxing water, but it was useless, for he would never again think of bathing in quite the same way.

The sigh turned to a groan as Gray realized that more than one of his personal habits had undergone a change since his first meeting with Kate. Even more disturbing than that acknowledgment was his growing suspicion that nothing in his life would ever be the same again.

# Chapter Seven

Kate rolled over and stared at the ceiling. Although she had gone to bed at her customary hour, weary after a long day, she had lain awake, tossing and turning for what seemed like forever. Try as she might, sleep would not come, for whenever she closed her eyes, she was taunted by visions.

Visions of Gray.

Despite her best efforts, Kate kept seeing him sprawled in her papa's bed or arrogantly at ease in the drawing room, as if he had been born to such surroundings, as indeed he had. Worse yet was the jarring image of him in the kitchen, his coat off and his shirtsleeves rolled up to reveal the dark hairs on his arms as he had helped her and made Lucy, for once, do her part.

Releasing a low moan of irritation, Kate finally swung out of bed. Naturally she was drawn to the marquis. He was the first man to enter her life since she had grown to maturity! Not only was he rich, powerful and handsome, but he gave off a heat that seemed to melt her insides—that made her do things like return his kiss and linger over his naked body.

Kate flushed at the memory. And if all that wasn't enough, there was the way he took control—of everything. His assumption of absolute mastery was seductive, perhaps more than anything else, but it frightened her, too. The temptation to give up some of her burdens—or at least share a few of them—was very great, yet Kate knew that she dared not.

Even if she ignored the complexities of her situation and the possible repercussions of trusting anyone, she had to consider the fact that Gray might well be gone tomorrow. Or the next day. Or the next. If he actually stayed to pursue Lucy's beau, then, once finished with his task, he would be off, back to London and a world so far removed from her own that it might as well be the moon.

The knowledge shook her, deep inside, in some part of her that only Gray seemed able to touch, and Kate shuddered. The bed held no ease, so she got to her feet. Some tea, perhaps. It had comforted her since the days after her father's death, when she and Mrs. Gooding shared a pot together in the kitchen during the nights she couldn't sleep. Nights when reality bore down on her so hard that she nearly collapsed under the weight of it. Only Mrs. Gooding and a hot cup had bolstered her up, giving her the strength to face her struggles again.

Mrs. Gooding was gone, sadly, but Kate could easily brew some tea. The night was pleasant, so she did not bother to cover her old nightgown or her bare feet, but headed toward the kitchens and the companionship of a fickle one-eyed cat. But when she reached the threshold, Kate stopped, her steps halted by the flickering of firelight. Why was it burning so brightly this late at night? She told herself that Tom might be finishing up the dishes, but it was too dark for that. She blinked at the sight of a single candelabra on the worktable and moved forward, drawn by something she could not have named. And before she saw anything more, she felt it: the heat, the moisture, and the subtle aura of a male presence.

Gray was there, before the hearth, in the old brass tub, his elbows resting casually on the sides and his head thrown back. Of course, she remembered now that he had asked her about a bath, but she had never expected him to go to all this trouble. She should have, for he was nothing if not unpredictable.

Kate stood, rooted to the spot, as she took in the sight of him, burnished golden by the light, like some pagan god. His eyes were closed, and dark strands of hair fell away from his face to gleam wetly in the candle's glow. Nothing disturbed the silence but the crackle of the fire and her pounding heart. It was so loud that she wondered he did not hear it, and the thought finally moved her sluggish limbs to action. She straightened, ready to flee, but it was too late. As she watched, wide-eyed, Gray slowly turned his head, lifted his lashes and looked directly at her.

"Kate."

The way he said her name seemed to draw the very breath from her body, and she sucked in a ragged draft of air to keep her lungs working. She strove for a calm, even tone, and words that would disguise her reaction. "Don't get your dressing wet," she warned.

His lips curved just enough to show her that he thought her concern amusing. "Come wash me, Kate," he said softly.

She shook her head, her cheeks flaming at the outrageous suggestion. If he had been anyone else, she would have found her tongue and apologized for her intrusion, but he seemed to rob her of the power of speech. Like someone drunk or dazed, she could only gape at the broad expanse of his chest, remembering the feel of it beneath her fingers.

Apparently he, too, recalled those days and nights she had spent tending his body, for she saw an answering flicker in his bedroom eyes. "I've been dreaming of you, Kate, dreaming of you touching me as before," he whispered.

Kate shivered as his voice flowed over her. Deep and rich and potent, it threatened to melt her resistance even as she searched for words to deny his memory—and her own. Her lips parted and stilled, too dry to be of use. She wet them slowly with her tongue as she watched a drop of water trail down his throat and disappear into the shadowy pelt below. Overcome by a wild desire to follow it with her fingers, to taste it with her mouth, she could only stare in fascination.

"Come, join me, and I shall return your favors. Shall I bathe you, Kate?" he asked, his tone low and seductive. The very idea made her knees weak, and she grabbed at the corner of a nearby cupboard to keep her balance. For one startling instant, she imagined herself going to him, sliding her modest night-gown down her body and climbing in beside him. The warmth. The water. His hands. On her. Shaken to the core, Kate closed her eyes against the image and the lure of it. Was this how Lucy had fallen from grace? Had someone like Gray taunted her with his male beauty, melting away her good sense with his hot promises? Tempting her?

Kate's eyes flew open in swift denial, but Gray was still there, his strong body relaxed in its naked-ness, his gaze smoldering as it touched her, moving from the high neck of her nightgown downward. Her limbs grew heavy under his perusal, and her breasts felt swollen and hard, chafed by the restricting ma-terial. She longed to take it off, to free herself of all clothing, all inhibitions, all responsibilities.

But she could not.

Slowly, without taking her eyes from his, Kate shook her head again, more firmly. It was all that she could manage, for anything more might reveal just how close she had come to accepting. Not trusting herself to speak, she pressed her lips together and, with great effort, turned away from Gray and all that he offered her. Her heart still pounding from the struggle to subdue a side of herself she had not known existed, Kate fled back through the house, to the safety of her room and her duty.

Gray roused himself slowly, the memory of a dream lingering just enough to tantalize him, but gone now, beyond his reach. Unused to such elusive visions, he probed his memory, and groaned when he realized what had triggered his restless night. His bath. And Kate, virginal and erotic in a white nightgown that had revealed her beautiful bare feet and slender ankles to his curious gaze. With her wide eyes and tousled curls, she had looked like a sleepy siren, and he had wanted nothing more than to see her, all of her, naked and flushed as she joined him.

Of course, a gentleman would have begged her pardon and sent her away, and a well-bred innocent like Kate should have fled at the first sight of him. But neither of them had played his proper role, proving to Gray just how well suited they were.

Something had passed between them there in the hot darkness, something that went beyond simple wanting. Gray's body surged to life as he recalled the outline of her small, hard nipples. Dark and alluring through a veil of pristine white, they had told him her desire matched his own.

Damn! Gray sat up abruptly and swung his feet over the side of the bed. Sunlight shone in through the windows, where he had deliberately left the drapes open. He had planned to rise early, but not quite so painfully, he thought with a wry grimace. Although he usually slept past noon, as did most of his peers, today he intended to explore before anyone else was about.

He needed some answers, and, fueled by what had almost occurred in the kitchen last night, his search took on a new sense of urgency. Standing, Gray stretched, wincing as his shoulder protested. Then he eyed his only set of clothing with disgust. He did not consider himself to be abnormally fastidious, like that idiot Wycliffe, or a dandy like Raleigh, yet he found himself loath to continually don the same ragged garments.

The problem provided him with yet another highly effective incentive to solve the puzzle of this strange household. This afternoon, he decided, he would send word to his valet for clothes, perhaps even a servant or two, or know a good reason why not. His patience was running thin, and he had no desire whatsoever to pluck his first fowl.

Slipping from the room, Gray headed toward the stairway. The silence that met his descent was familiar now, the lack of footmen no longer unusual. In the spacious foyer below, he paused to let himself out, closing the massive front doors quietly behind him.

The morning was pleasant, the verdant green of the landscape the only sign of the past few days' rain. Slowly descending the wide steps, Gray followed the drive until it angled off toward the stables and a myriad of outbuildings, then strode across the grass. It was a little too long to be fashionable, and he wondered how the devil the three members of the household kept up with the outside work.

Although someone obviously tended the area, Gray could see signs of neglect in the bushes that needed to be trimmed and the undergrowth that encroached upon the lawn. Too bad, for these once had been very attractive grounds, if the paintings in the drawing room were any indication. Those images had struck him as so familiar that he knew a view of the outside would place them. Now a far distance from the house, Gray turned and lifted his gaze to the mass of stone.

Hargate. He recognized it at once, although it had been many long years since his first visit. Gray stood still, letting his thoughts return to a time when he was ten or eleven. His parents had still been alive, and summers had been filled with endless traveling from one great home to the next, parties and laughter.

They had come to Hargate to celebrate the birth of the earl of Chester's first child, and Gray had been infernally bored for much of the stay, due to the lack of companions his own age. With the jaundiced eye of maturity, he recalled his pompous claim to an adulthood that would all too quickly be thrust upon him.

Searching his memory, Gray tried to picture the earl and saw an older, white-haired man. There had been whispers that he had married beneath him, but Gray had liked the countess, with her bright eyes and dark curls. Once, he had come upon her rocking the baby, and she had let him hold the infant. Smiling to himself, he recalled the warm and milky smell and the awe he had felt at such a tiny being. The little one had looked like her mama, with a thatch of soft, deep brown hair…

Kate. Gray drew in a breath as the realization struck him that he had held the poppet in his arms before. The discovery startled him, though it should not have. After all, having grown up among the titled and privileged, he had played with some of the country's reigning matrons. Still, the knowledge that he had greeted her so soon after her arrival and put her, alone of all the babies he would see, to his heart, seemed prophetic, somehow.

Gray's mouth twisted at such strange musings, and he shook off the odd mood, concentrating instead on Kate's history. The earl and his wife had seemed much like his own parents, wealthy and comfortable and happy together. Obviously there had been another child, the disagreeable Lucy, but then what had happened?

Ton gossip had held little interest for a youth, and then his own life had taken such a turn that he was occupied with too much else to wonder about one of so many acquaintances. Gray knew only that the earl had died several years ago, leaving the title in abeyance. What of the man's wife and daughters? Kate had mentioned a guardian, but where was he? Whoever it was ought to be horsewhipped for burying two lovely young girls in the country without a chaperone or servants, to fend for themselves like peasants.

It was unconscionable. When he wrote his valet, he would send a note round to his secretary, as well, with instructions to do some discreet investigating into the matter. Gray's jaw tightened at the thought of meeting whoever was responsible for Kate's veritable servitude. Meanwhile, he found himself anxious to hear her version of events, if only she could be induced to trust him.

Of course, with the discovery of their bloodlines came the knowledge that neither Kate nor Lucy could play consort to any man. One simply did not make an earl's daughter a mistress. Therefore, Gray must not only find the man who had ruined Lucy, but must

arrange her marriage, as well. And, as for her sister...
Gray smiled slowly. He already had plans for Kate.

Heading back toward the house, Gray sought the
study, where he helped himself to paper, pen and ink.
His directions to his secretary were clear and concise.
He had no idea whether his absence had caused concern or not, but he did not want the country up in
arms over his whereabouts.

Gray paused, his hand poised to continue, at the
thought that no one might even miss his presence.
Indeed, beyond his servants and a few close friends,
who would care? His loss would be felt throughout
the political arena, but personally? His lips curled
contemptuously at such maudlin musings.

Resting his palm against the foolscap, Gray contemplated the sum of his achievements. He took his
responsibilities seriously and executed his duties
well. He always had. He had held the title and all he
had inherited and had profited from his own investments. Perhaps he enjoyed less leisure time than his
peers, but he did not want for good food, good wine,
good company, or the pleasure of women. What
more could a man ask of life?

Nothing, he told himself firmly, and yet, he had
the distinct feeling that he had missed something,
some elemental mystery that idiots like Wycliffe had
discovered. Absurd! He took a deep, steadying breath
to gather his wits about him, and began writing in
his distinctive, elegant hand.

A separate note to his valet followed, with explicit
instructions. Gray wanted to send for his entire staff,
but without more details on the situation at Hargate,

he thought it best to wait. In the meantime, perhaps he could at least bring on a cook, to spare himself the dreaded fowl stripping.

Once finished, Gray folded one paper inside the other and sealed it, pressing his heavy signet ring into a dab of wax to ensure delivery. He had found the stub of wax in the desk drawer after some effort, for the girls obviously did not do much corresponding with the outside world. It angered him, the way they were cut off from everyone, like social pariahs, prey to smooth-talking seducers.

Although Gray could not picture the hardheaded Kate succumbing to honeyed words, there were many unscrupulous men who would not wait for agreement from a woman alone, especially one clad in breeches. The danger she was in—had been in for God alone knew how long—made his temper flare, and he looked down to find his hand balled into a fist.

For a moment, Gray stared at it, as if the white knuckles belonged to someone else. His acquaintances would be surprised to find him so stirred, for he preferred to keep a level head. But when he considered what might have happened to the innocent... The fist banged down upon the desk, rattling both the ink jar and his composure.

Drawing in a deep, steadying breath, Gray deliberately flexed his fingers. Shuddering at his own lapse, Gray blamed his wound and the illness that had followed. Telling himself that he had not yet fully recovered, he ignored the mocking inner voice that wondered if he ever would.

When sufficiently composed once more, Gray

went to find Kate. He did not have to go far, for the aroma of baking bread led him to the kitchen, where she was busy making breakfast. The sight of her there, working over the hot hearth in worn trousers, produced a violent response in the depths of his being, and so he spoke more sharply than he intended. "I want you to hire some help from the nearest village. Chesterton, is it not?"

Tom made a choking sound over his food, while Kate turned to gape at him. "You know," she said dully. Her face was flushed, but whether it was from the fire, surprise, or the memory of their meeting the night before, Gray could not tell.

"Know what? That this is Hargate, and that you, the daughter of the earl of Chester, are reduced to little more than a scullery maid? Yes, I know, and I should like to discover who is responsible."

Tom and Kate both stared at him, silently, with stubborn, angry eyes, and Gray cursed himself, the master of political finesse, for blundering so badly. He could not help it, for the very thought of Kate's gentle hands hard at work made him lose all sense of perspective.

"We get along," Kate said, turning away from him, her back stiff and straight. She had pride, and Gray had pricked it. He wanted to apologize. Damn! He wanted to kiss her and make it better. But most of all he wanted to shake the truth from her, so that he could avenge himself upon her alleged guardian.

Alarming. Positively alarming, this excess of emotion. Gray let out a low breath and seated himself at the table. Perhaps it would be best to concentrate on the most pressing problem first. "Yes, you do very well," he admitted smoothly as Kate placed before him a plate piled high with eggs and fat sausages and fresh slices of toast.

"Hmm. Wonderfully well," he said, the delightful aroma making him realize just how hungry he had grown. "However, a little help does not seem amiss. I will take care of the expense," he added. Before Kate could protest, he turned to Tom, who was gaping at him, his food unattended. "I have some messages for you to deliver to my town house today."

The old man shut his mouth and gave Gray an assessing look. "And just how do I know you aren't going to call in the authorities because of the little nick Katie gave you?"

Gray lifted his brows as he picked up his fork. "That little nick is more like a good-size hole in my shoulder, but Kate and I both know it was an accident. And unless you plan on murdering me outright, you had better let me contact my staff. Although I've been known to disappear into the hells before, on a gambling bent, sooner or later someone's going to wonder where I am. The longer you delay, the more hue and cry there will be, and I'm sure you do not want to draw unnecessary attention to the earl's daughters."

The implicit threat stilled any further protest from Tom, and Gray turned to Kate as she seated herself at the worn table. "How did you know?" she asked quietly. She neither burst into tears nor flew into a temper, and Gray realized just how much he admired her poise. Despite her size, she was strong. And sensible. And beautiful.

"As I told you, I have been here before," he said. "When I went out this morning, I recognized the north face at once."

Tom's snort of disbelief made him shoot a swift warning glance at the older man. Obviously Tom had forgotten the understanding they had reached the night before. "Did you say something?" Gray asked coolly.

With a glum scowl, the old man shook his head, and Gray looked back to Kate, waiting until she lifted her incredible eyes to his before speaking. "We were here to celebrate your birth," he said softly. He wanted to say more, to describe the baby she had been, to reveal the history that lay between them, but Tom was watching.

For her part, Kate appeared neither surprised nor pleased by the information. She simply nodded as if the news were just another burden to add to those already weighing down her delicate shoulders. Her lack of faith disappointed him, and Gray found himself annoyed by her closed expression. Did she think so little of him?

There was a fine line between keeping her dignity and shutting him out, and though aware of it, Gray nonetheless chafed at that boundary. His jaw tightened, and he might have spoken injudiciously again, if Lucy had not chosen that moment to come wandering into the room. Obviously, she had just risen and had not lifted a finger to prepare the breakfast she served to herself.

One look at her told Gray that despite whatever misfortunes had befallen the Courtlands, Lucy still managed to play the part of an earl's daughter. Unfortunately, she had turned her own sister into a drudge to do it, and that knowledge put a damper on Gray's appetite.

Absurdly irritated by her languid pose, he felt like lurching across the table to throttle the stupid chit. Instead, he clutched his fork and tried to come to terms with this unusual temperament. He had argued for hours with lackwits in the government and never lost his head. What the devil was the matter with him?

"So you will be leaving now."

Kate's low comment pricked Gray further. Was she that eager to be rid of him? The females of the ton long ago had learned not to throw themselves at his feet, for such behavior only earned his contempt. He preferred to be the aggressor, or at least to be on the receiving end of a more subtle approach to his bed. Never, however, had his attentions been rebuffed, even in his youth. He was not accustomed to being denied, and he did not like it.

"I am not leaving until I find out who has been using my name," Gray said, with surprising vehemence. In actuality, he did not have to see to the business personally. He could have a Bow Street runner investigate or put his unlimited resources of money and manpower to work finding the culprit, but he had already rejected those options. Even the most highly paid and discreet searcher might let something slip, and Gray did not want news of this imposter to get out. He had a position to uphold, and he had no intention of letting some country lout make a laughingstock of him.

Still, he did not have to stay at Hargate when he had a hunting box nearby. As Gray recalled, it was small, but well-appointed, and he could have a staff at the ready in but a few days. The idea was appealing, but he rejected it, as well, for he did not want to alert his prey. Better to remain hidden here at Hargate, he thought. His decision, he told himself, was purely logical, and had nothing to do with his reluctance to leave the poppet alone with none but a surly old bastard and a spoiled shrew.

Lost in his own musings, Gray suddenly realized that Lucy was sniffing delicately over her breakfast plate. "What the devil is the matter with you?" he snapped. Unaccustomed to weepy females gracing his table, he still might have spoken more gently, if the woman in question had been anyone but this vain creature.

She glared at him with blue eyes that were but a pale imitation of her sister's. "You cannot stay! I will not allow it!"

Gray heard Kate's soft admonishment, but ignored it. "Pardon me, but I would think you would like me to discover the identity of your child's father," he said.

Lucy gasped and stood, a picture of feminine distress. "And then what?" she cried. "What happens when you find him? You'll clap him in irons. You'll hang my beloved!" Then she burst into tears and rushed to the door, leaving it standing open as she raced into the garden.

The silence that followed her departure was almost palpable, and Gray saw Tom and Kate exchange helpless looks before turning toward him. Tom's expression was blackly accusing, while Kate's held a mixture of exasperation and censure that made his jaw tighten. Swearing silently, he realized that he really had no choice.

With one last look at his mostly untouched meal, Gray got to his feet and went after the brat.

# Chapter Eight

Gray had seen such dramatics before, of course. London was full of spoiled young misses and matrons, some with real problems caused by husbands, lovers or gambling debts. Once in a while, he stepped in to pay off some vowels, but he was not the sort of man to give comfort, and women did not seek it from him. They knew better.

Struggling against his growing annoyance, Gray made his way to a tall alder, under which the tearful girl was ensconced on a stone bench. He told himself it was the first step in his investigation. She was distraught, and he could use that to his advantage as he pried the truth from her. Cool and calculating, as usual, he told himself his actions had nothing to do with the look on Kate's face or how he would like to remove one of her many burdens from her delicate shoulders.

He approached slowly, and when the brat did not acknowledge his presence, Gray took a seat beside her. "I assure you that I have no intention of putting your *beloved* to death," he said.

"So you say!"

"Yes, so I say," Gray repeated. Then he deliberately softened his tone. "Suppose you tell me exactly what happened."

She had her back to him, and she sniffed softly. "What will you do to him?"

He smiled cynically. "I will make sure that he does not use my name again," he answered, without letting on exactly how he would accomplish that. Of course, a dead man could not don a disguise, but the fellow might have other uses. "And I would do my best to see that he marries you," Gray added, *providing he does not have a wife and five children already.*

Lucy whirled to face him. "He will not need to be forced! We would be wed already, if not for some mishap that has prevented his return," she said, her voice breaking. "Something has happened to tear him away from me, I know it!"

"Then let me help," Gray coaxed. She succumbed, nodding reluctantly as she dabbed at her eyes. For one so stricken with grief, they were remarkably clear, and Gray wondered just how much of her outbursts was theatrics, designed to gain attention.

She lowered her eyes and frowned daintily. "You cannot know what it has been like here since Papa died."

"Tell me," Gray urged.

Lucy lifted her damp lashes in a move calculated to gain his sympathy, not knowing that he was notorious for his very lack of that commodity. "Oh, it has been positively horrid, locked up here, seeing no one, having nothing! I could not bear it!''

"You have your sister," Gray pointed out.

"Kate! She has no care for fancy dresses or balls or handsome beaux! She doesn't mind working like a servant, cleaning and baking until her hands are ruined.'' Gray could have argued that point, but he restrained himself. Lucy was talking now, and he did not want to halt her confessions with the reminder that Kate, being the eldest, had no choice but to take care of her. She had done so, too, without complaint, and, apparently, with little enough reward.

As if sensing his disagreement, Lucy pouted prettily. "Oh, nothing bothers Kate! She is invulnerable, I assure you, but I am possessed of more delicate sensibilities. I could not stand such a harsh existence, so I began walking farther and farther afield, trying to escape my…prison! And then, one day, he came upon me in the woods.''

Gray remained silent, hoping for clues to the imposter's identity, as Lucy continued. "He said he had a hunting box nearby and…that I was the most beautiful thing he had ever seen. We began to meet daily.''

"Where?''

She looked blank for a moment, then frowned, as if annoyed at the interruption. "The woods, I told you!''

"So you never actually entered the hunting box.''

"No!'' Lucy said, as if shocked by the suggestion. "He did not want the servants to talk, but there was an abandoned cottage nearby, and we...often went there."

At least the house had not been broken into, but the lout had seduced an earl's daughter in some old hut, as if she were a common strumpet! Gray's jaw tightened. Although he cared little enough for Lucy, he could not countenance such treatment, and by God, he would like to get his hands on the man responsible.

Still, he kept his face carefully neutral as he fished for more information. "And then?"

Lucy had the good grace to blush and look away. "And then I began to suspect my...condition. When I broke the news to him, he seemed startled, but he was just as kind as always," she hastened to assure Gray. "He told me not to worry, yet I could see that he was concerned. I think he was worried about my guardian," she said, her voice low and angry.

"And who is that?" Gray asked, willing her to respond.

She did, with a vehemence that surprised him. "Uncle Jasper!"

"Your mother's brother?" Gray guessed, since no one had assumed the title. She nodded. "And where is he?"

"Who knows? Vienna? Rome? We have never seen him! He leaves addresses, and Kate writes, but he rarely answers."

"What of your solicitors?"

Lucy shrugged. "Kate went to see them after Papa died, but Uncle stands guardian until we marry." He saw her eyes narrow slightly. "I knew even

Wroth…or rather, my beloved…would never gain permission. I wanted to elope, but he said that he would not hear of it. He did not want to damage my reputation," she added, in a voice that dared Gray to disagree. Then she lifted her chin in a gesture that revealed her resemblance to Kate. "And now, I fear that Jasper has done some mischief to come between us."

Gray's jaw tightened. Jasper had already been up to plenty of mischief. It sounded as though he had taken the girls' inheritance and left them with nothing but a house that required an immense amount of upkeep. Obviously, it was entailed, or he probably would have sold it right from beneath their feet, Gray thought grimly.

His musings were interrupted by his companion, who chose that moment to burst into tears again. She fell upon his chest, and Gray absently lifted a hand to her shoulder, while he anticipated his first meeting with the infamous Uncle.

"Hush. I will take care of Jasper. Now tell me what your young man looks like," Gray urged.

Lucy sniffed. "He is young and handsome, with light brown hair and blue eyes, and he is not at all cruel, like some I could name."

"Describe what you mean by 'not cruel,'" Gray said dryly.

"He does not have your insufferable arrogance, nor does he talk to me in a way that makes me feel inferior," she replied, pulling away to glare at him through wet lashes.

As she spoke, Gray began to form a suspicion

about this estimable fellow that made his lips curve wryly.

"Don't you dare laugh at me!" Lucy snapped. "Oh, I don't care what you think! I hate you!"

Far from being insulted, Gray contemplated the ungrateful little chit with a lift of his brow. "Oh?"

"Yes! I hate you!" she cried. "Because you are not *him!* You have ruined everything." She sobbed. "You have destroyed the last of my illusions."

Gray drew in a sharp breath. He would never have expected to hear such honesty and insight from her pink, sulky mouth. He studied her anew, as she bent her head, her auburn curls falling forward to hide her face, her hands coming up to cover the sounds of genuine sobs. Maybe Lucy was more like her sister than he thought. Maybe not.

Whatever her disposition, he was bound to help her find her missing man, for her sake and his own. Gray frowned at the thought, for if his suspicions were correct, by the time he was through, Lucy would have even more cause to despise him.

Kate stared at the door for a long time. She wasn't sure what was more astonishing: that the marquis of Wroth had gone after Lucy, or that she had let him. But she stayed where she was, frozen in place, secretly relieved to have one fewer onerous task.

"Bloody high-handed bastard," Tom grumbled.

"Yes," Kate agreed softly. A smile tugged at the corners of her mouth, for she had grown to like Gray's imperiousness. His haughty stare, his very arrogance, had begun to appeal to her. *Come, bathe me, Kate.* The memory of those words, and his heavy-lidded gaze, made her blush. Even the soft request had sounded like a command, and she, who never took orders from anyone, had nearly obeyed. Kate shivered, forcing such thoughts aside when she noticed Tom eyeing her sourly.

"You aren't going to let him go after her, are you?"

Kate almost flinched at the harsh accusation. She was so weary of doing everything, of being looked to for each decision. What harm was there in letting Gray tend to Lucy? And yet, wasn't this the very thing that she had feared? Already she was giving ground to Gray's strength, Kate realized, with something akin to panic. It would be so easy to let him take charge of the household and of herself, but then what? She shuddered at the consequences, knowing she could not give in to temptation.

"He'll do more harm than good!" Tom warned.

The coachman was right, of course. Gray was hardly one to cater to Lucy's wayward moods; he was more likely to terrify than to soothe her. Forcing herself to think of her sister, Kate straightened her shoulders and rose to her feet. Although she had no desire to spend an exhausting hour petting Lucy, she had no choice. It seemed as if she had never had any.

Making her way through the garden, Kate noticed its neglect and mentally cataloged the slew of chores that awaited her. She would never get them all finished before autumn, and the knowledge threatened to weigh down her already heavy mood. She brushed it off, telling herself instead to welcome the sun that had finally decided to show itself.

Blinking in the light, Kate saw Gray and Lucy seated together on the bench under the old alder, and she climbed the gentle slope toward them. Her steps slowed, however, when she watched Lucy throw herself against Gray. His arms closed around her, and Kate stopped dead at the sight of the intimate embrace. For a long moment, she simply stared, too stunned to make sense of the scene.

To her knowledge, there was only one reason for a man to hold a woman, and she knew from personal experience that Gray's appetites in that direction had not been hampered by his recent injury and illness. Hadn't he tried, just last night, to coax her into his bath? Kate's cheeks flamed at the no-longer-pleasant memory. Had he really desired her, or had she simply been handy, a convenient receptacle for his lust?

Kate recoiled from the suspicion so violently that she swayed on her feet, but it made far too much sense for her to ignore. Nor could she deny what she was seeing with her own eyes, a truth that she should have recognized long before now.

Of course he would want Lucy.

Lucy was beautiful and fine. She had pale, soft skin and lovely clothes. She did not wear a boy's garments or ruin her hands or tire herself with menial work. She was always fresh and delicately perfumed. Gray would be able to smell her, for her hair was tucked beneath his chin, and his mouth was moving as he murmured some endearment.

He was touching her, his gloveless fingers gliding

along her shoulder, and Kate felt the breath leave her lungs. Her chest hurt, and she struggled for air, taking deep gulps to compose herself. Finally, she wrenched her gaze away, telling herself that the little scene she had just witnessed did not matter at all.

Just as *he* did not matter. Tom had been right all along. Noblemen were anything but noble, and this one, although adept at disguising his base nature, was no better than the rest of them. She had been fooled, but was none the worse for it, only wiser. Like so much else in her life, Gray was beyond her control, and Kate could hardly fault his judgment.

Of course he would want Lucy.

Tom found the servant's entrance easily enough, and knocked loudly on the door, annoyed at having to play errand boy for the high-and-mighty Wroth. *Gray,* Katie called him, Tom thought with a snort of disgust. The man had wormed his way into their household, right enough, and if Katie didn't watch out, he would worm his way right under her skirts, or breeches, as it were.

And all the man's fancy assurances be damned! Muttering a curse, Tom banged again, more forcefully. He didn't care what the fellow said, he had eyes in his head. He could see well enough, and he saw the way the marquis looked at Kate—like a starving man contemplating his next meal! For all the nobleman's cool disdain, he wanted Katie, and Tom was going to make sure he didn't get her, even if it took his last breath. As well it might, he thought

grimly, remembering the way the man had slammed
him up against the drawing room wall.

Tom shook his head. He never would have imagined a lord could be so fierce, but this one was known
to be dangerous. You didn't cross Wroth, or you
lived to regret it, they said, and Tom was already
ruing the day he had let Katie climb into the marquis's study. Aye, he was regretting aplenty.

"May I help you?" Tom jerked his attention to a
heavyset female who stood where the door had been,
wiping her hands on a wide apron.

"I got a message from His Lordship. It's for his
valet, a Mr. Badcock," Tom muttered.

"You have something from Wroth, you say?" the
woman asked him excitedly.

At his nod, she drew him inside through a hallway
and into a large kitchen area, where various servants
were taking their dinner. "We have news!" she
cried, happily, and everyone surged to their feet, talking at once.

"Joan, fetch Badcock!" she called out.

A petite servant girl shouted, "Yes, Meg," and
rushed off without hesitation. Then the large woman,
whom he deduced was called Meg, pushed him down
onto a long bench, insisting that he join them. Glancing down at the startling array of food, Tom eyed
her in confusion.

"What are you doing, emptying the larder while
Wroth's away?"

Meg laughed, as if he had made a fine jest, and
slapped him on the back so hard that he nearly fell
forward into a plate someone had shoved in front of

him. Since it had been a long time since he saw such bounty, Tom eagerly helped himself to some cold mutton and kidney pie, while Meg thrust scones and tarts at him, too.

By the time Mr. Badcock arrived, Tom's mouth was full. Digging into his pocket for Wroth's letter, he handed it over without a word. He refused to squirm as the valet looked down his long nose at the message. Gad, but the fancy-dressed, stiff-backed servant looked more like a lord than Wroth did!

The valet read the missive without response, as far as Tom could tell. It was hard to judge from his expressionless face. He called out for a footman to deliver a note to "His Lordship's secretary," then turned toward Tom. "Wait here," he said, in an arrogant tone that set Tom's back up. If it weren't for the food piled high on his plate, he would have refused—just for the hell of it. Instead, he nodded carelessly and continued eating, his eyes narrowing when the snooty fellow took Meg with him.

Once those two were gone, the remaining servants peppered Tom with questions, but he shook his head. He wasn't about to get Lucy and Katie into trouble by revealing Wroth's whereabouts to a bunch of gossipmongers.

"He's well, though?" a footman asked, with a fierceness that forced Tom to answer, and he grunted an affirmative, nearly choking when the man praised God for that good fortune.

Puzzled, Tom glanced around at the grinning faces, listening to the speculation that the master had got himself into some deep gambling, was planning some shrewd political move or had finally fallen in love. Abruptly Tom wondered if their interest in Wroth went beyond that of most employees. They didn't actually like the man, did they?

The thought put him off his food, and he slowed his pace. He did not stop eating, but he enjoyed it less, as he watched the people around him talk happily about Wroth. Damn the man's hide! He could ruin a fellow's appetite even when he wasn't around.

His stomach full, Tom pushed his plate away just as Meg returned, snapping orders at several of the girls apparently under her charge. Obviously, the woman had other things on her mind than a visiting coachman. Tom frowned and rose to his feet. Heading toward the hallway, he nearly collided with the valet, followed by some footmen with trunks. "Load these onto the...gentlemen's conveyance," the snotty fellow said.

"Now, hold on a moment. What's all that?" Tom protested, following the group out the door.

"His Lordship requested his personal effects," the valet answered.

Two trunks' worth? Tom scowled, but let them strap the infernal things to the old coach. He climbed up to his seat as Meg hurried forward with more boxes.

"Meg, is your daughter still looking for a seamstress position?" the valet asked.

"Yes, Mr. Badcock, indeed she is," the woman said, all smiles.

"Then we shall endeavor to take her with us."

"Oh, thank you, Mr. Badcock! God bless you and

His Lordship!'' she said, before trotting back into the town house.

Tom nearly fell off his box. "What's this?" he shouted down at the valet.

The manservant looked up at him with a bored expression that made Tom want to throttle him. "We shall go directly to Mrs. Leeds's lodgings in Little Man Row. She is one of Meg's daughters, a seamstress by trade, and can advise us in our purchases."

"What purchases?"

"Why, the bolts of cloth that the marquis requested."

Tom gaped, growing more confused by the minute. "Don't Wroth have enough clothes in those trunks?" he asked. Badcock only eyed him blankly. "Are you telling me that the girl is supposed to sew some more for him?"

"Certainly not!" Badcock replied. "His Lordship's garments are made by the very finest of tailors."

Tom's hands itched to close around the fellow's stiff neck. "Then what the hell are we buying?"

"The material we are to purchase is for two young ladies it has not been my pleasure yet to meet. Mrs. Leeds will be in charge of dressmaking for them."

"Now just wait a minute there, Noddycock!" Tom shouted.

"Badcock."

"I don't care what your name is, I don't have any orders to take a female back with me!" Tom protested.

"Of course you do," Badcock replied, tapping a

finger on Wroth's letter. "His Lordship specifically requested that I bring a seamstress with me."

"With *you!* And just where are you going?"

"To attend the marquis, my good man," the valet answered. Before Tom could protest, Meg returned, wearing a battered hat and carrying a large satchel. At first, Tom thought she had only brought out some food for the journey, but Badcock helped her into the coach. "Now, let us be off!" he called as he joined her inside.

Tom listened to the door close and ground his teeth. He didn't take orders from Wroth, or his snooty manservant! He was his own man, and he and the girls had done just fine for years without His High-and-Mightiness's interference. Why, he ought to climb down from his box and toss that fancy-pants out into the street! The more Tom considered it, the more he liked that notion. The only thing that stopped him was the thought of Kate in her old, worn-out trousers, and Lucy in those made-over gowns.

And then there was Meg. Tom could still taste the large woman's excellent cooking. There was no doubt that she would be an asset to the household, even if just for a while. As long as Tom kept an eye on Wroth, what harm could come from a few extra servants?

Snorting at his own misgivings, Tom snapped the reins, but he had the distinct impression that his regrets concerning the marquis were only beginning.

Gray rose to meet the returning coach, smiling at Badcock's shocked assessment of his person and the irrepressible Meg's squeal of greeting. Both the cook and the valet had been with him for years, and Gray knew he could count upon their loyal service. Once Badcock had recovered from the sight of his master in less-than-perfect attire, he introduced a young woman as Meg's daughter, Mrs. Leeds.

"Oh, my lord, call me Ellen, please," she said. "I am so grateful for the work! It's been hard since Jimmy died and all. Me mum is always singing your praises, so I'm thrilled to be doing whatever I can for you. And wait until you see the lovely things we brought!"

She turned to drag a bolt of cloth from the coach. It was a violet silk that would set off Kate's eyes to perfection, and Gray reached out to finger the texture. Oh, yes. It would do nicely. He pictured the poppet draped in nothing but the smooth material, and his pulse quickened. "Thank you," he said, taking the bolt in hand. "I'll let Tom show you to your quarters."

Ignoring the coachman's black scowl, Gray nodded to his servants and headed into the house in search of Kate. She had kept to herself since this morning, and he found himself eager for her company. Although he had never taken much interest in women's fashions, he wanted to see her in new clothes: low-cut silks, lacy chemises, and smooth stockings with ruffled garters. Dressing and undressing for him.

Gray's lips were curved into a wry smile by the time he reached the kitchen. He paused on the threshold, surprised by the jolt of awareness that shot through him when he saw her. His desire for her was becoming more pronounced. Indeed, he had never known such want as this slip of a girl inspired in him, and he was hard-pressed to keep himself in check. His gaze wandered from the brush of her curls against her nape down her slim back, to the tantalizing curve of her buttocks, and anticipation seized him. His colleagues had always praised his patience, but right now Gray did not know how much longer he could wait.

As if sensing his presence, Kate turned slightly, but barely glanced at him. "Tom has returned," Gray said, carefully controlling his reactions.

"Good."

"My valet, Badcock, is here, along with my London cook and a young widow who—"

She raised her head at that, and although her face revealed nothing, Gray saw the flash of anger in her eyes. "We cannot afford to feed extra mouths."

Gray lifted a brow, surprised at her vehemence. "I'll send Tom into the village to buy provisions. Of course, since they are my responsibility, I'll see to the expense."

"Oh, you will, will you?" She seemed almost belligerent.

"Yes, I will."

"Can't you live without your valet?" she asked, scornfully.

"I believe I have proved that I can, but I would rather not," Gray replied.

"And the girl? What service does she provide that you cannot do without?" Kate taunted.

Gray's eyes narrowed. "She is here to make a new wardrobe for you and your sister," he said, tossing the bolt on the table. It unraveled like a river of violets across the worn surface, but Kate barely spared it a glance.

"I don't need any of your fancy gowns!" she snapped.

"What the devil's gotten into you?"

"Nothing's gotten into me. Maybe I just prefer my own clothes," she said, lifting her chin, and Gray wondered if he had pricked her pride again. Surely she would not prefer her rags to new garments? He had thought her sensible, but he was having his doubts, as she fixed him with a cool stare.

"And just what kind of payment are you expecting for these gifts?" she asked. "Perhaps you think because Lucy is already ruined, she is a prime target for your lusts, but I will not allow you to use her further."

For a moment, Gray was so stunned that he simply eyed her in amazement. Then he threw back his head and laughed. She watched him with a determined expression that told him she would fight to the death for her sister's weathered honor, and Gray's amusement fled. He was proud of her, so strong and righteous in her indignation—even if it was misplaced. "I assure you that I have no interest in Lucy," he said.

She eyed him warily, and Gray wondered how he

would ever earn her trust. "I saw you this morning in the garden," she said.

Gray lifted a brow in contempt. "From the accusatory looks you and your coachman gave me, I thought it my duty to soothe your sister's ruffled feathers. What you saw was my untutored attempts at comfort, but I will gladly refrain from approaching her ever again." He paused to smile wickedly. "Especially if it makes you jealous."

Shaking her head in denial, Kate stepped back, but her thighs came up against the edge of the table and Gray moved forward, bearding her with his gaze. "This talk of Lucy is nonsense," he muttered. "I think we both know where my lusts, as you so quaintly put it, are focused."

Her eyes widened, and Gray tilted her chin upward, his fingers sliding to rest over the rapid beat of her pulse. Gently stroking the smooth skin, he watched her eyes turn dazed and warm and her lashes drift downward, proving his case. Then he lowered his mouth. Brushing his lips against hers softly, he sought to banish all thoughts of her sister and mark her as his own.

That was all he intended, but Kate insisted upon more. He felt her arms slide around his neck, pulling him down to her, and he smiled against her mouth, pleased at her response. The feel of her tentative kiss robbed him of his good humor, however, and he met her lips eagerly, urging her to open for him. When she did, all hell broke loose, as his tongue plunged inside.

Gray usually had more finesse, and he was vaguely

conscious of his lack of restraint. He was an excellent lover, skilled and patient, but when Kate moved up on her toes, pushing her breasts into his chest, his control was tested to its limits. He slid a hand down her back to cup her buttocks and lift her upward so that his erection pressed into the very heart of her. Her startled sigh only heightened an excitement that was almost foreign in its intensity.

"Yes, poppet," he murmured. "Put your legs around me."

He helped her, lifting thighs encased in soft material, stroking, sliding, and anchoring them at his back, and then she was against him, tight, and he felt as if his head were spinning, his wits scattered, his whole being throbbing with want for her. Without thinking, Gray laid her down upon the table, on the cloth that had spilled from its bolt. Her arms were limp at her sides, her short, dark curls had fallen away from her face, and she blinked at him with eyes heavy with desire. Her lips were moist and parted, her slender legs spread wide for him.

Right here. Right now, Gray thought. His breathing had escaped his usual mastery, and he could hear it, loud and ragged, while the blood rushed past his ears, urging him on. Right here. Right now. He could pull down her breeches, open his own and be inside her, her maidenhead be damned. Exhaling harshly, Gray placed his hands on her thighs, caressing them lightly, and then he brought her up hard against him. She sighed, her eyes drifting shut, and his fingers tightened their hold, his control straining as he rubbed himself against her. Here. Now.

Just as he thought he might burst, Gray heard a low, startled sound from across the room. His head snapped around in time to see Badcock standing in the doorway with a carefully blank expression on his face. "Having an early supper, my lord?" he asked.

Slowly, as if groping his way out of a fog, Gray removed his hands from Kate's thighs and helped her to a sitting position. His body did not care for this course, and he drew in a sharp breath as it was deprived of her warmth. Although still painfully hard, he stepped back, away from her, and managed to speak.

"No, Badcock, just trying out the cloth you brought along. Good choice," he said coolly, though he felt aflame.

"Just so, my lord," the valet answered as Kate slid from the table and fled. Helplessly, Gray watched her go, while the realization of what he had nearly done sank in. He had been ready to take Kate's virginity in the common kitchen, where anyone might come upon them, and, indeed, he might have, if it had not been for Badcock's interruption.

Stunned, Gray glanced back at his impassive valet, unsure whether to thank the man or kill him.

# *Chapter Nine*

Gray watched as Kate excused herself from the breakfast table, irked that she refused to look at him. He could follow her, of course, but he had learned that the most successful negotiations were conducted after tempers were allowed to cool, and Kate's was still burning brightly. In fact, she had been treating him like a leper ever since yesterday, when he had nearly taken her maidenhead on the kitchen table. Obviously, she was not the sort to enjoy such public behavior.

But, then, neither was he.

He was not sure what had possessed him, but he was immensely relieved that Badcock had interrupted before things went any further. He was also keenly aware of the good fortune that had caused his valet, and not the protective Tom, to come upon the scene. Had the irate coachman been there, Gray's pleasure might have been halted by a carving knife buried in his back. He probably would never have felt it, either, considering the state he was in. The memory made him uncomfortable in more ways than one, and he shifted in his seat.

The movement drew Tom's attention, but instead of scowling, the old fellow actually grinned. Pushing away his clean plate, he patted his belly. "I'll say this for you, my lord, you know how to pick a cook."

"I agree that Meg is a treasure, but I cannot take credit for her employment. That was my mother's doing. As always, she showed both impeccable taste and good sense," Gray said. Tom obviously took no particular delight in chicken plucking either, and would rather eat the food than prepare it.

"Now that our most immediate needs are provided for, I would like to ferret out my imposter," Gray said, studying the coachman carefully. "What do you know of the rendezvous point where Lucy met her lover?"

Tom gaped at him, his face turning red. *"What?"*

"Lucy told me she met him in the woods, in an abandoned cottage near my hunting box. Can you take me there?"

Tom eyed him suspiciously. "Why?"

Gray met his gaze coolly. "I would like to have a look at the place. Maybe it can tell us something about the man's identity."

Tom snorted. "I know where it is, all right. I've been there. I waited for the bastard night after night when Lucy told us, but he never came back. He's gone. Make no mistake about it, and there's nothing there that will lead you to him."

Gray lifted a brow. "You'll pardon me if I would like to see for myself."

"Suit yourself," Tom said, with a shrug. "I'm to take Meg into the village for supplies, but I can show you where it is first."

Gray nodded his agreement. Since he put absolutely no faith in Tom's investigative skills, he was not discouraged by the man's pessimism. If his suspicions concerning the imposter were true, there was a good chance the bastard had left a trail.

And Gray hoped to find it.

An hour later, Gray had to admit that the dim-witted coachman might have been right. The tiny cottage where Lucy had supposedly trysted with her lover was bare of all but a narrow bed, a table and chairs, and a few implements. Gray walked around the interior once, twice, then strode to the bed and pulled back the blankets.

"Lucy's," Tom said smugly. "She brought 'em from Hargate. And this set is fresh."

Gray frowned and tucked the linens back into place. He looked beneath the bed and found nothing but great clods of dust. Obviously, Lucy was not a vigilant housekeeper, either at home or at her love nest. Abandoning that corner of the room, Gray moved to the table, studying its workmanship and eyeing the tin cups and plates for any clues to their origin. Unfortunately, the tableware probably was his own property, furnished from the hunting box some time ago.

Next, Gray stepped to the hearth, hunkering down before it and poking through the remains of the fire with a stick, searching for a scrap of paper or telltale trace of wood, but there was only a blackened log and lots of ashes.

"Nothing," Gray said, leaning back on his heels in frustration.

"I told you," Tom said, but his words lacked their usual spite, whether because of his own interest in helping Lucy because of or his improved mood, Gray could not tell. "It's hopeless, my lord."

Gray lifted his head at that. "Nothing, Tom, is hopeless," he said. "If this place will not yield up an answer, then we must find it elsewhere. Let's look close at hand first. Here's Hargate." With a gloved finger, he drew an X in the dust of the floor, then a circle around it. "Now, I want you to tell me who lives within a ten-mile radius, all the way around."

Tom looked at him blankly, then turned belligerent. "Who's to say the fellow lives nearby? What makes you think it wasn't one of your noble friends having a lark?"

Gray eyed the coachman calmly. "Our imposter is no lord."

Tom snorted. "Why? Because of what he did?"

"No," Gray said. "Because of what he didn't do. He brought her no gifts, no trinkets of any sort indicative of wealth. And he wore no rings, no distinguishing jewelry, not even a watch."

Tom gaped at him in amazement, while Gray continued. "I questioned Lucy at great length yesterday," he explained. "And I discovered that the fellow did not even have a substantial wardrobe, so we can rule out anyone with money. Of course, it is conceivable that our man was some penniless aristocrat passing through, but if so, where did he stay? How did he live?"

When Tom did not answer, Gray went on. "No. I'll wager that our imposter is a commoner. But not too common. A local farmer or traveling tinker would not be able to fool Lucy into thinking him a marquis. Therefore, I suspect him to be a member of the area's gentry, or someone of similar circumstances who was visiting for a time. Let us hope for the former, so that he can be more easily discovered."

"I'll be damned," Tom muttered, staring at him. "You are a clever one."

Gray's mouth curved wryly. "High praise from you, of course. Now, tell me of our suspects."

Tom looked down at the markings in the dirt and crouched down across from Gray. "Well, saying as this is north, there is nothing up that way but the old earl's land. And west is your fancy place. South is the village, but there are few gentry living there." He scratched his beard. "The squire's house is a bit east of it."

"Does he have a son?" Gray asked.

Tom grinned. "Aye, but he's too young to be chasing skirts."

"Any other young men living there?"

Tom frowned thoughtfully. "Well, that's the trouble. You see, my lord, I'm not so sure of local gossip as I used to be, seeing as how we keep pretty much to ourselves these days. I think there's a nephew or a cousin, someone in charge of the home farm at the squire's, but I'll have to check."

He paused. "Then there's the vicar. He's got five

boys, three that might be of an age. He lives east of the village, too,'' Tom said, pointing to a point on the circle. ''His sister has a house nearby. And there's the small manor next to it. I'm not sure who's living there now.''

Gray studied the small marks on his makeshift map. ''Then that area, southeast of Hargate, must be a focus of our investigation. The squire or the vicar and his people might have had guests for the winter, to say nothing of the residents of the manor.'' He lifted his head to fix Tom with a steady gaze. ''I hesitate to show myself in the village, so I will have to rely upon you for the time being.'' To his surprise, the coachman nodded and puffed up his chest like a toad.

''Start today, when you take Meg in for supplies,'' Gray said. ''She can help you. She has a good ear for gossip. You can let it be known that she is the new cook, and hint at a change in fortunes at Hargate. Then perhaps our imposter, if he was frightened off by the girls' lean circumstances, might come sniffing around again.''

As he waited for the coachman's assent, Gray wondered if he was entrusting his investigation to the wrong man. Obviously, there was no love lost between Tom and himself. He had considered sending Badcock instead, but the valet was a stranger and might have difficulty getting the villagers to talk to him. A local would be best, and Tom was it.

As if sensing his misgivings, the old man scratched his beard. ''You're a smart one, make no mistake,'' he said, shaking his head. For a moment,

Gray thought he would refuse the task, but then his wrinkled face split into a wide grin. "You're even beginning to make me think that you just might find the lad."

Gray acknowledged the compliment with a jerk of his head, but he could not help lifting a brow at the coachman's lack of faith. "Of course I'm going to find him," he said with complete conviction. "I do not fail."

After Tom and Meg left for the village, Gray sought out Kate, only to find that she and her sister were busy being fitted by Mrs. Leeds. If not for Lucy, he might have tossed all decorum to the winds and sat in on the session. Then again, the sight of a half-naked Kate draped in silks and satins would have sorely tested his control.

Instead, he took the opportunity to walk through the house while Badcock took notes on its furnishings, condition, and potential problems. Obviously, the place had been neglected for years, and on top of that, various improvements, such as a bathing room, were sorely needed. Again Gray noticed the telltale signs of paintings that had been removed, and he was reminded that he must question Kate later about the missing items—and about her guardian's dubious financial support.

They ended their tour in the study where he had taken pen to paper yesterday, but now Gray looked the room over more thoroughly. Although he had no compunctions about opening drawers and checking contents, he could discover no letters from the infamous Jasper, or correspondence of any kind. What he did find, neatly tucked away, was the household account book.

Laying it open upon the desk, Gray saw, with some surprise, that the most recent entry was payment for one pig, already butchered. Livestock normally was a part of an estate this size, if not held by the property owner, then raised by the tenant farmers and easily traded for a portion of the rent owed. Running a finger up the page, Gray skimmed over meticulous records of small purchases, mostly of food, until he reached an entry for income. Then he stopped and swore under his breath.

Written in the same delicate hand was the sale of one black basaltware urn by Wedgwood for little more than pocket change. Glancing quickly through the columns, Gray cursed loudly at the loss of several busts, one by Bernini, and a portrait by Lely. All had been let go for far less than their worth. And all to one man.

Squire Wortley.

"What is it, my lord?"

Gray looked up to find Badcock studying him with some concern. "I have discovered where the missing items are, and it's worse than I thought."

"Oh?"

"Yes, some very valuable things were sold for absurdly low amounts to the local squire," Gray said.

"Perhaps he is their only source of funds, my lord. There cannot be many other residents of the area who could afford to buy the earl's possessions," Badcock suggested reasonably.

Yes, Gray thought, unless the girls had a contact in London, where they could get higher prices for their goods, the squire probably was their only hope. Still, he did not have to cheat them so baldly. There was a difference between getting a bargain and fleecing innocent women, between transacting business and stealing from ladies who were above the lowly squire's station. As the embodiment of local authority, Wortley should have been watching out for Lucy and Kate, instead of... Suddenly, Gray wondered if the bastard had put pressure on the Courtlands to obtain their treasures.

"My lord?"

Gray glanced up, startled by the look on Badcock's normally expressionless face.

"The, ah, accounts, my lord."

Gazing downward, Gray saw with surprise that he had crumpled a page of the book in his fist. Slowly, he released his grip, and pressed the paper flat once more. He really had to get himself under control. Wherever Kate was concerned, he reacted with gut instincts that had little to do with civilized behavior. It was becoming rather alarming.

Releasing a harsh breath, Gray thumbed through the rest of the volume, but he could find no references to income, other than that acquired from Wortley. As far as he could tell, the earl's daughters were not receiving an allowance of any kind from their guardian. Nor were they collecting any rents from the vast estate's tenant farmers. Indeed, they appeared to be paying for all their food, what precious little there was of it.

Gray found himself growing angry again, and made a deliberate effort to remain calm. The thought of Kate struggling not only with the drudgery of daily cooking and cleaning, but with the juggling of nearly nonexistent funds, as well, filled him with violent impulses. Mentally, he added Squire Wortley to his list of matters to attend to, right after the unmasking of his imposter and his confrontation with Uncle Jasper.

It appeared that he would be busy with Courtland business for some time to come, Gray thought, smiling grimly. But the notion invoked other images, of unfinished dealings with Kate that had nothing to do with money, relatives or neighbors. Only the two of them. Alone. Naked.

His first pleasant musings of the day were interrupted by a loud knocking at the study door that heralded the return of Tom and Meg. The cook was positively beaming at the success of her covert mission, and even the coachman seemed in good spirits as Gray urged them to sit. Glancing around the room, he had to suppress his amusement at the sight of the odd group. Never before had he engaged a coachman, a cook and a valet for an investigation, but he had long ago learned to be flexible when it came to resources. And he knew he could trust all of them, with the possible exception of Tom.

Right now, the old fellow appeared honest enough, as he prepared to report what he had learned in Chesterton. "Well, there's good news and bad, my lord," he said, seriously. "There's been some activity everywhere this spring, at the manor, the vicarage and the squire's house. People popping in and out as if they haven't homes of their own, from the sounds of it.''

Gray was not surprised. ''I'll admit that seems discouraging, but if we discover the identities of the guests and the length of their visits, I'm sure we could narrow down our list of suspects,'' he said.

The coachman looked skeptical, but nodded. ''As for the vicar's boys, one is too fat and one too fair. That leaves Ezra, the eldest, and only one other local who fits Miss Lucy's description, the squire's nephew, Archibold Rutledge.''

Gray put a finger to his lip and rubbed it absently. ''Very good. You have done well.'' He paused, his gaze flicking to each of them, in turn. ''I do not need to tell you that we must keep our activities quiet for the time being. I do not wish Miss Lucy to get her hopes up,'' he explained, giving Tom a particularly sharp look of warning. To Gray's surprise, the coachman nodded, without argument, and hurried after Meg to unload her supplies.

When the door shut behind them, Badcock shook his head. ''The culprit could be anyone, long come and gone, my lord.''

''Perhaps,'' Gray answered thoughtfully, ''but I have found it best not to overlook the obvious.''

''What next, then?'' Badcock asked.

''Next, we shall set a trap,'' Gray answered, his lips curling in satisfaction, ''and see what we catch.''

Kate swung the buckets beside her, glad of the freedom of her trousers as she followed the edge of the woods up to where the blackberries encroached upon the old pasture. The air seemed especially fresh and clean after the stifling hours spent with Mrs. Leeds.

All that poking and prodding had served to remind her of another existence, a lifetime ago, that no longer served her. Oh, some of the materials had been as smooth and delicate as a butterfly's wings, but what use would they have in her world? Kate snorted aloud. Where would she wear such finery? There were no balls or social calls on her calendar, only work that needed to be done.

Lucy, who clung tenaciously to her past, had been ecstatic over the fittings, so Kate had gone along, unwilling to spoil her sister's happiness. And Meg's daughter had been kind, carrying on over the sisters as though they were still heiresses, and not impoverished beggars. But Kate knew the truth, and no amount of dressing-up could change it. They were hanging on, just barely, and needed another hog to butcher far more than elaborate gowns.

But one did not argue with the arrogant marquis, and if he thought them too shabby for his taste, then let him provide them with different garments! Gray had never mentioned a price in connection with Mrs. Leeds's services, nor had Kate any intention of paying one. He claimed he had no interest in Lucy, so she no longer worried about him exacting a toll from her sister. The marquis was not the sort to lie to her face, whatever his shortcomings.

And Kate had discovered a few. In addition to his arrogance, he was possessed of a devilish whimsy that had prompted him to kiss her yesterday. Apparently he had been trying to prove his point concerning Lucy, but Kate did not appreciate the lesson. Her belief in his veracity did not extend to his implication that *she* held his attention. Never would she be convinced that such an elegant, handsome, powerful man could be attracted to a grubby girl in boy's trousers.

Obviously, the marquis enjoyed testing and teasing her, but his actions in the kitchen had gone too far. Kate's face flamed with the memory of his untoward behavior and her own wanton reaction. She took the last few steps at a run, as if to distance herself from the recollection, and tossed down her buckets angrily when she reached the blackberry bushes.

It was all his fault! A gentleman would never have put her in such a situation. The incident with his bath was one thing, for she had come upon him accidentally, and though he had taunted her about joining him, he had made no move. The events yesterday, however, had been precipitated by him. Gray had started it, and if she had been responsible for fanning the flames with her own eager response, Kate refused to blame herself. He had no business toying with her for his own amusement.

He should have apologized, at least, but he had not seemed at all contrite. In fact, he had conversed with Badcock as if nothing had happened. The thought made Kate swallow hard, for she realized that the experience that had been so momentous, if disastrous, for her probably had meant little to him. Her hand shook as she reached for the ripest fruit, embarrassment and a prickly sort of dismay engulfing her. She had melted in his embrace, so bereft of her good sense as to lie back shamelessly on the table like a serving of dessert, while he had appeared totally unaffected.

It was degrading. And such had been the way of it since the marquis's arrival, for he had maintained his cool control while sending hers spinning to the winds. Kate blinked as misery threatened to engulf her. Her life was difficult enough, without the added problems posed by her visitor.

The silence was broken by the sound of movement, and Kate turned, unsure who or what would seek her out in this secluded spot. Her anger resurged abruptly at the sight that met her eyes, for climbing up the slope was Gray, impeccably dressed, from the tops of his shiny boots to his elegant coat. Despite the warmth of the day, he looked perfectly composed, without even a drop of sweat across his brow to mark his exertions.

Kate felt like knocking him down the bloody hill, dirtying his superbly cut clothes and wiping that look of restrained power from his darkly handsome face. Her lips tightening in disgust, she turned her back to him and continued picking berries, yanking on the stems hard enough to test her gloves.

"Kate." His voice weaved its way under her skin, all warm and compelling, but she refused to acknowledge it. "I've come about Lucy," he said, a trace of amusement in his tone that set Kate's teeth on edge. Had he no intention of begging her pardon for his behavior of yesterday, or had it meant so little to him that he had forgotten it already? The thought made her squish a ripe berry between her fingers, and she looked down, surprised at the mangled fruit.

"Careful now. You don't want to get pricked," Gray warned, and Kate glanced over at him, annoyed to see the slight curve of his lips. Was he toying with her again? Refusing to rise to his bait, she gave him a cold look and turned back to her task.

"I've begun my search for the imposter," he said. "Meg and Tom gathered some gossip in the village today, and we have a few promising leads, but I do not want Lucy to know what we are about."

Kate kept her eyes on her work, while trying to come to terms with the wealth of information in his simple statement. "You're afraid she might interfere."

"Well, yes, she seems to be a bit headstrong, overly emotional perhaps," Gray admitted.

*Not like me,* Kate thought grimly. Not sensible Kate. Yet right now she felt anything but sensible. Although she could well appreciate Gray's efforts and what they might mean to her sister, Kate could not stifle a wholly unreasonable anger that he was so eager to be done with Hargate and everyone in it.

"Very well. I won't tell her," she said, trying to maintain some semblance of the control that had marked her life for the past few years. Unfortunately, Gray seemed to tug at the loose threads of her nerves, unraveling them like a skein of wool. Instead of responding calmly to his announcement, Kate wanted to rage or cry or do something—anything—to destroy his perfect mastery of every situation.

"Good. I think it will be best, at least until I can

discover what sort of man he is,'' Gray said, and then
he stepped closer. ''Here, let me help you.''

Alarmed, Kate shot a swift glance at him, dismayed to see him reach for the edges of his claret
superfine. ''No! That isn't necessary,'' she protested,
unable to tear her gaze away. *Please don't take off
your coat! Please don't take off your coat!* Although
the words screamed in Kate's head, Gray did not hear
them. He shrugged out of the elegant material to
stand before her in his shirt and waistcoat, and while
she watched, he rolled up his sleeves, exposing a
dark dusting of hair.

Kate had seen him in far less, certainly, but the
sight of his bare forearms in the sunlight nevertheless
made her feel warm and weak and wanting. As if
oblivious of her stare, Gray picked up the other
bucket and moved toward the bushes. He wore no
gloves, but reached for the fruit with his well-formed,
well-groomed hands. When his long, masculine fingers caught a berry and rolled it gently from its
perch, her breath caught.

Kate looked away, her cheeks flaming, her blood
pounding. ''You will stain your skin,'' she snapped,
when she could speak.

''No matter.''

She should have known. For all his elegance, Gray
seemed at ease anywhere, anytime. She could easily
imagine him as a great Norman knight, or a Viking
warrior, strong and bold and... Clearing her suddenly
tight throat, Kate tried to ignore him, concentrating
instead on filling her bucket as quickly as possible,
so as to escape his heady presence. For a moment,

all was quiet, except for the sounds of rustling branches and calling birds, and she thought to regain her composure at last. Then he spoke.

"I regret any discomfiture I may have caused you yesterday," he said, and Kate jerked, dropping a berry.

Discomfiture?

"You'll have to take my word for it, but I am usually not so impulsive," he added.

Impulsive?

"You appear to have a peculiar effect on me, poppet."

Peculiar?

Kate needed no reminder of her own extraordinary circumstances. "Just so long as you understand that these gowns you insist on having made are to be given to us freely, with no expectation of payment of any kind." She turned to give him a cold glare, but it was wasted on him, for he only lifted that dark brow of his disdainfully.

"You insult me, Kate. You don't actually believe I would try to bribe you? Do you think I've ever had to pay for sex?"

She colored hotly, turning away to reach for fruit with shaking fingers, cursing his casual tongue.

"I delight in your blushes, Kate, but I thought you believed in plain speaking," he said, his tone revealing his amusement.

"I do, but even I have my limits."

He leaned close, his breath brushing against her hair as he spoke. "Do you, Kate? I wonder," he whispered, as if reflecting on something else entirely.

His nearness, his heat, his low, liquid voice, made her want to melt, and in furious rebellion, Kate turned to push him away, her outstretched palm landing squarely in the middle of his expensive gold-embroidered waistcoat. It squished beneath her fingers.

Snatching her hand away, Kate caught her breath at the sight of the dark stain spreading across the pristine silk. Dismayed, she glanced up at his face, steeling herself against his anger, for what arrogant lord would not decry the loss of such a fine garment?

Apparently Gray would not. His brow cocked in surprise, and then his lips curled in a subtle threat more menacing than any rage. "Katie, love, I don't believe you thought this one out in your usual sensible fashion." Reaching down, he plucked a dripping berry from his chest and flicked it at her. It plopped against her throat and sank down to her collar.

Kate swallowed her gasp of outrage when his gaze, dark with promise, lifted to hers. "I'll get that for you," he said, his lashes drifting downward.

"What are you doing?" she cried. A gentleman would have left in a huff, but, as he had proved before, Gray was not a typical lord. He was more unexpected. More dangerous. As Kate watched in astonishment, he dipped a thumb in the fruity mess and lifted it to her mouth. She would have backed away, but there was nowhere to go. And then he touched her.

He rubbed gently, tracing the outline of her lips with his thumb, while she stared, stunned into silence by the heat that flowed from that simple contact. He cupped her chin, his fingers sliding along her neck, and Kate nervously darted out her tongue to wipe away the trail of juice.

"You missed some." His voice was deep and rich, and Kate felt her limbs grow weak as he leaned over her. He moved at an unhurried pace, as if to tease her until she ached for his touch. And she did. When he licked her lips, it was so deliberate and so delicious that she wanted to cry out. Her fists rose to seek purchase on his upper arms, for she was melting away under each slow glide of his tongue.

His leisurely exploration drove her to madness, and she opened her mouth, forcing the issue and sighing softly at the familiar greeting of his tongue, twirling, sucking, and sliding so skillfully against hers. His hands lifted to her face, his fingers tracing her brow, her cheeks and the tender ridges of her ears before dropping to the throbbing pulse beneath.

And still he kissed her, each new slant of his lips and weight of his mouth an exquisite sensation to be experienced. Heat dazed her, and Kate felt the glide to the ground as a respite, the grass cool beneath her back. Before she knew what he was about, Gray had tugged the shirt from her trousers and slipped his palms inside, atop her shortened shift. Kate drew in a ragged breath as his palms moved upward, his thumbs flicking against her suddenly hard nipples. His lips traveled down her throat, over the twisted folds of her shirt, and lower, until they closed over the worn linen.

Gad, she could feel him, hot and moist, through

the cloth. His mouth was gentle, soft, tantalizing, tugging…and then it was gone. Kate opened her eyes, a sound of protest dying in her throat as she saw him dip a hand into the bucket beside her. His fingers came out black as berries, and he put one to her mouth.

"Taste me, Kate," he whispered. He was leaning over her, his handsome face dark with intent, and she could no more deny him than she could herself. Hesitantly she touched her lips to one dripping digit, and she watched his eyes flare in response. Then he nudged her lips until she took the tip of his finger inside, sucking away the sweetness.

His breath came out in a harsh exhalation, perhaps even a curse. Kate was too benumbed to decipher it. The heat from him was scalding, and when he slid up her shift and laid his palm upon her chest, it was a miracle of relief to feel the air brushing her wet skin. He spread the juice over her breasts, his mouth following in a dizzying rush of warmth and coolness and heightened desire.

Gray moaned, the sound so at odds with his skillful caresses that Kate shivered. Then his wet hand splayed over her ribs, roaming in a less practiced motion as his mouth closed over her nipple. Kate cried out at the bright, sharp shaft of pleasure, and then he was over her, his mouth rough on hers, his heavy body pressing into her, right between her thighs. His weight was a joyous thing, his tall form a wonder of muscle and heat, and the hard ridge that pushed against her core the answer to all her restless yearning.

In a flash of unclouded insight, Kate knew just what she wanted. She had seen it before, though it seemed to have grown alarmingly since then, and it throbbed now at the juncture of her legs with the dark promise of fulfillment. But at what price? Kate's hot delight faded with the cold realization that she was as wicked as her sister, perhaps more so. Could she give herself so easily to a man who would be gone tomorrow, who toyed with her for his own amusement?

"No." Kate pushed at his chest, and he lifted his face above hers. For one moment, she saw a naked intensity that took her breath away, a glimpse of a voracious appetite so at odds with the calm, controlled marquis as to be frightening, and then it was gone. His expression was carefully shuttered once more.

"I seem to have developed a penchant for the most inappropriate locations," he said, moving smoothly to her side. Kate was certain, then, that she had imagined his tortured response, for he spoke with barely a hitch in his breathing to mark what had passed between them.

## Chapter Ten

Gray stalked into the kitchen, calling for his valet so loudly that he startled Meg and earned a glower from Tom, who was ensconced on a stool in the corner.

"And what's got your back up?" the coachman asked.

"My back is not 'up', as you so quaintly put it," Gray said, glaring at the old fellow. Unfortunately, it was another part of his anatomy that was giving him trouble, rising with alarming frequency, whether he willed it or no. Gray adjusted the coat he held in front of him, cursing the member that he had thought well under his control since his youth. Apparently it was defecting at this late date.

"Yes, my lord?" Badcock appeared in the doorway, and Gray welcomed the distraction.

"Take the tub from the buttery up to Kate's room and make sure she has enough hot water for a bath. Get Tom to help you, since he has nothing to do."

"Here, now!" Tom protested, straightening at the brusque order. Then his eyes narrowed. "And just why does Katie need a bath in the middle of the day?''

''She's been berry picking,'' Gray said, depositing the bucket he had stayed to fill on the table. He gave the coachman a look that made him squirm on his seat and then stalked from the kitchen, eager for the privacy of his own room. He needed to think, and he'd be damned if he could do it here, surrounded by a sea of expectant faces.

At his own homes, he never particularly cared what the servants did or did not see, for he had grown up surrounded by them. It was understood that they knew where lovers trysted, what children were sired by whom, and the most minute personal habits of those they served. It was a fact of life, and never before had he been concerned with it. He had no vices to hide, and he conducted his personal affairs discreetly enough, with women who knew what they were about.

But here at Hargate, instead of the usual staff, there was only a handful of people, very protective of their mistress. Gray could not fault them for it; Kate was not one of the ladies of uncertain virtue with whom he normally consorted. She was an innocent, and Gray found that he did not want the other residents of the house to know that he had been rolling around on the ground with her, spreading berries over her luscious body in a sybaritic scene that came very close to paradise. Perilously close.

Damn. Gray frowned as he tossed his coat onto a chair and stripped off his now purple waistcoat. He had gone after her to talk about his investigation; he had never planned to kiss her, let alone what followed. His heart tripped. The memory of Kate's slender body lying beneath him, covered with juice by his own hand, made him sweat. He was so hard that it hurt, and he wished that Kate had not stopped him. He wanted to finish it, *needed* to bury himself inside her and stay there until his reckless compulsion to have her eased.

Although a meadow was not his first choice for deflowering her, Gray had to admit that it would have done just fine, more than fine. The location didn't matter, as long as he mounted her at last, as long as she took all of him, deep, and she would, her passion rising to meet him...

Damn! Gray moved to the table, where Badcock had left a bowl and pitcher. He poured the water, spilling some over the side in his haste, and splashed it on his face. Once. Twice. Again. He stood up, dripping, to wipe away the moisture with a groan.

This was getting out of hand. He had been in control of himself, his emotions, his actions, his immense fortune and properties, since the tender age of twelve, and his tendency to lose that mastery in Kate's presence was unsettling, to say the least.

He liked her. He appreciated her quiet courage, her strength, her intelligence. Circumstances had conspired to give her an openness, lacking in her contemporaries, that was delightfully refreshing. She was dependable, loyal and logical—for a female, he thought with a smile—and beneath her sensible exterior burned a fire that had singed him more than once. She was an intriguing, appealing woman, like

Charlotte, only more so. More straightforward, more uninhibited, more everything. Maybe too much.

Gray swore again, viciously. Looking at it objectively, he was not sure he particularly liked what happened when he made love to her. He lost all finesse, all reason, all sense of himself. Just the thought of the way he had gone wild with the fruit made him swear loudly. And it wasn't just when he was touching her. Kate was affecting him even when she wasn't near him, in ways he never expected.

What had begun so simply had become more complex than he ever imagined. For the first time in years, Gray began to doubt his own judgment. He scowled at the water bowl, realizing that his plans for Kate, long laid, might have to be reassessed.

Three days later, Gray stood behind the doorway in the cottage, waiting for Lucy's lover. Since rumors of the Courtlands' new wealth had drawn no one, he set a trap, paying a village lad to give each of the local suspects a message, ostensibly from "the beautiful lady who lives at Hargate."

The fevered plea that "we meet this afternoon at the usual place" would hold little meaning for an innocent man, but the culprit might come running, if only to find out how his identity had been discovered.

Gray smiled grimly. He could just picture the kind of callous bastard who would so use an innocent girl. He had seen such men before. Of course, he put no faith in Lucy's judgment; he was almost certain the kind and gentle nature she ascribed to her lover was just as feigned as his title. Unfortunately for this particular fellow, he had chosen the wrong name to use for his charade.

Gray's hand tightened upon the pistol he held at the ready, one of a brace that Badcock had brought down from London. Although he would rather use his fists, his shoulder was in no shape for a brawl, and a cornered man might easily become dangerous. Gray believed in preparing for any eventuality, and to that end, he had posted Badcock among the trees outside, ready to spring should the villain slip through his fingers. Tom, whom he could not trust to follow orders, had not been informed of this little adventure, and presumably had not moved from his cozy spot in Meg's kitchen.

A noise from outside roused Gray to instant alertness, and he flattened himself against the wall. Someone was here, and from the sound of it, the fellow was not adept at stealth. For a moment, he feared that Lucy had gotten wind of their scheme, but then the door opened and a distinctly male body stepped in.

Light brown hair, medium height and build. So far, the fellow fitted Lucy's description perfectly. Gray slid in front of the door, shutting it neatly behind him. The young man—and he was young—turned abruptly, his mouth opening in surprise, his blue eyes bright with alarm. He was dressed neatly enough, but not in the exquisitely tailored clothes of the ton.

Imposter.

He stood there, gaping at Gray, until the silence became annoying. "Well? Have you nothing to say for yourself?'' Gray snapped. Was the man an idiot? A coward? ''I could kill you for this, you know.''

His words finally produced an effect, for the young man fell into one of the chairs and buried his head in his hands. ''I know. I know. And it's no more than I deserve,'' he moaned.

Gray stared at the boy in disgust, outraged that this baleful pup had passed as himself. ''Do you know who I am?'' he asked, his tone rife with menace.

The young man lifted his head, frowning in confusion. ''Miss Lucy's guardian?''

Gray laughed harshly, the sound echoing eerily in the close confines of the cottage. ''I am Wroth,'' he said, and he had the distinct pleasure of watching every bit of color fade from the young man's face.

''My lord! I... Forgive me, I never planned to...''

''Steal my name? Just how far did you take the charade? To Chesterton? To London? Is this debauchery the sum of it, or have you run up bills to my accounts?''

''Debauchery! Now—now wait a minute, my lord!'' the young man stammered.

''No, you wait a minute,'' Gray said savagely. ''You used my name for sex, taking a green girl who knew—''

''Stop!'' The young man surged to his feet, took one look at Gray's face and then sat back down, slowly, obviously thinking better of his brief show of temper. ''Do what you will to me. Shoot me right now, if you like, but don't drag the lady into it,'' he said with a tight frown.

''A little late for that, isn't it, boy?''

Gray was relieved to see the young man's quick flash of anger. Apparently Lucy's beau was not totally spineless. He drew himself up and met Gray's eyes evenly for the very first time. "My name is Archibold Rutledge, my lord. And you have no cause to malign Lady Courtland. She is an innocent in all of this."

"Not anymore," Gray said softly.

"No," Rutledge said, dropping his gaze. "But it's not what you think. I...I had been out scouting property." He glanced back up at Gray, his expression too earnest to deny. "I manage the farm for my uncle, Squire Wortley, and he had been talking of buying more land. I came upon her in the woods, and she was like an angel, a fairy, so beautiful and fine." He flushed and stared at his boots. "When she said she was one of the earl's daughters, I knew she wouldn't think much of some poor relation to the squire. So I lied. I knew the marquis's—" He paused, swallowing nervously. "I knew *your* hunting box was nearby, so I said I was Wroth. It was just for the day, and I didn't think any harm could come of it."

"But you saw her again," Gray said, prompting him.

"Yes," Rutledge admitted in a low voice. "I couldn't help myself. She was so lovely and regal, like a queen, but gentle, too, and sweet." Gray lifted a brow in skepticism, for he had yet to see that side of Lucy's nature.

"Each time I told myself it would be the last, but it was like a fire in my blood, this need to see her,"

Rutledge explained, lifting his head as if to seek understanding. Gray refused to give it to him, but shifted uncomfortably, as the boy's raw admission struck perilously close to his own obsession with Kate. "I love her, my lord."

The stark devastation on the youth's face made Gray heartily glad that he did not subscribe to such nonsense. "Then why did you leave her?"

"What else could I do?" Rutledge asked. "I have no money, no prospects, no title, *nothing* to offer a lady like Lucy."

"Still, a man who claims to care for a woman does not abandon her, or his child, to the Fates," Gray replied. "The Courtlands are in dire enough straits, without the burdens you have added."

Rutledge's startled look made Gray release an impatient breath. Apparently Lucy had not been exactly candid about her circumstances, either. "I just thought her guardian would marry her off to someone…better," the boy muttered, burying his head in his hands again.

Privately, Gray doubted there was anyone better suited to Lucy than this besotted youth who, no doubt, would be willing to spend a lifetime worshiping at her feet. The lady in question was known to have a mind of her own, however, and it rarely was in accord with his. And though Gray would like to put her life in good order, he had no desire to be blamed if her grand romance turned sour.

It was time for Lucy to make her choice.

Gray found her in the garden, sewing daintily under the shade of the large alder. Calling softly to announce his approach, he walked toward her, stopping to lean a hand against the tree trunk. She gave him a sulky nod of acknowledgment that did not wound him in the least. If all went well, he would soon be rid of the chit.

"I have found him," Gray said, without preamble, and her eyes flew to his, bright with astonishment.

"His name is Archibold Rutledge, and he is nephew to Squire Wortley, managing the farm there," Gray explained. He saw the swift play of emotions cross her features: hope, dismay, disappointment, and a building anger. Before she could work herself into a fury, he went on. "He claims to have taken my name to impress you, without meaning any harm. He says he loves you, and would marry you, if he had prospects."

Her face fell, and Gray saw what looked to be real tears pool in the corners of her eyes as she faced the truth. "If you want him, I will give him employment managing one of my estates," Gray said, amused to see her dainty mouth drop open in surprise. "If you do not, then I can try to arrange a suitable marriage for you, but we don't have much time."

She sighed, glancing down at herself with a sad smile that made her seem less spoiled and shrewish, and Gray wondered at the side of her that Rutledge saw. Then she eyed him warily. "This...Mr. Rutledge. He wants to marry me? You are not forcing him?"

Gray shook his head. "I have not told him of the job offer."

Lucy pursed her lips, then rose to her feet in decision. "I would see him."

Gray nodded. "He is close at hand." Turning, he whistled toward the trees, where Badcock waited with the heartless villain, who had turned out to be little more than a frightened boy, running scared from his responsibilities. Although Gray could not condone Rutledge's actions, he no longer was determined to run the fellow through. Let him be saddled with Lucy for life; that was punishment enough, Gray thought with a wry smile.

Rutledge climbed down the slope to fall to his knees at Lucy's feet, which only reaffirmed Gray's thoughts. He shot a glance at Badcock as the two lovers held a tearful reunion, but the valet's expressionless face revealed nothing.

With a jerk of his head, Gray summoned Badcock to him, and they made their way back to the house. "Badcock," Gray said, his lips curling in contempt as he fled the romantic scene, "if I ever become so besotted as to beg a female for her favors, please shoot me."

"Yes, my lord." Something in the valet's voice rang false, drawing Gray's attention, but Badcock looked so sober that he decided he must have imagined the man's amusement. Distracted, the ever-watchful marquis missed his servant's wide grin.

Kate sat in the corner, feeling oddly out of place in her own kitchen. She had come in to help with supper, but Meg claimed that Tom could assist her, and her daughter, too, if need be. "As the lady of the house, you should not be soiling your pretty hands,'' the cook had said.

Reason told Kate that she should be relieved at one less responsibility. God knew that there were plenty of other tasks for her at Hargate, and yet she had lingered, her sense of displacement growing as she listened to the easy banter between Tom and Meg.

''Here, now, watch out for that hellcat!'' Tom said suddenly, hopping up from his perch on a worn stool, as if to come between the cook and where Cyclops slept, atop the bricks of the hearth.

''What? This old love?'' Meg asked, reaching up to pet the one-eyed cat. To Kate's astonishment, the feline let her stroke it a bit before turning in a circle and settling down once more.

Another defection, Kate thought, then frowned at her own selfishness. She should be glad the cat was warming up to someone besides herself, and that Tom had taken a liking to the friendly cook and that some of her burdens were lifted, albeit temporarily. Yet she had to restrain herself from shouting out at the uselessness of caring for people who might well be gone tomorrow.

As if he had heard her thoughts, the source of her distress appeared in the doorway. His height was such that he nearly was forced to duck, his shoulders seemingly too wide for the space, and Kate wondered churlishly why he was even coming through the kitchen. She would have expected a great lord like Gray to stay above stairs, which was one of the reasons she had been keeping company with the servants.

Kate had been avoiding him ever since the Berry Incident, which had quickly surpassed the Kitchen Incident and the Bathing Incident as her most excruciating source of humiliation. Just one look at his tall, lean body was enough to bring it all back. The amazing rush of sensations. His mouth. His hands. His tongue, *tasting* her!

Kate tore her gaze away and tilted her flushed face downward, willing him to pass by her, but, of course, he did not. Must he torment her at every opportunity? She saw his boots move into her line of vision. They were polished to a black sheen and led up to thighs that she knew were thick with hard muscle...

"I believe a celebratory supper is in order, Meg," he said, and Kate glanced up in surprise. "Lucy's beau has returned to claim her hand."

Kate stared at him, stunned, while Meg squealed in glee and Tom peppered him with hostile questions. Gray held up his palm to stem the flow of curses from the bloodthirsty coachman. "He is just a boy, Tom, confused and smitten by the lady."

"Who is it? Wortley's nephew?"

"Precisely," Gray answered. He turned to look back through the doorway as Badcock fell in behind him.

"Here they come, my lord," the valet said.

Kate pasted a smile on her face, but her thoughts were chaotic. Lucy marrying? Who was this boy? And why had he not come forward sooner? Although she had once yearned for someone to solve her sister's problems, now Kate found herself strangely piqued to know nothing of this abrupt resolution.

And then Lucy rushed in, breathless and flushed, with a young man in tow. Kate's first thought was how very little he resembled Gray. He was much younger, barely more than a gawky boy, shorter, less sturdy, with an uncertain expression that was a far cry from the real Wroth's cool confidence.

How could Lucy have thought him a marquis? Kate's smile faded, but she stepped forward to offer her congratulations, nonetheless. Tom, who had once threatened to deprive Lucy's lover of his privates, slapped the youth on the back jovially, and Kate felt as if the whole world had gone mad. She grasped at her own last few wits as she studied the man who would marry her sister.

"And how will you support a wife and child, Mr....Rutledge?" she asked, her voice of reason bringing silence to the room.

"Oh, that!" Lucy answered with a wave of her hand. "Wroth has offered Archibold a position managing one of his properties."

"It will not pay a fortune, but enough to set up a household," Gray said. He gave Lucy a stern look, but she only nodded happily.

"Oh, I don't want for much, after living here!" Lucy hastened to assure him, and for some reason, the careless remark stung Kate. She had done her best with what little she had. Did that not count for anything? "What of our guardian?" she asked, compelled by something she could not have named. "Surely, you realize that Lucy is underage." When she saw Lucy's bright happiness pale, Kate wanted to take back her words, but wasn't it best to get it all out now?

"According to my sources, your guardian is out of the country," Gray said. "Post the banns. Once they are read by the local cleric for three Sundays, you may wed. I doubt if your guardian will even hear of the notice, let alone place an objection." And if he did, he would have the marquis of Wroth to deal with—that much was evident in the disdainful lift of Gray's dark brow. He cast a glance at Kate that told her not to doubt him.

Instead of being reassured, Kate found Gray's confidence annoying. She turned to Lucy. "Still, I would like to make certain that this is in my sister's best interests. Lucy, may I speak with you alone for a moment?"

Nodding reluctantly, Lucy sent Rutledge a brilliant smile and told him to meet them in the drawing room in a few minutes. "Send some tea up, will you, Meg?" she asked, waving a languid hand.

Kate wondered if Gray's new position came complete with cook and housemaid, but she knew the answer immediately. All but the poorest of homes had servants. All but Hargate. She pursed her lips and pulled her sister into one of the smaller rooms off the gallery.

"Are you certain that this is what you want, Lucy?"

"Yes, and I hope you are not going to spoil it for me, Kate."

The taunt hurt, for Kate had done nothing except

struggle to keep her sister content these past few years. "I only want what is best for you, and I must admit that your...gentleman seems rather young. Will you be happy with him? In a smaller home, with a child to care for?"

Lucy sighed, pouting prettily. "Would you have me prefer it here, slaving like a servant to hang on to a house that means nothing to me? A legacy that has left me nothing?" Kate flinched, startled by the vehemence in her sister's expression, but then it softened, as if Lucy were having second thoughts.

"Katie, I know you've worked hard for us, but I'm not like you. You were always the smart one, the strong one, the brave one. You can ride and bake and do accounts. *Anything!* I used to hate you for it, but now I've finally got something of my own. Oh, Wroth offered to arrange another marriage for me, but I'm comfortable with Archibold. He won't tuck me away in some corner while he conducts affairs, as those arrogant lords are wont to do. He'll pay attention to me. Me, Katie. And I won't have to do anything but look pretty."

Kate swallowed, her throat suddenly thick with uncommon emotion, her eyes smarting under the pressure of tears at her sister's revelations. She had never dreamed that Lucy might be jealous of her. And for what? Kate could only blink in dismay, still disbelieving.

But Lucy was right about one thing. They had heard about ton marriages, in which infidelity was common for both spouses, and Kate deemed it better that her flighty sister be out of temptation's way. Although technically a mésalliance, her union with Mr. Rutledge was hardly lowering, considering their current circumstances. Indeed, Lucy would probably be better off than at Hargate, where every day was a struggle.

Kate choked back a sob as Lucy caught her up in a tight embrace, the first sign of affection she had received from her sister in a long time. There was so much she wanted to say, but before she could even form the words, Lucy was gone, moving back into the gallery, chattering excitedly about her wedding, just as if the poignant moment between them had never occurred.

Drawing a deep breath, Kate leaned dazedly against the doorjamb, trying once more to sort out her chaotic emotions. Everything seemed to be happening so fast, when only a fortnight ago her life had been quiet and predictable. What had changed? Kate wondered dizzily. The answer came all too swiftly.

Gray had appeared, and nothing would ever be the same again.

## Chapter Eleven

Gray was disappointed. He was not sure what he had expected from Kate at the news of her sister's nuptials, but not this calm acceptance. Hell, he received more admiration from his political opponents! Even the most dim-witted of them could not deny his intelligence, his negotiating skills and his expert juggling of finances. And rarely did his efforts touch their personal lives. Yet he had just found a husband for Lucy, salvaging both her reputation and her romantic notions of love, and what thanks did he get?

Although Gray kept his face carefully composed, he felt the slow burn of annoyance. He did not want Kate to fall at his feet, prostrate with gratitude, but, at the very least, she could pretend to be impressed by his clever deductions. He had come to respect her opinion. It mattered to him, in some inexplicable way, yet she had remained silent and sullen through supper, giving him only a brief nod of acknowledgment, as if to say, "Fine work, my lord. Now be off with you."

Gray's nostrils flared at the thought. Oh, no, his

little poppet would not be rid of him so easily,
whether she willed it or not. His irritation grew. It
was one thing for him to consider leaving, quite another for her to push him away. Gray was unaccustomed to such behavior, and rebellion surged through
him in a most startling fashion. He had always taken
what he wanted. He was Wroth, and none dared gain-
say him.

The doubts that had plagued him for the past few
days disappeared in a rush of covetousness. He
wanted this woman, not only physically, but to share
with him her thoughts, her laughter, her passion,
never retreating. It was a hunger, surprising in its
intensity, and when he saw her turn to go, Gray was
seized by the unheard-of desire to throw her over his
shoulder like some primitive and carry her off to his
hut. Or at least his hunting box.

"My lord, if I could have a word with you?"

Tom's voice broke through the uncivilized urges
that had overtaken his thoughts. Blowing out a slow
breath, Gray turned his attention to the coachman,
who was eyeing him with a thoughtful expression.
"What?" Gray asked.

"A walk in the garden, if you would?"

Gray's mouth tightened. The last person he wanted
to stroll around the grounds with was Tom. Normally, he would think the feeling mutual, so the
coachman's unusually friendly behavior roused all
his senses to alertness. Now that he had outlived his
usefulness, did Tom plan to waylay him? Hardly. He
doubted that even Kate would be able to get the best
of him again. Still, he flexed his arm to test the

strength of his bad shoulder and, with a swift nod to Tom, strode toward the doors. It would not hurt to stay awake on every suit, and although he did not expect another bullet, Gray believed in being prepared for any eventuality.

The evening was warm and delicious, the air heavy with scents, the sky brimming with stars. It was a night for lovers. Unfortunately, his companion was no comely maid, but a grizzled old servant, for whom Gray harbored few charitable emotions. But it was not the first time he had been forced to associate with those who fared low in his estimation, so Gray kept his expression carefully neutral as he fell into step with the coachman.

"I...I just wanted to thank you, my lord," Tom said, startling Gray with his admission. "I know that I haven't always treated you as you deserved, but I had my girls to consider, you know. Now that I know you meant right by them all along, I have to say that I never did see a cleverer piece of work."

Gray's pleasure at the old man's words was tempered by his natural wariness and his desire to hear similar sentiments from a certain female member of the household. But he nodded graciously and continued walking.

"Aye, if not for you, Lucy would never have had her man, and for that we are all grateful. However..." Tom paused, as if considering his next words, and Gray's foreboding deepened. Now that his task was finished, had Kate given the old man instructions to run him off? For the first time in years, heat stained his cheeks, making him glad of the darkness. If she thought to send him packing so callously, she had better think again! He was not through with Kate yet, not by a long shot.

"We still have a bit of a problem," Tom said, scratching his beard. "And since it's on account of your being here, I thought you might see your way clear to remedy the situation, so to speak." The old man fell silent, and Gray wondered what the devil he was referring to. He was in no mood to decipher the fellow's cryptic comments.

"Perhaps if you could be more explicit?" Gray put in. He saw the slash of Tom's grin in the darkness and halted his steps. The coachman's smile was even more ominous than his flattery, and Gray tensed. His practiced eye scanned the garden, but nothing moved in the stillness except the leaves above them.

"Uh, you see, it's a matter of some delicacy," Tom said, rubbing his beard. "I admit that I misjudged you, my lord, but you've proved me wrong. And now I'm expecting you to do what's right."

"And what precisely would that be?" Gray asked, lifting a brow.

"Well, the thing of it is, my lord, you've been staying here for some time, without any proper chaperone. Of course, there was once a paid lady, but when the money ran out, she took herself off, and then the servants went, until there was none but me and Mrs. Gooding. After the good Lord took her last autumn, it was left to me, you understand. That's the best we could do, even though I knew it weren't proper."

Gray nodded, although he was still not quite sure which direction the coachman was heading with this lengthy speech.

Tom eyed him cannily. "I admit that you didn't exactly come here of your own free will, but it was your decision to stay, and you and I both know what your fancy friends would say of that. Why, you've ruined my Katie for sure, just by being here with no female but Lucy."

Gray nearly laughed aloud when he realized just what the coachman was suggesting. He hid his amusement, but relaxed his heightened vigilance. Now it was Tom who appeared distinctly uneasy, as he hurried to explain himself further.

"Don't go practicing your boxing on me, my lord," he said, holding up a hand, as if to ward Gray off. "I don't want to quarrel with you, but I think you ought to do right by Kate, and the only way to do it is by marrying her. She is one of your own, an earl's daughter and all, and you couldn't do no better were you to go after London's finest, I'm sure of that," the coachman added. "If you take yourself off, what with all that's happened, Kate will be the one looked down on, not Lucy, even though she's done nothing to earn it."

Gray's thoughts quickly strayed to several examples of Kate's behavior that could hardly be called proper. Indeed, although the coachman was, thankfully, ignorant of these instances, Gray recalled them most vividly. He was well aware that he had thoroughly compromised Kate in a variety of locations, from the kitchen table to a grassy hillside.

Mindful of the coachman's close scrutiny, Gray pushed the heady memories aside. He had to admit a grudging admiration for the old man's loyalty—and nerve; not many servants would presume to suggest a wedding to their betters. Gray's lips curved at the thought, and, despite their often-acrimonious encounters, he was tempted to put the old man's worries to rest.

"I assure you, I have no intention of leaving Miss Courtland in the lurch," he answered. Unfortunately, it seemed lately that Kate, her burgeoning passions aside, might rather be left, and Gray's own feelings on the matter were far from steady.

Tom scowled, apparently unsatisfied with such a vaguely worded pledge. "What's that, then? Are you saying you'll marry the girl?" he asked.

Gray hesitated. He was a skilled gambler, and he was not yet certain that he wanted to reveal his hand. His original plans had come under renewed scrutiny recently, though the doubts that assailed him had a tendency to flee in the presence of the woman in question.

Drawing in a deep breath, Gray gazed out into the summer night. He was cognizant of the coachman's concerns, for they had once been his own, yet he knew he was under no obligation to marry Kate. None but a few trustworthy servants were aware of his presence here, and no one need be the wiser if he left.

He could still pursue Kate's uncle and wrest control of her inheritance from his hand, putting it under the wardship of someone more trustworthy. And, once properly outfitted and chaperoned, Kate could have the London season that had been denied her. Gray pictured her there in some crowded ballroom, surrounded by suitors, and his hand tightened into a fist.

She was no longer the innocent she had once been, of course, and his deeply ingrained sense of honor called him to account. Yet Kate was none the worse for what had gone between them. Gray had unleashed her passion, but she would still gift her husband with her maidenhead.

And, abruptly, that was what determined Gray's decision, not a lifetime's worth of weighing options or exploring alternatives, but a violent gut reaction to the thought of anyone else making love to the woman he had chosen for his wife. Possession, pure and primitive, rocked him, along with a jealous rage at some nameless, faceless male that was so fierce it twisted his insides into a knot.

And so, the man who had been described as brilliant, cynical, ruthless, but never impulsive, blurted out a response without even considering the possible repercussions of his actions, for both himself and the young woman who so often seemed displeased with him. "Yes, I'm marrying her," he said, practically growling his response.

Tom's grizzled head bobbed furiously in approval. "Ye gods, but that's good news, my lord. Good news, indeed. Wait till I tell Meg! She'll be a happy woman, make no mistake about it!"

"Yes, I'm sure everyone will be ecstatic," Gray said dryly,

*Everyone, that is, except the intended bride.*

* * *

Kate stood in the darkened kitchen, thinking she'd be safe there from prying eyes. Meg had gone off to bed, so as to be up early, but Kate had no reason to rise at dawn anymore. She swore softly, angry at herself for sulking. She should be pleased. Lucy had her man, and he had turned out to be not a brutal cad, but a scared young man who loved her. No longer did her sister face an uncertain future as a penniless, unwed mother. She would have a husband with an income to support the coming baby. Her happiness was assured.

So why did Kate feel as though someone had torn out her heart? She had never been jealous of Lucy in her life! Until now. And mixed in with the burning envy was a desperate desolation, as she realized that Lucy would soon be gone. Suddenly, the sister who had more often than not seemed a spoiled shrew stood between her and total isolation.

The little household that Kate had struggled to hold together for so long would be split into pieces, with Lucy off to her new life, and Tom leaving, too, perhaps. It was no secret that the coachman had grown quite cozy with Meg, and Kate knew he should make the trip back to London with the cook. She would have to speak with Gray about it. Although the marquis was not exactly fond of Tom, he ought to be able to find a place for the man in his stables, so that the coachman could be near the woman who had taken his fancy.

And then she would be well and truly alone. Tears

threatened, and Kate gripped the edge of the worn table as if it were her lifeline. What if she became ill, here by herself? She would have to establish some kind of contact with the village, but who there could she talk to? She could not let it get out that she was here by herself!

"Kate?"

The sound of Tom's voice made her blink and choke back a sob. She didn't want him to find her like this, or he would never consider following his ladylove to London. Kate whirled around, glad of the dimness in the kitchen.

"Oh, Tom!" she said hurriedly. "I was looking for the last bit of that wonderful cherry tart of Meg's."

"Sorry, but I finished it off myself," Tom declared, without a bit of remorse. "But let's have a taste of that wine His Lordship bought. I've a mind to celebrate." He lit a candle from the smoldering fire and turned to face her.

"Yes, it is wonderful news, isn't it?" Kate said, forcing a smile. "We should have all toasted Lucy's happiness! And to think her gentleman was so close, all along."

"What? Oh, Lucy's chap. Aye, I'll have to admit His Lordship was a clever one, no doubt about that. I've wronged him, Katie."

His words so startled her that Kate nearly dropped the bottle. Meg certainly had mellowed Tom's enmity toward the marquis, but Kate had never expected such complete capitulation.

Tom grinned at her shock. "Well, you understand

as how I had to watch over my girls, and what did I know about this fellow, except that he was ruthless and dangerous and rich as Croesus?'' he asked her with a chuckle. "Not much to recommend himself, especially when I was thinking he was one of those fancy London lords. But he's different, Katie.''

Kate's neck prickled. Why did she get the feeling Tom was not so much trying to convince himself as to persuade her? She poured the wine, then watched him intently over her glass. She had known the old coachman long enough to judge well his moods, and she could be forgiven for distrusting his sudden change of heart.

"Aye, he's a fine lad. Clever as they come, and he knows how to do the right thing when given a little nudge.'' Tom winked at her and drank down his portion.

"And he's not one of those milk-and-water fellows, but a fine, strapping specimen who will sire many sons, I'm guessing.''

Kate blinked at that. She did not care to think of Gray siring anything—on anyone. She swallowed a sip of a delicate vintage such as she had not tasted in a long time.

"Aye, he'll make you a fine husband,'' Tom said, slamming down his empty glass.

At the unexpected words, Kate nearly spewed out the drink in her mouth. Swallowing quickly, she coughed before regaining her composure. Even then, a bright surge of something indefinable swept through her that made it difficult to speak. Surely Tom was mistaken. "Husband?''

"Aye. I've convinced him to do right by you."

Kate's glow of surprise dimmed, chased away by an altogether different sensation, and a coldness settled into the very midst of her being, directly around her heart. "Do right?"

"Aye. He was very reasonable about it. I simply explained that him being here without any proper chaperone wouldn't look the thing to his peers, and he agreed with me. Never even argued."

That was Gray. Reasonable. Clear-thinking. And he would do what was expected of him, because he was an honorable man. He would take her to wife, whether he wanted her or not. The thought made her shiver.

Kate had no illusions about herself. Her worth was in her hands and her mind. She could cook and plant and tally accounts, but she could not flutter a fan or carry a tune. Although an earl's daughter, she had never taken her place in the vaunted sphere of the ton. Instead, she had struggled to keep her little family alive, and it had changed her irrevocably. She was ill-suited for anything now but simple country living.

And as for her other attributes... Kate knew she was not as lovely and delicate as Lucy, and she could imagine well the kind of sparkling beauties Gray had waiting for him in London. The thought of them made her gulp down her drink. Gad, she would not be an object of pity! Anger gave her strength, and she put down her own glass with a loud thump.

"Well, he can take his noble, self-sacrificing offer and go hang!" Kate said, her voice ringing with emotion.

"Now, Katie, don't get yourself in a taking. This is good news!" Tom protested.

"Good for whom?" she asked. "Did you force this on him, so that you would feel free to run off with Meg? Well, I have no intention of holding you here, Thomas Beane, nor do I need you, so you can do whatever you like, without feeling responsible for me."

Despite her best efforts, she was nearly shaking with outrage, and she could see Tom was stunned by her reaction. "Now, Katie, it weren't like that at all. I thought... Hell and damnation, I thought you had taken a liking to the man!"

"You must have been imagining things," she snapped. "I appreciate Wroth's efforts on Lucy's behalf, that is all. And there is no way I am going to let him shackle himself to me, when I'm the one who broke into his study and shot him, thanks to Lucy's incorrect identification!"

Unaccustomed anger and humiliation and despair boiled around inside Kate until she felt like some foreign mountain ready to erupt. She could hardly make sense of it all herself, let alone explain it to Tom, who stood gaping at her with a shocked expression.

"Now, Katie, be reasonable—"

*Reasonable? Sensible?* Suddenly Kate wanted to be none of those things. She wanted to lash out at everything and everyone for disrupting her placid existence, robbing her of those she cared about, taking away the duties that had become her life and making them meaningless, and the final indignity, handing her a sham wedding, while her sister married for love.

"No," she said, her voice a low, thready sound in the dim kitchen. "I do not want to hear another word about your ludicrous scheme, Tom. Go on to London with Meg, but don't try to tie me up in a neat little package, like some loose end."

"Katie—"

At another time, Tom's mournful tone might have touched her, but not tonight. Kate was so enraged, her head throbbed with it, and if she didn't make her escape soon, she feared she would lose all decorum and explode right there in the kitchen. Not daring to put herself to the test, she stalked past the coachman with a regal air worthy of Lucy.

Then she hurried toward the servants' stair, praying that she did not come upon anyone else, especially Gray.

After a night spent tossing and turning and twisting her sheets, Kate remained in a foul mood. Somewhat calmer, she nonetheless found her cheeks stinging every time she imagined Tom forcing the marquis into offering for her. Her first inclination was to hide in her room all day, feigning illness, but she had never been one to ignore a problem, and so she finally put in an appearance, determined to show nothing of her turmoil.

It was afternoon by the time she arrived in the dining hall, but the remains of a breakfast still stood on the sideboard, and Kate picked at the food desultorily. Obviously, Meg had no need of her in the kitchens. Perhaps today she could coax Badcock into helping her clean some of the first-floor rooms. Although Gray's valet, he seemed more than willing to help out wherever necessary, and Kate had no intention of seeking Tom out, only to hear him harp upon her threatened reputation. Ha! She had long ago ceased caring about such intangibles, when matters of daily survival took precedence.

She was just rising from the table when a girl in a starched apron came in. "Can I get you anything more, my lady?" she asked, with a pretty bob of her head.

Kate stared for a moment before catching herself. "Who are you?" she asked in surprise.

The girl smiled. "I'm Dora, my lady, the new housemaid. His Lordship sent me up from London, and I never seen such countryside before!"

*The new housemaid?* Kate felt a surge of outrage at the high-handed marquis. She opened her mouth to speak, but shut it again quickly, unwilling to heap the imprecations that sprang to her tongue on the head of an innocent girl.

"No, thank you...Dora," Kate said, pasting a smile on her face. She walked to the doorway and watched absently while the housemaid cleared the table. Obviously, the girl was here to clean, so there was no point in interrupting her. Pursing her lips, Kate decided that instead of working inside, perhaps she should tackle the gardens, while the weather held.

An old shed held most of the implements Kate required, but one look at the flower beds told her she would need a shovel to remove some of the bigger weeds. With a sigh, she went round to the stables for one, halting suddenly at the sight of a stall freshly filled with straw. A glance into the nearby pasture told her that the only two horses they owned were happily dozing in the field.

Odd. Kate's irritation grew as she began to feel like a stranger in her own home, completely unaware of what was happening around her. Spurred to action, she strode to the kitchen and poked her head inside, where Meg was busy at the old table.

"What is going on in the stable?"

"Oh, Lady Kate, you startled me!" Meg said, putting a hand to her ample bosom. "Why, I believe that Mr. Badcock and Mr. Beane went to London to get one of His Lordship's horses. They brought Dora back with them, and I must say it will be nice to have some more help around here."

Kate flushed. The cook's casual comment held no censure, and yet she felt it, the same old gnawing guilt, that the sad state of Hargate was somehow her fault. She stiffened. "And just where is this beast?"

Meg looked up, eyeing her in some surprise. "Why, I understand that His Lordship took the animal out himself, to check on the tenants."

*The tenants? Her* tenants? Kate seethed. Not trusting herself to speak, she nodded curtly and closed the door. Then she stomped back to the stables. How dare he! Admittedly, she had not talked to the people who worked her father's land lately, because she no longer had any power over the estate. Uncle Jasper controlled the rents and the collections, as he did everything else. But what gave Gray the right to meddle?

What made him think he could poke his nose into everything? The more she thought about his arrogant usurpation of her role here at Hargate, the angrier she became. Although she had once longed for someone with whom to share her burdens, she had never had any intention of relinquishing all her responsibilities, indeed, her very existence to some overbearing lord. It was bad enough that Gray had taken over her household, installing his own servants, without asking her permission, and throwing the contents of his deep pockets around, but now he was acting as if he owned the very land beneath her feet, hills and pastures that had been in her family for centuries!

Kate would have taken off after him, but she had no idea in which direction he had gone. And so, she could do nothing but wait near the stables, hoping to catch him when he returned. As she stalked back and forth, her frustration mounted. How dare he! He was nothing to them. Nothing! Not a blood relation or a guardian or even a...suitor, Tom's ridiculous efforts be damned! His only connection to them was the imposter who had used his name, and that was a tenuous bond at best. What gave him the right to barge into their lives, disrupting everything, taking over all her duties and leaving her with nothing?

With a strangled moan, Kate sank down upon a hillock and buried her face in her hands as resentment and rage and despair welled up inside her, threatening to spill out. Gad, what was happening to her? How often had she rued her position as head of the faltering family, cook, maid, groom, grounds-keeper and general jack-of-all-trades? Ever since her father's death, she had taken on more and more duties, until they became overwhelming.

But better to be overwhelmed than not to be needed at all.

Kate had nothing to do, nothing important anyway, and it frightened her, because her work was who and what she was, and without it, she felt as nothing. She was little more than a well-bred oddity, an earl's daughter who wore breeches and mucked around in the dirt or the ovens, who could swear like a sailor and tend her own horse, but who had no place in the noble world into which she had been born.

In her own sensible fashion, Kate recognized that she could not go back. She could not don a fancy gown and turn into a lady again. She could not spend her days watercoloring and playing the pianoforte and prattling on about *nothing*. She could never fit into that shallow and glittering world again, because she was too different. But if she could not go back, and had lost her place, what was she to do? How was she to go on?

Kate was not certain how long she sat there, immersed in her own misery, but the sound of hoofbeats finally roused her. She quickly straightened, dashing away the telltale tears. She would certainly never let Gray see her cry. She was not a weepy-eyed whiner like Lucy. She was made of sterner stuff, and he was about to find out just what.

"Kate!" Ignoring the warmth that spread through her at the sound of her name on his lips, she turned on him, forcing herself not to watch the clean lines of his body as he dismounted: long legs, muscular thighs, wide shoulders. Surely there had never been such a handsome Judas.

"How dare you!" she asked him, as coolly as she could manage.

In response, he lifted that infernal brow of his, and she wanted to yank the dark hairs from his head. Instead, she kept her gaze level, her tone even. "You overstep your bounds, my lord."

"Did I? I was not aware that you had set any bounds for me, Kate."

Kate could feel her cheeks blaze, but she refused to be drawn into another one of his games of taunt and parry, one of his sophisticated London plays of flirtation. She would have none of it! She crossed her arms over her chest and glared at him. "Damn you, you have no right speaking to our tenants."

She had his complete attention now, for both brows went up, and his eyes glittered. "I was trying to discover just how they fare, Kate. Yesterday I came across one of your families leaving the land because of their ill-usage. I would think you would like to see your uncle called to account for his greedy practices before he destroys your heritage."

Kate blinked. How had he found out about Jasper? And why had he said nothing of it to her? Of course, she wanted her uncle brought to justice, and she was both grateful and envious of his efforts, when her own had come to nothing, but he was running rough-shod over her, and she refused to be dashed into the ground. She glared at him; he was so cool and contained and fine-looking that he made her constraint snap.

"Damn you and your high-handed ways!" she cried, lashing out at him physically. She struck his broad chest with one fist and then the other. Long held back, her anger exploded with the pain of so many humiliations, including the marriage offer forced from him by her coachman, which he had yet to discuss with her.

Gad, but she was not a creature to be pitied, or a ninny to be shunted aside while all her decisions were made for her! Her rage unleashed, Kate pounded on him furiously, though her blows had little effect upon that hard expanse. Finally, he grasped her wrists and held them up, his gaze sharp and questioning. "What is this all about, Kate?"

"You have no right! Who are you to come in here and take over? Can't you see what you are doing, you arrogant beast? No, you just stand there, as stiff as your valet, without even blinking. Don't you feel anything?"

His eyes narrowed. "I feel. I feel too damn much, where you're concerned." Gray growled out the words in a low, threatening tone that pulled her up short. Kate glanced at him, startled by the taut fury that showed on his features, the dark, dangerous stance of his strong body. Too late, she wanted to recall her hasty words, and she tried to step back, away from him, but he held her fast.

The gray depths of his eyes glittered, and Kate watched, stunned, as he lifted one of her wrists and pressed his open mouth to her racing pulse. She shivered, although it was heat that rushed through her, making her limbs weak. When he pressed his lips to the other wrist, she swayed on her feet, and would have fallen if he had not swung her up into his arms. The world careened dizzily around her as Kate clung to his neck, the ground moving swiftly below. She was dimly aware of the shadows of the stables closing around her before she tumbled backward, out of Gray's embrace, and landed with a soft jolt in the fresh hay that filled the empty stall.

Kate gasped as she looked up at him. Gone was the marquis that she had come to know. This man stood over her like a stranger, his hair wind-tossed, his face hard and his eyes wild. As she stared, he stripped off his gloves and threw them aside, then yanked off his coat. His fingers, always deft and assured, fumbled with the buttons of his waistcoat before it, too, was flung aside.

Gad, was he going to take off everything? Kate's heart thundered in her chest. She had seen him naked before, but not apurpose, and certainly not in this manner, tearing off his garments like a man driven by demons. It was as if the cool veneer that had encased him for so long were being cast away with his clothing.

And although she had wanted to discompose him, this was not at all what she had had in mind. She drew in a deep, ragged breath as he pulled at his shirt, drawing it up to reveal his broad chest, the hair dusted across it, the puckered red mark of his wound and the dark thatches beneath his arms. Thrusting away the fine linen, he paused to look at her.

Kate shivered, half in fear and half in delicious excitement, as he came down on top of her, his mouth finding hers with luscious abandon. She knew not what fueled him, anger or madness, or whether he was toying with her still, but she could no more deny him than she could the swift spark of her own escalating passion. She had forgotten the feel of the clean lines of his torso, and she slid her hands up his chest, delighting in the play of his muscles, the soft hair, the hard nipples, the smooth skin of his back. He groaned, pressing closer, and the weight of him settled against her until all she knew was his hardness.

And the heat. It surrounded her, from his body, his lips, and his hands as they cupped her face. His fingers traced the whorls of her ears, laced through the curls of her hair, kneaded her scalp and glided down her throat, leaving fiery trails behind them. His tongue danced with hers, a simmering, swirling waltz of taste and texture that fired her desire. His palms glided over her breasts before he pulled impatiently at her shirt, whispering curses.

Gone was the smooth, polished lover from the hillside, and in his place was a man whose hands trembled when they touched her bare stomach. He kissed her there, his tongue dipping into her navel and startling her with bright pleasure before moving on to skim the flesh beneath the edge of her trousers. Kate was filled with a sweet, giddy warmth, and smiled to hear him swear again as he fumbled with the fall.

Her amusement fled when, above the harshness of their breaths, came the sound of a button popping and landing against the side of the stall while he ripped the material asunder. And then she felt him. Kate sucked in a breath of shock and delight as his hand slid inside her pants to touch the thatch of hair that covered her nether regions.

"Kate. God, Kate," he murmured against her stomach, and his hand dipped lower, over the hidden place between her legs as he nudged them open. "You're wet. Ready for me." He shuddered, and lifted his head to look at her. His eyes blazed with a fire that she had never seen before, a wildness that held her in thrall. He loomed above her, his tall body still as he trapped her with his gaze, and the air simmered around her, heavy with anticipation.

And then she felt it, the slow insinuation of one of his long fingers, into her, up high, and she cried out, closing her eyes at the unholy pleasure, so…fine, so intense, so… She lifted her hips, meeting his knuckle, and he rocked his finger deep, pressing his thumb tight against her. A noise escaped her throat, and Kate gripped his muscled arms, her nails digging into his skin as she sought purchase. Her head fell back, and she gasped for air, while the heat grew in intensity until it exploded within her, an amazing rush of flame that left her body boneless and melted.

For a long moment, Kate lay there, unable to move or think, until a snuffling sound finally made her open her eyes. She saw Gray and, over his shoulder, a large dark shape. His horse, obviously tired of waiting for a nonexistent groom, was nudging his back. Muttering a curse, he pushed the animal's head away, but it was insistent. Although Kate wanted to laugh, the expression on Gray's face stopped her. He looked down at her with such naked emotion that she blinked, and then it was gone, and his features were shuttered once more. He stood, leaving her there, with her shirt pushed up and her trousers gaping open, and grabbed for his shirt.

"So now you know," he said in a hoarse whisper. "Now we both know the passion that rides beneath the surface."

# Chapter Twelve

Silently, Kate let Mrs. Leeds help her into the first of her new gowns to reach completion. Although she was tempted to refuse it, Kate could hardly insult the young widow, who was justifiably proud of her work. The garment fitted her to perfection, the silk flowing over her body seamlessly. Smooth and light as a cloud, it was finer than anything Kate had ever owned, and she touched it with something akin to awe.

At Mrs. Leeds's urging, she stood before the mirror in Lucy's room, amazed by the reflection that met her eyes. The girl who stared back at her looked nothing like the drudge she had become, but resembled a younger, more carefree version of herself, slender and pretty, her dark curls gathered in new ribbons.

"It's lovely, Mrs. Leeds," Kate said softly, fingering the soft material. The color was beautiful and seemed oddly familiar, like a field of violets spread before her, fresh and... Kate stiffened and jerked her hands away as she remembered Gray laying her down upon this very fabric, draped over the worn oak table in the kitchen like some hedonistic carpet.

"His Lordship chose the bolt himself, to match your eyes, he said, and he was right," Mrs. Leeds said, smiling happily. "You look fair as a summer morn, lady."

Kate turned away from the mirror, her brief pleasure in the garment destroyed by the mention of Gray. She had spent the better part of the night lying awake, wondering how she could have been so wanton with him, how in just a few moments he had transformed her anger into desire. Kate blushed to recall her behavior, arching into his hand, crying out her pleasure in breathy sobs! And then, after giving her the most intense experience of her life, he had left her lying half-naked on the floor of the stall.

She had watched Gray stalk away from her, his fists clenched at his sides, and she had felt as if they were closing around her heart. She had tried to goad him into feeling something, but it was she who had ended up shaken to the core. If he had meant to teach her a lesson, he had succeeded. She would never again try to pierce his cool exterior, for fear of cutting herself. And yet, he had felt *something*, she would have sworn it. But what? Lust, longing, disgust?

And even as she rued what had gone between them, Kate wondered what, if anything, might have happened if they had not been interrupted. The other time, on the hill, she had possessed the strength to end it, but yesterday that resolve had dissolved in the pulsing heat of his touch. Would he have sought satisfaction himself? Or did she repulse him so that he could not bear to go farther?

Kate shivered, suddenly cold, and rubbed her arms.

"Here, my lady, you're not used to baring so much, are you?" Mrs. Leeds said with a chuckle. That was true enough, for instead of a man's shirt, her arms were covered only with tiny puffed sleeves, and an alarming expanse of her chest seemed to be displayed before the neckline made an appearance.

"I'm sure we brought along just the thing! Here!" Mrs. Leeds said, turning to hand Kate a spangled shawl that matched the elaborate trim of her gown. It sparkled like spun gold, and although she told herself she had no business wearing such finery, it slid over her shoulders delightfully, in a sensuous glide that reminded her of Gray's touch. Gad, could she think of nothing except the man?

"Are you all right, my lady? You've turned a bit pale, but here now," Mrs. Leeds said, reaching up to pinch Kate's cheeks. "That's better. Now, I've orders from my mum to let her see you first off, so we must make a stop in the kitchen, if you don't mind."

Mumbling her assent, Kate dutifully followed the seamstress down the servants' stair and let Meg exclaim over her daughter's handiwork. Then she was shooed off to the dining hall, where Lucy waited, presumably breathlessly, for her gentleman, who seemed to spend nearly all his time at Hargate lately. Although Kate forced herself to put aside such petty resentments, she was still assailed by the same combination of joy and sadness that accompanied any thoughts of her sister's wedding.

Kate tried to put on a brave face as she walked along the gallery, but, in truth, she was not looking forward to the celebratory meal that Meg had planned for tonight. Supper the evening before had been a stilted affair that left her feeling dismayed by the changes in her little household.

Tom no longer ate with them, but joined Meg and her daughter, Badcock and the new maid in the kitchen. Kate could hardly blame him, for the atmosphere there had to be more convivial than above stairs, where Lucy preened for Rutledge and he petted her in return. Neither one of them had eyes for anyone else, which left Kate to entertain the other guest, Gray.

She refused to do it. The haughty marquis presided over them all as if he owned the place, so she left him to his own devices and concentrated on eating what little food she could manage. Thus, silence reigned at their places, for Gray spoke little. She often caught him glaring at her, as if she were to blame for…something, while at other times he studied her as if she were some sort of oddity, which, of course, she was.

Kate did not appreciate the reminder.

She took her leave as soon as manners permitted, and Gray did not seek her out to apologize, explain, or otherwise converse with her. Despite Tom's claims, the marquis had never offered for her, either, and instead of feeling relieved, Kate knew an odd, painful disappointment. Her face flamed when she wondered, as she had so often during her sleepless night, whether the proposal was a hoax, a jest to satisfy Tom while Gray amused himself.

Embarrassment and anger surged through her once more. Surely Gray was not so cruel! And yet, what did she really know of the marquis? He was a man, and, as such, a mystery to her. He was dangerous and powerful and arrogant and was ordering her very existence, though she knew not why.

She knew only that she couldn't go on like this anymore, unsure of her place in her own household and embarrassed by the passions that Gray seemed to stir in her so effortlessly. Kate swallowed hard. Although she appreciated what the marquis had done for Lucy, she saw no reason for him to linger here. Each day he stayed made it easier for them all to lean upon him, and would make it all the more difficult to accept the inevitable parting when it came. For the others, Kate clarified. Personally, she would be glad to be rid of the haughty, heartless lord, for then she would resume her life.

Without him.

Drawing in a deep breath, Kate resolved to have it out with him today. Although she would rather conduct such a conversation in private, she knew better than to meet with Gray alone. She would speak to him after dinner, with Lucy and Rutledge present to lend their dubious support.

Her determination was shaken when she spied him ahead of her in the gallery. Although she halted, Gray must have heard her, for he turned and stood, awaiting her approach. Kate had no choice but to walk toward him as he watched her, his eyes seeming to strip her of every bit of clothing, including the underthings hidden beneath. Suddenly, acutely, aware of the fact that it was his coin that had purchased them, she felt oddly wicked and yet strangely excited.

Against her better judgment, Kate's eyes strayed from the top of his wide shoulders, down his broad chest, to his muscled thighs, encased in tight doeskin. She shivered, determined to set her mind on a more appropriate path. It would do no good to moon over the marquis of Wroth, for he would be leaving soon, as she had always known he would.

If only he weren't so tall, so handsome, so self-possessed, so supremely male, Kate thought, dizzy with regret. If only he didn't threaten her peace of mind...

If only she didn't threaten his mastery over himself, Gray thought as he watched Kate walk toward him. Clad in the violet silk, she looked more beautiful than ever, and he struggled against the desire that raged through him. Desire, hell! This lust for Kate had gone beyond that, as his performance in the stable had proved. It was a wild, primitive need to mate.

Nearly uncontrollable.

And so far, nothing in Gray's life had ever defied his dominion. He was not sure he liked this ragged, raw sensation of want. But as he saw the filmy material flow over her curves, dipping low beneath a milky-white expanse of breast that he had tasted and remembered all too well, he was not certain he had a choice.

He held out his arm. She gave him a cool smile that belied the passion he knew he could ignite. With a curt nod, he led her in to dinner, but Meg's dishes held no interest for him, as he became absorbed with Kate. Her every moment seemed unerringly erotic: the lift of her lashes, the dip of her head, the brush of her curls against a nape that drew him like a magnet.

Shifting in his seat, Gray deliberately eyed the other members of the party, just to prove that he could, but Rutledge's fawning admiration for Lucy was an uncomfortable reminder of his own obsession with Kate. He let out a ragged sigh. He would be glad when the two lovebirds were ensconced in one of his more remote properties, never to be seen again.

After the meal, Gray led a coolly aloof Kate into the drawing room, and grew annoyed at himself when the light touch of her hand on his arm sparked an overheated response. Dangerous, he thought with a frown. His pursuit of the poppet had assumed more importance in his mind than was warranted. He never had wasted so much time contemplating a woman's charms! It was ridiculous, he thought, even as he caught himself staring at her mouth and craving the hot, sweet taste of her.

If Kate noticed his discomfort, it was not apparent, for she simply found her own place and turned toward him, her expression somber. "I assume, now that your work is done, that you will be leaving us," she said, with an expectant lift of her head.

The words made Gray stiffen, though he disguised it, raising a brow in question. "Are you so eager to be rid of me, Kate?"

She blushed and shot a glance at the other two people in the room, but they had gathered together on a sofa and were raptly staring into each other's eyes. "I simply would like to know how long you plan to stay," she said. Was he imagining it, or did her voice falter?

"I feel responsible for you now, and would right this situation with your uncle," Gray answered, deliberately keeping to practical matters and not the vagaries of his own thwarted desires.

"Oh, thank heaven!" Lucy piped up, tearing her attention away from her lover. "Perhaps you can get me a dowry!"

Gray tilted his head toward Lucy in acknowledgment, but his eyes were on her sister. Although accustomed to reading people, he found nothing in Kate's chilly expression that hinted at her desires. Did she want him to remain? Gray had yet to meet a woman who rebuffed him, and despite her distant behavior now, he knew he could rouse Kate's passions as he had so effortlessly in the stable. He stared at her, willing her to give him answers to questions he could not put into words.

"Kate!"

The sound of a shout brought them both around, and a short, rotund man burst into the room, followed by an apologetic Badcock.

"There you are!" the man said loudly as his head swiveled toward Kate.

"I beg your pardon, my lord," Badcock said, his expression tight with disapproval. "But this... gentleman insisted upon seeing Lady Courtland."

"Squire Wortley," Kate said, her greeting decidedly unenthusiastic.

"Uncle!" Rutledge exclaimed, jumping up with a look of alarm on his boyish face.

"And you!" the squire sputtered, turning toward his nephew. "What's all this nonsense about you marrying?"

Squire Wortley. Gray fixed his contemptuous gaze on the little bastard who had so swindled the innocent Courtlands. Already annoyed by his recent exchange with Kate, Gray found himself only too ready to take on the squire, preferably by slamming him into the wall.

"Squire Wortley," he said coolly, rising to his feet. "What a propitious meeting. I have been most anxious to speak with you."

Wortley swung toward Gray. "And who the devil are you?"

Gray's lips curled grimly. "I am Wroth."

"Wroth?" the squire asked, looking puzzled. "The marquis?"

At Gray's nod, he swallowed noticeably. Obviously, even Wortley had heard of him, and Gray took some pleasure in his reputation. He tilted his head in acknowledgment. "And you, Squire, have arrived at a most opportune time. Let us speak, privately."

"Privately, eh? What's this? Katie?" The man shot Kate a panicked glance, but she ignored his pained expression with such regal grace that Gray paused a moment to admire her. Then he nodded to Badcock, and without blinking an eye, the valet assumed the duties of a butler, leading the marquis and his reluctant guest to the study and closing the doors behind them.

"Please, be seated," Gray said, waving his hand toward one of the threadbare chairs that stood near the empty grate. As he moved to a place behind the desk, Gray took the opportunity to assess his opponent, and experienced a vague disappointment. The squire was like so many of his class, a fleshy, red-faced little man with pretensions to a higher station, but lacking the intelligence to better himself.

Gray eyed the short, squat fellow, whose bulging belly told of his fine table and whose expensive rings and watch fob spoke of his prosperity, and he suddenly wondered whether the bastard had sold the items he took from Hargate in order to realize a tidy profit. At the thought, Gray felt his fingers clench, and he purposely spread them, steepling them before him as he fixed the squire with a cool gaze.

"I, uh, really, my lord, I do not see what business you could possibly have with me," the man muttered. "I came to see Ka—uh, Lady Courtland—about a matter involving my nephew."

"Ah," Gray said, "the impending nuptials, I assume."

Wortley's head swiveled toward Gray, his small eyes bulging in surprise. "Yes! I, rather... It is most unusual, most unusual—"

"Surely you can have no objection to the marriage," Gray said.

Wortley's gaze darted about nervously as he cleared his throat. "I hardly think it is a matter for my lord's interest."

"Oh, but you are wrong. I am very much interested," Gray said smoothly.

With a scowl, Wortley abandoned his manners. "Dash it all, the boy has but a small allowance from his grandmother, and God knows the Courtlands have no money. I have allowed him to live with me, out of respect for his father—"

"A viscount's younger son, I understand."

The squire colored. "Well, yes, but blood hardly signifies, when there are pockets to let. As I was saying, I have allowed the boy to live with me—"

"And received his management skills free of charge."

"Now, see here!" Wortley sputtered, apparently reaching the end of his patience. "I would like to know what connection you have to this household!"

Gray smiled slightly. "Very well. Although it is not common knowledge, considering the circumstances, I will take you into my confidence." He leaned forward, as though bestowing a favor upon the portly squire. "The elder Lady Courtland and I are betrothed."

Gray sank bank in his chair while Wortley gasped in astonishment. "But, but, how? When? She has not spoken to me of it!"

To avoid speculation concerning the sudden betrothal, Gray lied easily. "It is an old engagement, arranged by our families when she was just an infant, and one that was kept secret until we were both sure of our feelings.''

Wortley looked stunned, but swallowed the tale whole. "Why, this is astonishing news, my lord," he said, nodding as if he had decided that such a scheme could benefit him. "Puts quite a different light on things, I must say." He smiled eagerly.

"I thought it would," Gray said, dryly. "So, you shall have no objections to the match between Lady Courtland and your nephew?"

The squire cleared his throat again. "Well, now, as I was saying, we haven't the room for a new family at the house, but if you are going to provide a living for the two of them—"

"Their income need no longer be your concern, Squire, for Mr. Rutledge will be moving from your household to take employment with me."

Wortley sputtered some more, undoubtedly regretting his hasty words, now that his nephew would be brother-in-law to one of the wealthiest men in the country, but Gray paid him no heed. Leaning back in his chair, he eyed the man coolly.

"But that is not why I asked you here, Squire. I understand that you have borrowed some pieces from the estate, and I would like them returned as soon as possible."

Wortley turned bright red, his eyes practically popping their sockets, as he spat out a denial. "Borrowed? I purchased those items, my lord!"

"Did you, now?" Gray asked, fixing the squire with a gaze that made him squirm in his seat. In the silence that ensued, Gray casually picked up a silver-handled knife used to break the seals on correspondence. It was a trifle that Kate once might have sold to the man across from him, and he fingered the blade suggestively while Wortley's crimson cheeks lost their color.

"Well, then, perhaps you can return these missing goods as wedding gifts to the Courtland ladies, your neighbors of long standing, as a sign of your goodwill," Gray said, feigning a smile.

Wortley squeaked out a protest, but Gray disregarded it, as if the man had not spoken. "Very good. I knew we could come to an agreement. Now, I'm sure you will want to attend to that at once. Shall I have a full accounting prepared for you?" he asked, rising to his feet.

"No! I recall every item, but—"

"Badcock," Gray called out, and the vigilant valet immediately opened the doors to the study. "Show the squire out, will you?" he asked.

"Very good, my lord," Badcock said solemnly, leaving Wortley no option but to follow behind.

Watching the fellow turn tail and flee, Gray's lips curved slightly. Now he had only Uncle Jasper to run to ground, and his business with the Courtlands would be completed—with one glaring exception. His smile faded.

There was still Kate to contend with.

Resting his hands against the back of one of the few chairs that still graced the long hall, Gray stood pondering her increasingly factitious behavior until he realized that his knuckles had turned white. Damn.

Deliberately lifting his hands from their position, he stretched his fingers, then turned to rejoin the others. Perhaps it was time he settled things with the poppet.

Gray had nearly reached the drawing room when the sound of raised voices drifted to him from the foyer. Was Wortley giving Badcock trouble? He ought to have wrung the little bastard's neck! The annoyance and frustration that dogged him so much lately made him swing on his heel angrily, determined to test his fists on the squire's red face. Stalking back along the gallery, he strode into the tiled entranceway, only to halt in his tracks.

Wortley was gone, but in his place were other visitors, two men and two women, to be exact, and Gray drew in a sharp breath as he recognized the gentlemen. They were all talking gaily as Badcock tried to fob them off, and for a moment Gray thought he might escape unnoticed, but it was too late. One of the men glanced his way and gave up a happy shout. "Wroth!"

Inwardly groaning, Gray could do naught but make the best of the situation, all the while wondering what had brought Raleigh and his cronies to Hargate. He stepped forward as the other man, a rather obnoxious character named Pimperington, ogled him curiously.

"Wroth? Is that you? What the devil are you doing here, I'd like to know! Egad, man, the whole town is abuzz with speculation as to your whereabouts." He turned to Raleigh. "I say, where the devil are we? Who owns this place?" Slightly deaf, he spoke in a loud tone that Gray now recalled all too well.

"You are at Hargate, the ancestral home of the earls of Chester." Gray stiffened at the sound of Kate's calm, cool voice, and total silence fell as all four visitors, including the incessantly giggling females, stopped talking to stare at the woman who stood in the doorway. She was beautiful, of course, and had more dignity than any of them, Gray thought proudly.

"Eh, what? Who's this?" Pimperington shouted.

"Indeed!" Raleigh echoed, lifting that ridiculous quizzing glass of his to gaze at Kate boldly.

"Lady Courtland," Gray said, moving swiftly to her side. "May I present Viscount Raleigh, Mr. Pimperington, and..." He trailed off.

"Oh, yes, of course!" Pimperington blustered. "Gels," he said, motioning to the females. "This lovely widow is Mrs. Parker and her sister, Miss Collier."

"Lady. My lord." Both women simpered and fluttered their eyelashes at him in a manner that made Kate's cool composure all the more appealing, by contrast. How easily he had forgotten the very differences that drew him to her.

"Wroth, you wretch!" Raleigh cried accusingly, dropping the quizzing glass to stare unabashedly at Kate. "I wagered a small fortune that you had discovered some new gambling den! Lud, no one will win in the betting books, for who would have ever thought you to rusticate in the country? But I can see why you're here," he added, bowing low to Kate. His usually amusing charm suddenly grated.

"Eh, what's that? Oh, I should say so," Pimperington agreed, edging closer. The ladies, not to be outdone, crowded in, too, and began to pepper Kate with questions.

"Why is it we have never seen you in London?" the widow asked coyly.

"Eh, what? Yes, what are you doing, buried up here in the country?" Pimperington asked.

"Perhaps she thought to keep the marquis all to herself!" Miss Collier suggested, and Gray knew he had to put a stop to such speculation immediately, before it grew out of hand or Kate, taking offense, said something regrettable.

"Or perhaps Wroth thought to hide this diamond from the rest of the world," Raleigh said, coming to Kate's defense in a way that irritated Gray. He felt a primitive urge to lay claim to her, to announce his possession in no uncertain terms. Schooling his features to reveal none of the aberrant emotions that surged through him, Gray leaned toward her.

"Indeed, I'm afraid that you have found me out," he said, his brow lifting slightly. "I've been enjoying a respite from town with my future bride."

# Chapter Thirteen

Gray's announcement was met with varying degrees of shock, not the least of which passed across the face of his intended. She recovered her composure quickly, but the other females gasped and gaped rudely, while Pimperington ogled her in a most unseemly fashion, his rapt gaze moving over the white expanse of her breasts with an interest that made Gray livid.

Raleigh was the only one who did not stare at Kate as if to determine exactly what she possessed that had managed to ensnare the marquis of Wroth. Instead, the viscount was watching Gray, his usually languid gaze bright with interest.

"This is splendid news!" he said, with a broad grin. "Should have known you'd snatch up such a goddess without giving the rest of us mortals a chance! May I be the first to tender my congratulations," he added, bending low over Kate's hand. She nodded rather dazedly.

"And when is the wedding to be, my lord?" Mrs. Parker asked slyly as she raised her fan to flutter about her face. "We have heard nothing of your engagement in town."

"It is of long standing, arranged by our families when Kate was but a child," Gray said, fixing the nosy woman with a fierce gaze that made her step back. "Now that we are both of an age and mind to wed, I suspect the ceremony will be held very soon."

"Marriage? Wroth? I say, this is something! Now none of you can complain about me getting us lost! Like to take up the reins, you know," Pimperington said to Kate. "Had to try out my new curricle, you see. Must have taken a wrong turn somewhere, but all's well that ends well, as the Bard would say!"

"But we've been traveling forever!" Miss Collier complained.

"And still would be, if we hadn't spied the house chimneys," Raleigh muttered.

"Well, we can certainly set you to rights again," Gray said, cursing the ill luck that had brought them to Hargate. As much as he would like to send them on their way with all speed, common civility demanded that he offer them something. "If you are in a hurry, I can show you the proper route at once, but if you would care for some rest and some refreshments, you may join us in the drawing room."

"What's that? Refreshments, you say? Just the thing to revive us!" Pimperington said loudly, and Gray had no choice but to lead them into the gallery.

To his surprise, he felt a restraining hand upon his arm. "You go on ahead," Raleigh said, waving to Pimperington and a pale-looking Kate. "I want to speak with Wroth for a moment."

As he watched the rest of the party disappear, Gray resigned himself to a brief interrogation. Although he had no patience with some of Raleigh's dandified antics, beneath the frivolous exterior beat the heart of a genuinely kind friend, a rarity among the ton, and Gray knew he could rely upon the viscount's discretion. Striding toward the study, he motioned Raleigh to a seat and shut the doors behind them.

"Well?" There was no mistaking the humor in the viscount's tone.

Gray turned. "Well, what?"

Raleigh laughed. "What are you *really* doing in this godforsaken place? And with a gel who looked as surprised as I was to hear that she's to wed you!"

Gray frowned. He did not know why Kate had seemed so startled. Did she think he would have seduced her nearly to the point of consummation if he entertained no thoughts of marriage? The idea annoyed him. Though he knew he was under no obligation to her, the notion that she expected the worst of him was not comforting.

"Circumstances brought us together," Gray said, refraining from explaining just how Kate had snuck into his study and shot him. "As you know, I've been considering taking a wife for some time now, and Lady Courtland meets all my requirements."

"Which are?" Raleigh asked, his mouth drawn up in amusement.

"She is intelligent, attractive, and of good lineage," Gray hedged, not wanting to reveal too much, even to Raleigh.

Even to himself.

Raleigh straightened in his seat. "Lud, Wroth, that's a little cold-blooded, even for you! Are you saying you have no affection for the girl?"

"I hardly think that is necessary for a good marriage," Gray said, rounding on his friend. "Lady Courtland has a number of admirable traits—honesty, strength, and a poise that defies all hardship. Such qualities are more to be valued than some passing flirtation."

"Hmm." Raleigh's smile returned. "Not a case of opposites attracting. I'll wager you and the gel are too much alike to have an easy time of it. And from the looks of her, she's got a will to match your own, which should prove a bit uncomfortable for a man who has gotten his way since he was in leading strings!"

Ignoring Raleigh's foolish prattle, Gray walked to the windows and stood looking out. "I had thought that we could have a companionable existence together, but..."

"But?"

Gray turned around. "Now I'm not so sure."

Raleigh whistled long and low. "Lud, this is serious. The great Wroth himself having *doubts?*"

Gray disregarded the jest and stalked past the desk. "I knew from the first that she was suitable. More than suitable," he amended. "But she seems to have a peculiar effect upon me, a loss of composure, if you will, that is most unsettling."

"What's that you say?"

Gray turned his head to fix his friend with a meaningful stare. "I've been smashing things." The violence was part of it, but there was more that was harder to articulate, even to Raleigh. He walked back to the windows and stared out. "I've lost all finesse, Raleigh. Clarinda wouldn't recognize me," he admitted softly, referring to one of his most famous mistresses.

"Deuced, but it's positively alarming," Raleigh said, sounding highly entertained. "I fear for your sanity. Why, next you'll be beating your breast like a gorilla and swinging the gel from a chandelier!"

Gray frowned at Raleigh's amusement. "I don't like it," he said.

"You're still the same man," Raleigh argued.

"Am I?" Gray turned to face him. "I wonder."

Raleigh eyed him soberly. "You've been restless, searching for something. Perhaps you've found it."

Gray did not reply. He had been seeking peace, or at least a sort of quiet companionship, not this disturbing passion that threatened his very mastery over himself.

Raleigh sighed. "Well, you're going to have to marry her now, or do some fancy maneuvering. Pimperington's not the type to ignore a juicy *on-dit*. He'll have the news all over town within the week."

"I know," Gray said softly. He had thought the open declaration would settle his mind, but he still had nagging doubts about himself—and about Kate.

As if reading his thoughts, Raleigh gave a snort of laughter. "And what about your counterpart? She don't look too thrilled to be betrothed to the most eligible bachelor in the kingdom."

"She's too stubborn for her own good," Gray

muttered. "Of course Kate will marry me. She'll do what's sensible."

Raleigh shook his head. "Not every female will put up with your high-handed ways, Wroth, not even for the privilege of being a marchioness. And this one doesn't appear interested in your wealth or position—or your considerable physical charms." He flashed an irreverent grin.

Gray frowned. Of course, Kate didn't care about such things; that was one of her most appealing traits. Yet surely she would not refuse his name. And now he had announced their betrothal, she could hardly deny him!

"She must marry. Her uncle is going through her fortune like water," Gray said grimly. "According to my inquiries, he's been throwing money away on women, gambling and elegant trifles. He's in Scotland now, having fled the country after a certain unpleasantness with a lady of quality."

"He's not the earl."

"No, her father made a mésalliance. The marchioness was lovely and sweet, but her brother is not. Jasper Gillray imprisoned the girls here to fend for themselves, without a chaperone, without even proper servants!" Gray felt the familiar sure of rage and released a harsh breath. "I would like to kill him with my bare hands, Raleigh," he said, turning to give his friend a glimpse of his fury.

"Hmm," the viscount mused. "Better to channel all that excess of emotion into your marriage bed. Less chance of being arrested for murder! I'd say a special license is in order, if the gel's of age."

"She is," Gray said, feeling some of the strain leave his body.

"Then, do it!" Raleigh said, rising to his feet. "If only to have mercy on my spinning head, for I can't stand to watch you pace a moment longer!"

Gray halted his steps to glare at his friend. "I never pace."

Raleigh grinned. "Just so. Beastly trait, isn't it? I believe Wycliffe used to say the same thing."

Gray glared at him. "Do not liken me to that idiot Wycliffe and his wife, for my marriage will be entirely different."

"Oh?" Raleigh said, raising his quizzing glass.

"Yes! The two of them fancy themselves in love, while Kate and I are embarking on a sensible arrangement that will benefit us both. She will have her fortune returned to her, along with my name and my title, while I shall have a wife to get me heirs. It is as simple as that. And put down that ridiculous thing," Gray said, knocking Raleigh's glass aside as he stalked past him and out of the study.

Simple. Business. A contracted marriage, Gray told himself, even as the sound of Raleigh's laughter followed behind him.

Kate went through all the polite motions, ringing for tea and cakes and making introductions, just as though she were the lady of the house and not its poverty-stricken tenant. Although the unwanted guests could, no doubt, guess at Hargate's decline, Kate told herself they had no way of knowing that the servants were here only temporarily and that there was no chaperone in residence. She spoke loud enough for the odious Mr. Pimperington to hear, deflected Mrs. Parker's barbed questions, and watched Lucy preen for a new audience.

For once, she wished she had some of her sister's vanity, for despite her new clothes, she felt as drab as a mouse next to the visitors. The man she pegged as a dandy, decked out in satins and silks of every hue, with a high starched collar and dangling watch and flashing rings. He nearly outshone the ladies, who were less colorfully, if no less splendidly, attired, in low-cut gowns that made her own seem modest. They wore elaborate hats with plumes and feathers and carried beaded reticules and fans that they twirled and snapped and fluttered as in some sort of mysterious communication.

And in between taking tiny nibbles of their cakes, they stared at Kate, their eyes narrowed, their mouths turned up into smiles that were patently false. They were like the illustrations of exotic vipers in one of her papa's books—both beautiful and deadly—and Kate felt like tipping them over in their chairs and pouring tea upon their heads.

Instead, she gave them cool nods and ignored the voice inside that told her this was the world she had left and to which she could never return, no matter what that arrogant tyrant Gray said. And when her thoughts tended to drift to the pain his abrupt announcement had caused her, she refused to acknowledge it, concentrating instead upon holding her own against the company.

"But surely you know Lady Bradley? She is most

famous for her entertainments! Why, everyone has been to Bradley House!'' Mrs. Parker said. It was on the tip of Kate's tongue to put a halt to this devious conversation and begin some plain speaking, but just then Gray returned, bringing the other dandy with him.

"Kate has not been to London recently," he said easily, coming to stand behind her chair. "She spent several years in mourning after her father's death, and has not had the heart for such frivolities."

"But you must bring her to town soon!" Mrs. Parker protested as she lifted her fan.

"Perhaps after we are married," Gray answered, and Kate was startled to feel the tips of his fingers brush her shoulders. "You will forgive me if I am a bit selfish about what is mine."

Kate saw Mrs. Parker's mouth drop at Gray's possessive claim. "And now, let me direct you back to town. I'm sure you are in a hurry to finish your journey," he said smoothly.

Although Raleigh would be denied his refreshments, he did not protest. He only watched the interchange with a slight smile on his lips before urging the others to depart. Good. Kate had seen enough of them! Rising to her feet, she bade them farewell, all the while aware of Gray hovering closely near her back, as if to claim proprietorship over her.

Then they were gone, as remarkably as they had arrived, in a flurry of loud speech and giggling, and Kate breathed a long, slow sigh of relief before she turned to face Gray. She was acutely aware of how alone they were, Lucy and Rutledge having escaped into the garden with the departure of the guests. And, suddenly, she felt very ill-prepared for her confrontation.

The marquis said nothing, but eyed her with an intensity that disturbed her, as if he would see into her very soul. Kate glanced away, unwilling to let him know her feelings, for despite her anger and humiliation, her heart had leapt briefly when he described her as his betrothed. Luckily, her brain had quickly put a stop to that romantic nonsense, and now she was determined not to agree to such folly. Nor would she admit that her affections were engaged, for Gray was much too sure of himself already.

Drawing a deep breath, she turned to face him. "No," she said firmly.

"No, what?" Gray asked, lifting one of those infernally expressive brows.

"No, I'm not going to marry you!"

"Of course you are," he said, walking toward her.

She stepped back. "You cannot be serious! I appreciate your efforts to uphold my reputation, but it is not necessary, I assure you. I shall never see those dreadful people again, nor do I care what they say about me."

His mouth tightened for a moment before curving into a slight smile. "Ah, but I do."

"Well, then, that is your problem, is it not?" she asked defiantly.

"And yours, too, I fear."

His control exasperated her. "No. It is yours. I

simply wish to return to my old life, without any further interference from you.''

His mouth hardened again. "It is too late for that, Kate, and you know it.''

She turned away. "I cannot do it, don't you understand? I cannot be...them!'' she said, waving a hand toward the window.

"Who?''

"I cannot go to London and play at conversation with wretches like that, smiling when I don't mean it, waving fans—''

"What? Pimperington and his ilk?'' Gray dismissed them with a contemptuous snort. "They are idiots, not fit to grovel at your feet!''

Kate's heart threatened to melt at his quick defense, but she would not allow it. "I cannot pretend to be a part of that world. I am a cook and a groom and a maid. I am no longer a lady.''

Gray gave a low growl of laughter that made her turn toward him again. "You have more integrity and dignity than any so-called lady! You can be whatever you want, wherever you please, Kate. After what you've done here, you can do anything!''

His faith in her was daunting, and perhaps, with his help, she could reenter that glittering existence, but that was the least of her reasons for refusal. "No matter, for I will not do it. Nor will I marry you.''

"Don't be ridiculous,'' Gray said. "You're a sensible girl, Kate.''

She nearly flinched at the word, which had become onerous. When had she ceased wanting to be prudent? When she marched into the marquis of Wroth's study with a gun in her hand? Or when she first looked upon his face…touched his body? Kate had a fleeting, outrageous desire to be flighty and reckless, to dress as a boy and flee the mastery of this man, tossing away the house and the birthright that meant so much to her.

"You want respectability for your sister. How could you want anything less for yourself?"

Kate glanced at him, so arrogant in his assumptions, and she felt as though she were unraveling. They had begun their odd relationship on even ground, both of them independent and assured, and now… Gray stood before her as haughty as ever, her heart in his keeping, while she had nothing, not even her composure, to call her own.

"You have no idea what I want," she managed.

"Oh, I think I do," he said, his lips curling into a provocative smile that sent tendrils of heat twining throughout her limbs. The involuntary reaction made her stiffen, and she glared at him.

"I don't want you."

He lifted a dark brow in arrogant amusement. "You positively wound me, Kate."

"If only I could," she whispered. Straightening her shoulders, she walked past him, intent upon her own company and her own whirling thoughts. Behind her, she heard his low, seductive voice, taunting her with its power.

"I shall procure a special license, so we can be wed as soon as possible," he said. Kate's steps faltered at the suddenness of it all, but she should have known that a man like Gray could accomplish anything with all speed—even an unwanted wedding ceremony.

Her lips pressed together, as what she once would have admired left a bitter taste in her mouth, and Kate resumed walking, not even turning back when she heard his last thinly veiled warning.

"I'll expect you to do what's right, Kate."

Watching her go, Gray felt helpless, an uncharacteristic condition that both annoyed and dismayed him. He knew he ought to go after Kate, to make sure that all was settled between them, but he was feeling unaccountably raw and exposed by her adamant refusals.

Refusals! He stalked across the drawing room. How could she possibly deny him? The very idea was ludicrous. Any woman in her position would be a fool not to snap at his offer! Not only was she in need of his wealth and power to redeem her heritage, but he had compromised her and publicly announced their betrothal. How the devil could she say nay?

Gray strode to the windows and stared out at nothing. Obviously, Kate felt ill-equipped to be his wife, and he should go to her, if only to reassure her that she need not waste her time among the ton's dubious company. They could travel or make their home at his country seat—at any number of houses. Hell, they could stay at Hargate, for all he cared.

And he would have gone after her in an instant to tell her so, if he had not sensed there was more to her refusals than a reluctance to enter society. Kate was too brave to risk her future on such a trifling excuse. From her wary, defiant expression, he knew she had other reasons for tossing his proposal back in his face. But what? Gray walked to the threshold, only to stop abruptly, uncertain of himself for the first time in years.

Common sense and his own experience with negotiations told him that he should seek out Kate and wrench the truth from her, but Gray felt an uncommon reluctance to do so. In all his life, he had never known rejection, and he did not want to ask her any more questions, especially on the eve of their wedding, for one simple reason.

He was not sure he wanted to hear the answers.

## Chapter Fourteen

In the end, Kate decided to be sensible, as usual. It was pointless to fight against a will stronger than her own and toss away her only chance for a future not mired in toil and deprivation. She had to weigh the possibility that Uncle Jasper might never return, that Hargate might be lost and she forced to make a living out in the world. Faced with such visions, marriage to Gray seemed the lesser of evils, and so she ceased her arguments.

She approached it logically, telling herself that she was entering a marriage of convenience, for that was surely how the marquis saw it. He would expect nothing of the union, and she must not, either, for such were the ways of the ton, where legal ties meant little and fidelity even less. If she was lucky, Gray would be satisfied to tuck her away at Hargate, while he returned to London. Then the only difference between her old and new life would be a slight change in circumstances among the household and one small document that bound her to a man who did not care for her.

And if her heart was broken in the process, that could not be helped. It would mend someday, as had every other hurt in her life, making her stronger. She drew upon that strength to maintain her composure throughout the brief, lifeless ceremony, and the parody of a celebration that followed.

Only later, when Gray hinted at retirement and the little maid led her to her mother's old room, did Kate balk. Her cheeks flamed at the thought of consummating this farce, for she knew that he had offered for her only out of his own nobility, after Tom pressed him to do it. Whatever kisses he gave her in the past had been purely for his own amusement, and Kate refused to provide him with any more.

She halted before the door, disinclined to enter, but Dora's presence kept her from protesting. Although the servants were undoubtedly privy to the reasons for the sudden nuptials, perhaps these new arrangements were meant to quiet their wagging tongues. A useless effort, Kate was sure, yet she swallowed her arguments and stepped over the threshold. She let Dora help her from her new gown, just as if she always slept here, but once the fancy dress was hung in the wardrobe, she dismissed the girl, whose bright blush and sly smiles were a painful reminder of what this night should have been.

Clad in her shift, Kate bent down to remove her slippers and stockings. She was accustomed to doing for herself and needed no assistance donning her old nightgown, but when she pulled open the dresser drawers and peeked in the cupboard, it was not there.

Although some of her clothing had been moved, she could not find that serviceable garment.

Turning, Kate glanced around the room irritably until she spied something laid out upon the bed. When she moved closer, she drew in a sharp breath at the sight of the gossamer-and-lace confection waiting for her. She picked it up, ignoring the delicious texture to glare at a material so sheer it would hide nothing. She had never thought to wear anything like it in her life, and she certainly was not going to do so now, when her wedding night was only a mockery of what it should be.

The longer she looked at the absurd attire, the more Kate wanted to wring Gray's neck with it. All her rage at his arrogant machinations, and all the hurt she felt at this pretense she must endure, surged up in her chest, clogging her throat. Gad, he was probably getting a good laugh out of the prospect of her flaunting herself before him in this filmy fabric!

Gripping the loathsome thing in one hand, Kate marched over to the door that linked the two rooms and yanked it open, her rage carrying her to the middle of the worn carpet. Gray, who was standing near an old settee that he had scavenged from another part of the house, turned in surprise, and despite her anger, Kate swallowed hard when she saw him.

He had removed most of his clothing and stood before her wearing only his breeches. She had forgotten just how beautiful his body was, from the mass of hard muscle and dark hair that was his chest to the clean bones of his feet and taut calves. For a moment, she was speechless.

"Kate?" His voice, low and amused, brought her gaze back to his face, where one of his dark brows lifted in question at her intrusion.

"My belongings have been moved."

That infernal brow only climbed higher as he gave her an arrogant nod. "It is customary for a husband and wife to have adjoining rooms, although I would be happy to share this one with you." He smiled—a small, erotic curving of the lips that left Kate short of breath. Dimly she was aware of his tendency to steal her wits, but not this time. She refused to be the object of his charity or the butt of his humor.

"No."

"No?" He looked slightly bemused.

"No," she said, more firmly. "And I am not going to wear this...this *thing*, either!" She tossed it at his chest, and it slid down his body in an arresting manner that nearly made her forget her anger. Drawing in a deep breath, Kate recaptured it quickly. "So you can take that smirk off of your face. This marriage is a sham, and we both know it, so there is no need for you to pretend otherwise."

"A sham? I assure you it is not. It is entirely legal and binding." He looked so cool, so composed, standing there half-naked, that Kate wanted to punch him. Instead, she sought desperately to match his mood of detachment.

"Do you think me a fool? I realize that you only wed me because you had to, because of what people would think if you did not."

Did surprise flicker in his eyes, or had she imagined it? One side of his mouth quirked upward.

"Kate, I assure you that I have never worried in the slightest about the elusive thoughts of others. Do you really believe that the inane prattle of creatures like Pimperington would concern me enough to make such a sacrifice?"

Although he seemed as arrogant as always, Kate noticed a sharpness around his mouth that spoke of some strain. "But you said—"

He cut off her protest with an impatient sound. "The arguments I used to convince you to accept my proposal had nothing to do with my offering it," he said. "My position and wealth are such that I would be unaffected by any scandal, short of murder."

"Perhaps so," Kate admitted, as she tried to harness her wayward thoughts. What was he saying? She felt oddly edgy, and the tension in the room was palpable, as though the great Wroth himself were similarly afflicted. "But you have a sense of honor, a code that made you marry me because you stayed here without a proper chaperone. That's what Tom said. He told me that he made you…do the right thing." There. It was out, the worst, most humiliating aspect of the whole business. Now, let him deny it, Kate thought, lifting her chin.

To her surprise, Gray gave a low growl of laughter that seemed to skim along her exposed skin, teasing her senses. Abruptly she realized that she wore nothing but her shift.

"You insult me, Kate! Do you really think that I would order my life on the whim of that feeble-witted coachman?" Gray asked. His brow traveled upward in a manner that made her feel foolish for listening to Tom. But, if neither Tom nor gossip had forced Gray to wed, then why…?

Gray took a step closer, and Kate knew a sudden warmth, though he still stood away from her. His gaze captured her own, and she saw no amusement, only sober truth. "I'll admit that my decision was hastened by the untimely arrival of Raleigh and his friends," he said. "But I assure you, poppet, that I married you for the simple reason that I wanted to do so."

"But why?" The words came out in a whisper, as shaky and uncertain as Kate herself.

"A variety of motivations, not the least of which has to do with that lovely gown I bought for you," Gray answered. He glanced down at the pool of sheer material on the floor, and then up at her face, his mouth taut, as if he were acknowledging a weakness.

Gray? The man had no frailties, no flaws such as those suffered by lesser mortals. He was all hard competence, all simmering power and intellect. Wasn't he? Kate shook her head, bewildered by what he was saying.

"I want you, Kate."

Well, that was clear enough, if she could only accept it. "But…but I thought you were teasing me before," Kate protested. "Amusing yourself."

Gray did not look amused. "No. Never," he said. He took another step toward her, and fixed her with his gaze, steady and confident once more. "I want you, Kate."

"I don't believe it," she muttered, half to herself.

"Believe this," Gray said. Then he took her hand

and pressed it to the front of his breeches. She started, for he was not as he had been before, when she bathed him. Beneath her palm, he was huge and hard, and he pulsed like a living thing, making her hot and breathless.

"Wh-what's happening?" she asked, staring at him in stunned surprise.

"A man's body changes when he wants a woman. It becomes hard. Erect," Gray whispered, in a voice that poured over her like warm chocolate. Slowly, he guided her fingers upward and then down again in a broad stroke of his amazing length, and the feel of him spread heat throughout her body in a delicious, languid rhythm such as only he could produce. It beckoned her, this melting desire that she had known before, but Kate snatched her hand away and stepped back.

"No," she said, denying even the physical evidence of his desire.

"Yes," Gray said, coming closer. "I want you, Kate, and only you."

She shook her head, moving backward once more.

"I have wanted you ever since that first night, when I discovered you were no boy. I wanted to feel you beneath me even then."

"No," Kate whispered, disbelieving, her flight halted by the edge of the bed pressing behind her knees.

"Yes," Gray said, grinning seductively. "I feel feverish again, Kate. Will you cool me?" His hands moved to the buttons of his breeches, and she flushed, remembering all too well how she had bathed him when he was ill.

"I was half out of my head, but I wanted you then," he declared. His fall came open, to free the turgid length of him, which was just as he had said. Hard. Erect. Upthrusting. Kate swallowed as his hands moved to his hips to slowly slide the breeches downward. "I could feel your hands on me, and I wanted to touch you, to taste you, to be inside you."

Kate knew her face must be crimson. Her breathing was low and ragged, her pulse thudding loudly through blood that seemed to thicken and slow as he stood before her, gloriously naked. He stepped forward, and she fell back upon the bed with a cry, only to find him leaning over her.

"And I have wanted you every moment since. In my bath. In my bed. In my life." As Kate stared, dazed, up at him, trying to absorb his words, his hands moved to the hem of her shift, and he raised it deliberately, his fingers brushing along her leg, her waist, her ribs, as he lifted it over her head.

He stared down at her, his eyes burning where they touched. "And now I will have you, Kate. Tonight and forever. Whenever and wherever I wish. However I wish. Beneath me, above me, in front of me." His eyes flickered with a brilliance that seared her. "Your breast at my mouth, your legs around my waist. Tight. Hot. Slick with sweat. Fragrant with your perfume."

Kate tried to swallow, but her mouth was too dry, her responses too sluggish. She slid her tongue out to wet her lips, and Gray took it in his mouth. Gently.

Slowly. All thought of resistance fled as she melted into him. Her own nakedness, which once would have alarmed her, became freedom, a recipe for liquid pleasure as he touched her, his fingers sliding down her body in the most exotic of caresses.

He stroked her hair, her shoulders, her waist. He placed hot, intense kisses on her palms, the curves of her arm, the arches of her feet. He drew her toes into his mouth, startling her with the raw sensation that spread upward, pooling between her legs. He massaged her calves and her thighs and buried his face in her belly. His tongue teased at her navel and her ribs and the underside of her breasts. And then his hands cupped them, pushing them together, so that his mouth could work its magic on her nipples. And all Kate could do was gasp her delight as she quivered beneath his expert handling.

Finally, when she began whimpering her need, Gray rose up on his knees between her legs. "What say you now, poppet?" he asked.

As if she could deny him! Lost in a whorl of sensation, beyond thought, Kate was unable to form the words to respond. She stared up at him, so glorious and strong and powerful, and she felt utterly helpless to resist him, now or ever. Whatever resentment she might have felt for his mastery dissolved in the moment she saw his body shudder—an involuntary display of his need that could not be feigned.

"Yes," she whispered.

He reached for a pillow and lifted her hips upward, so that he could slide it beneath her. She lay open to him then, but felt no shame as his hands glided to the juncture of her thighs and his fingers spread her wide. Watching in heady fascination, Kate saw him position his huge member, and then she felt the press of it, smooth against her. She let out a low breath and closed her eyes, her head falling back, but Gray's voice, softly insistent, drew her attention back to him.

"Look at me, Kate," he said, and she stared at him. His tall form was bathed golden in the candlelight like that of a beautiful god, his torso taut as he poised to enter her. And then he did, in a delicious, slow glide that made her gasp with pleasure. But she knew she had taken only the very tip of him, and she saw his body shudder again, as if protesting his pace. Kate wanted to lift her hips, to puncture his steely control as he would her maidenhead, but she could not, not when she sensed his need to control this, as well as all else in his life.

And so she remained still as Gray pushed deeper, though she felt stretched and full. He stroked her with his fingers, and she welcomed more of him, but it was not enough. He was breathing roughly now, his face harsh, his muscles strained and glistening with sweat. Kate felt the press of him, harder and harder, and then she bit her lip against a bright slice of pain as her flesh tore, giving way to the massive length of him. He tugged at her hips, and she was seated against him, his member buried fully within her.

"Yes, you are mine now, poppet," Gray said in a strangled whisper. His eyes glinted like that of a man possessed, and Kate wondered if hers held that same frantic, wild look.

"Yes," she answered.

"It will be better in a moment. Just let me catch my breath," he said, but he didn't. Instead, his head fell back, and he groaned as he pulled himself nearly from her.

"Kate!" he cried, though he was the one who had moved. Abruptly he hauled her back to him, thrusting so deeply that she bit her lip again. "Damn, I—" He struggled for words, and she felt him pulsing inside her, big and hard and... "No!" he shouted, and then his whole body began to shudder and shake. Grasping her hips in a frenzied grip, he ground his groin against her, and Kate felt the quakes that racked him deep inside her. A new sensation of liquid warmth at the point where their bodies joined made her wonder if their lovemaking was over.

His head dropped forward, and he drew in great gulps of air, as if spent. Had he spilled his seed inside her? Had he found ecstasy such as he had given her the other day in the stable? If so, he did not seem too happy about it.

Damn! Gray swore silently as he sucked in a deep breath. He had disgraced himself like an untried youth, something he had not done since a lovely and lonely married woman initiated him into the rites of love at a tender age. Never, in all his encounters since, had he failed to satisfy his partner before finding his own release. Never! Angry and disgusted with himself, Gray felt like stalking from the room, but he couldn't. Hell, he didn't even want to leave her body—because beneath his contempt for himself was the sizzling awareness that he had never experienced such bliss before in his life.

It was Kate's doing, of course. Lifting his head, he hazarded a glance at her and cursed himself again. She was looking at him with dazed eyes, questioning, while he brooded. No longer, he decided. Sliding his hands up her body, he lowered himself over her and took her mouth. The kiss, intended to both comfort and rouse her to passion once more, had quite another effect, as her passionate response quickened his own desire with startling intensity. Tentatively, he moved inside her, and then smiled against her lips.

Himself again, Gray pleasured her with deep, slow strokes, bringing her to the brink over and over as he watched ecstasy play across her beautiful features. This was the lovemaking he was accustomed to, and yet it wasn't, for instead of his usual detachment, Gray felt a deep, fulfilling…something for Kate that made their union more than just mutual delight. His perceptions seemed heightened, his body more alive than ever before, his mind more fully engaged. Perhaps it was because he had waited so long to have her, but that did not explain his continuing, driving need to claim her for his own and never let her go.

Gray surged forward at the thought, and she cried out, gasping and pulsing around him so wildly that the tenuous control he had regained snapped like a twig and his plans to delay his own gratification were gone with it. She called out his name, and he thrust deep, clutching her hips as he lost himself inside her, in blind, unthinking sensation.

Afterward, Gray lay awake for a long time, staring sightlessly up at the ceiling, while Kate dozed. He was used to sleeping alone, and the feel of her slender body curled up next to him, her hair brushing against his chest, was both strange and delicious. Annoyed, he decided to put her to bed in the other room, but when he moved, it was only to tighten his arm around her, pulling her closer.

Damn. It was worse than he'd thought. The want that he had thought to vanquish with his possession of her had only grown more pronounced, tipping perilously close to need. Gray's free hand clenched, for he would not admit to such a weakness. He ought to get up and go somewhere—anywhere—just to prove he could.

But he didn't.

He lay there and let the soft warmth of her breath brush his skin, the subtle scent of her perfume fill his head until he ached with desire once more. Although it was too soon for her, and he knew it, his body stiffened, ignoring the control he had known all his life.

Until tonight. Gray drew in a sharp breath at the reminder. He had acted like a boy, not the man he was known to be, and had lost mastery of himself not once, but twice. And instead of his usual articulate phrasing, he had been reduced to incoherent grunts and curses! Perhaps Raleigh was right, and next he would be beating his breast like a jungle beast.

He was behaving little better than one, and it galled him. Gray had always taken his superior intellect for granted, using it to harness his wealth, his influence, his life, certain there was no other force more powerful. But now, something was happening to him, *changing* him, and he did not like it.

It had begun here, at Hargate, a sort of disorientation that eroded his composure. Perhaps all he needed was a different venue, a return to his own milieu. He had thought retirement to the country would banish his ennui, and it had, but now it was time to go back to the familiar world of town and the responsibilities he had neglected.

Gray released a long breath as he considered such a course. He could present his new bride to the ton and take some amusement in their astonished reactions. He could begin proceedings to regain Kate's inheritance and retake the reins of his varied business and political dealings. Action. That was all he needed.

His certainty faded as Kate stirred in her sleep and slid a silky thigh across his. Gritting his teeth, Gray wondered if she would lose her luster among the glittering ladies of London. Perhaps then he would gain some respite from this endless wanting. He ran a hand over her shoulder to quiet her, but her knee grazed his groin, and he shuddered, remembering the exultation of possession. He had washed the blood from her thighs, as a gentleman should, yet even while performing that courtesy, he had wanted her, and felt dismayed by it. Would his craving for her never cease?

Maybe just one more time would ease it, Gray thought, now wide-awake and painfully hard. He stroked her back and turned toward her, letting his fingers roam her silky skin, his lips brush against hers. She sighed gently and opened her mouth for him, lifting her arms and parting her thighs to take him in, and he was lost again.

Kate turned, snuggling against her pillow and clinging to the remnants of a delightful dream. A dream about Gray. A dream in which their marriage was not one of convenience, but of mutual desire and... She blinked, a warm, slow awareness seeping through her at the realization that all of it was true.

Gray had not wed her out of pity or duty or amusement. He felt *something* for her. She had seen it in the depths of his eyes and in the taut lines of his body when he made love to her. At the very last, she had breached his composure, had watched him lose control because of *her*, because of his passion for her, and it had been wonderful.

Kate stretched, a long, languid sigh escaping from her lips, for she was happier than she had ever thought to be, happy beyond her wildest imaginings. The marriage that only yesterday she had viewed with grim resignation now loomed before her like a brightly colored package waiting to be opened. What a difference a single night had made upon her outlook!

Her pleasant musings were interrupted by the soft

sound of footfalls, and she looked up to see Gray entering from the other bedroom. Through the doorway she could hear Badcock's voice echoing behind, and she scooted under the covers. Surely the manservant would not come in while she was here!

"Ah, good. You are awake at last," Gray said over his shoulder as he walked toward the dresser. Something in his tone, a thread of brittle coolness, made Kate eye him carefully. He was fully dressed in the finest riding clothes, the very picture of the elegant lord.

Kate swallowed uncertainly. "Gray? You're up early," she said softly.

"Early?" he said, a faint mocking edge to his voice as he barely glanced at her. "I think not. You are the slugabed, for it's past noon."

Past noon? Kate sat up, pulling the blanket up to her neck as she watched Gray's fashionably attired back. She had never slept so late, but then, she had never spent the night making love, either. She flushed, embarrassed to be lingering among the rumpled sheets while Gray seemed so far removed from them.

"Since I've no dressing closet, I finally called Badcock into the adjoining room," he said, recapturing her attention.

Befuddled, Kate stared at his coat, wishing he would face her. "Badcock?"

He did turn then, to fix her with a dispassionate gaze. "He is my valet. I could hardly let him perform his duties while you're lying in my bed."

"I'm—" Kate broke off and took a deep breath

before attempting to understand what he was saying. "You do not want me to sleep here?" she asked in amazement.

Gray lifted a brow. "It makes for a rather inconvenient morning."

The air went hissing out of her lungs in a low rush as Kate felt the impact of his words like a blow. He did not want her to stay with him, after what they had done? After what had passed between them? Before Kate could gather her scattered thoughts, he headed toward the other bedroom. "No matter, but you had better call your maid, for we leave for London this afternoon."

"London?" Kate managed to halt him at the door.

"Yes. The town house is one of my principal residences, and I have some business to attend to that I have been neglecting of late."

Kate stared, struggling to speak to the man who stood poised on the threshold, casually arrogant. A stranger.

"What about Lucy?" she stammered.

"I've arranged for her to stay with the squire and his wife."

"Too bad she's not of age, or they, too, could be married in a day, and the business of their lives dispensed with as quickly!" Kate said, swinging her feet over the side of the bed.

Gray gave a startled growl of laughter, his gaze sliding down to her bare legs and then swiftly away. "Good morning, then. I shall see you at breakfast," he said, exiting the room without another glance in her direction.

As soon as he closed the door behind him, Kate sank down upon the bed, her brief show of strength spent, to bury her face in her hands. Who was that man? That haughty nobleman could not be the same person who had joined with her in the most intimate of acts, the lover who had spent hours caressing her body, the husband who had washed away her virgin's blood as if it were a sacrament?

A sob broke loose from Kate's throat. Things were far worse than she had ever anticipated when she spoke her vows. At least her marriage of convenience had raised no expectations within her, had not touched the emotions she harbored for the man she wed. But now she had had a taste of what a true union could be, had given herself in *love*, to this man only to have him ignore it.

Why had he made love to her? Why had he claimed to want her? For all his arrogance, Kate had never thought Gray a liar, but what else could she believe? His very demeanor today mocked her tender memories of last night, took her feelings for him and threw them back in her face, as if to say, "Really, poppet, do be serious. I've no use for your affection."

How could he do this to her? Her pleasurable fantasy that he had felt something for her had obviously been a delusion. After all, what did she know of the intimacies they had shared? What had been momentous to her had meant nothing at all to him. Less than nothing, for he wanted her out of his bed.

The very thought made Kate lift her head as anger crowded aside her despair. How dare he! Her lips pressed together tightly as she resolved that he would have no further worries on that score. She would never enter his bed again! And as for his peremptory commands... Kate waved her hand carelessly, a bitter smile touching her mouth. So he thought to treat her poorly and order her about, did he? Perhaps he had forgotten that she was the woman who had shot him. And she bowed to no man.

*That for your fine dictates, my lord Marquis,* Kate whispered. Snapping her fingers in disdain, she began to form plans of her own.

# *Chapter Fifteen*

**K**ate was out in the garden when he found her. She had avoided the dining hall altogether, slipping out the front entrance and walking around to the shed to get her implements. By the time Gray arrived, she had already dug up a large pile of weeds, her anger fueling her efforts with the shovel and trowel.

She saw him, of course, but, taking a cue from his own behavior, barely glanced at him while jabbing violently at the earth. She fancied an especially hard clod to be his heart—if he possessed one.

"What the devil are you doing?" His voice was rougher than usual, and Kate took some slight pleasure in his strained tone. Was the great Wroth angry? She smiled sweetly. "I am working, as I do almost every day. Yesterday put me behind, with the nuisance of that ceremony, you know."

She had the intense satisfaction of knowing she had upset his equilibrium, at least, for when she looked up, he was glaring at her fiercely. "You know damn well that you no longer have to act the servant.

Leave that for someone else and get properly dressed. We are going to London.''

Kate bent down to dislodge a particularly large specimen. "No," she said, straightening. "*You* are going to London. This is my home. I live here."

"No longer. You are my wife now."

*Am I? Am I really and truly your wife, Gray?* Kate thought, but she kept her query to herself, refusing to let herself feel anything but annoyance. Her other emotions ran too deep and were too painful to touch.

"By law, you must obey me."

Kate let loose an unladylike snort of laughter. "I'm afraid you married the wrong woman if you want that, you arrogant, pigheaded bully!" She tossed the epithets carelessly at his head while leaning on her shovel.

He ignored them, as if she hadn't spoken. "I'm not leaving without you."

"Then stay, but don't expect me ever to go with you. There is nothing for me in London." Because of him, there was nothing for her anywhere, but Kate would not admit it. She heaved a fat clump of weeds onto the stones with more force than necessary and watched them break apart.

"Do not push me, Kate." The warning rang with dark menace. "You do not wish to make an enemy of me."

Kate stilled, her fist closing around the handle as she met his gaze evenly. "And what will you do? Beat me into submission?"

His eyes flashed, his mouth tightening in a swift response that reminded her how dangerous it was to bait him. Yet she held her ground, knowing that if she gave way now, she would lose herself forever.

"I think you know that I would never strike you," Gray said, the words clipped, as if bitten off through gritted teeth. "But I could easily drag you off to London as you are. Would you like to make your first appearance in society dressed as an urchin, pulled kicking and screaming from the coach?"

"No, but I'll warrant that you would like it even less," Kate answered. "You would be the laughing-stock of the ton, for people would say what a pity it is that the great Wroth can't control his own wife."

For a moment, Kate thought she had finally goaded him beyond endurance. His eyes narrowing, he took a step toward her, and she saw him draw in a deep breath, as if he were going to explode. But then he growled out a low laugh, dispelling the illusion that he was anything other than his elegant and composed self.

"You nearly incite me to violence, poppet," he said, his mouth quirking as he turned from her. He walked casually around the pile of garden debris, a picture of male grace, before stopping beside her. "But, come now, Kate, you do not want to be viewed as a hoyden. Your reputation is assured. Why destroy it now, when you can take your place as a marchioness?"

He was tempting her again, with his velvet voice and the power of his personality, directed solely at her, as though she were the center of his life. As with his marriage proposal, he would make it all sound too logical too refuse. Kate swallowed hard and looked away.

"Come," he urged. "How long has it been since you've visited London? I'll show you the sights—the Thames, Vauxhall, the theater, Astley's, Almack's..."

No wonder he was such a good politician, Kate thought bitterly. He was so used to maneuvering people and swaying them to his indomitable will that, even knowing what she did, she found it hard to hold out against him.

"Surely you are not going to let a bunch of sapskulls like Pimperington intimidate you. You are the most courageous woman I know, Kate." The compliment was uttered in a soft, sober manner that defied her to disbelieve him. "You are not afraid of them, are you?"

He was making it into a challenge, Kate realized, and she lifted her chin in answer. All she was scared of was Gray himself, and what he could do to her hurt her further—if she let him. She would not.

"Come, Kate, you can do this."

The particular phrasing startled her, and Kate glanced at him sharply, but his hooded gaze revealed nothing. Was he talking about more than the trip to London, or was she reading things into his words that were not there, imagining what she wanted to, as she had done before?

"I dare you." His liquid tone caressed her, promising all sorts of things that had nothing to do with traveling. Obviously, he sensed that she was weakening. And yet, he was right. She had never turned away from a hardship. But this…this emotional test would be far worse than any of her struggles with Hargate or her uncle or Lucy. Her very heart was as stake, and it was already sorely wounded. Was his dare an earnest request to help him turn their soulless union into something more? Could she make this marriage work somehow?

Gripping the wooden handle of the shovel so tightly it hurt, Kate stared down at the ground. In a life of challenges, this was the greatest she had ever faced. Could she do it? Could she make Gray care for her?

"You can do it, poppet," Gray said softly.

Startled that he echoed her own thoughts, Kate gazed searchingly up at him. For an instant something flickered in his eyes, a dark plea that reminded her of what they shared during the night, and again she wondered if he was asking more of her than he would ever put into words. Foolish though it might be, Kate seized that glimpse and made her choice.

She let out a low breath. "All right," she muttered, and was rewarded with Gray's most wicked grin. The rogue! He knew how to get his way, that was certain.

Now the question was, would she be able to get hers?

In the end, Kate left Hargate willingly, but with a heavy heart. Her home was to be closed up while everyone went to London, and she could not help wondering just how long it would remain empty. Even the luxury of Gray's elegant coach, brought from town especially for the journey, did little to lighten her mood, for the spacious interior seemed isolating. Gray rode outside, the servants followed behind, and Kate, alone, watched the life she had known disappear forever behind the curve of a hill.

Although only weeks had passed since her furtive visit to Gray's town house, Kate's circumstances this time were far removed from those of that nocturnal prowl. Instead of climbing through the study window, pistol in hand, she walked through the front doors, carrying only a fashionable reticule, and was introduced to the servants, with much solemnity, as the new marchioness.

Kate was uncomfortable under the scrutiny of so many, all staring at her with interest. Although she knew that Hargate had once boasted such a staff, she could hardly remember those days, and so would have much to get used to during her stay. To her annoyance, she had barely arrived before Gray set a horde of modistes, led by a voluble Frenchwoman, upon her. Apparently her new position required innumerable gowns, all to be supplied as soon as was physically possible, and while Mrs. Leeds would continue to provide what she could, these women would work at a frantic pace to please the marquis.

The whole business was exhausting, and by the time the group had packed up their fabrics and pins and measuring things and left, Kate was tired and out of sorts. She tried to nap, but her strange surroundings kept her from sleeping, and finally she was roused by a young woman who claimed to be her personal maid. Kate let the stranger dress her for an early supper and followed one of the many footmen to the dining hall, where the long, gleaming table was set for two.

Everywhere, nameless servants attended her, observing her in a way that made Kate wonder how she had ever thought to assume the role of marchioness. And the few familiar faces she knew to be residing with her were nowhere to be seen, Tom presumably relegated to the stables, Meg to the kitchen and Badcock to his duties as valet.

Supper was a stilted affair, and although the endless courses of delicious delicacies would have tempted a saint, Kate could do no justice to the repast. Instead, she pushed a few bits of food around on her plate while sipping sparingly at her wine. Gray seemed to be as strange as the rest of the household, and the conversation that had once flowed effortlessly between them during his convalescence was now strained and sparse.

When Kate excused herself from the table and the evening, pleading tiredness, he nodded his agreement. "I'm sure you are weary from the journey. However, it is still early by London hours. I think I shall look in at White's."

His eagerness to desert her chafed at Kate's raw senses, although she was not sure what she had expected of him. She felt as if her usual optimism had been left behind at Hargate and her grand scheme to win his affections were a hopeless venture, doomed from the start. Too tense to argue with him, she let one of the footmen lead her back to her room, where she waved away the startled maid to attend herself.

Although far more luxurious and well-appointed than any of those at Hargate, her new suite felt cold and lonely. Everything was lovely and new, but nothing held meaning or sentimental value. Kate laid out her mother's silver brush and comb, but she had few possessions that would make this place feel like home. And already she missed Tom and Lucy, and even Cyclops, the one-eyed cat. More than any of them, the feline would be able to fend for himself, but she worried nonetheless, and her spirits sank even lower at the knowledge that none of them needed her anymore.

Once dressed in a more demure version of her wedding-night garment, Kate walked to the connecting door to Gray's room. She had no key to lock it, of course, so she tucked one of the shield-backed chairs under the handle. It wouldn't hold indefinitely, but the makeshift bolt would tell him that he was not welcome. Let him complain about her presence in his bed, then, Kate thought, but her triumph was bitter, and when she slid between the cold sheets, she lay awake for a long time.

Married two days, and while most people would still be celebrating, she felt more alone and miserable than she ever had in her life.

Gray had no interest in visiting White's; he went simply to prove that he could, that he was a normal man in control of his own actions and his own body. And because he knew that if he looked across the table at his wife any longer, he would have her right there, the servants and her own weariness be damned.

He had hoped to distract himself from the woman who seemed to have taken over his life by joining some deep play, for he always gave his complete concentration to the tables. But before he could reach his destination, he was hailed by several acquaintances demanding to know where he had been for the past few weeks and whether the rumor of his engagement was true.

The announcement that he had already wed raised some eyebrows, and Gray could have cursed his normally facile tongue, for what man would be at White's, instead of enjoying his marital rights, so soon after the ceremony? Only someone who had married a hatchet-faced she-dragon! Gray's mouth tightened, for he would hold with no talk about his wife. Deferring their questions with a cold gaze, he sent all but the most tenacious scurrying back to their own business.

"Wroth! Here now, Smythe, let me through, will you? I've need of private conversation with our newly married man," drawled Raleigh, waving a languid hand, as if to brush aside the others. Although Gray was well accustomed to holding court and fielding difficult queries, Raleigh's inane antics were a welcome diversion, perhaps because, for once, Gray was not entirely comfortable with the topic.

In arrogant dismissal of the others, Gray followed Raleigh to a pair of chairs in a secluded corner and let the viscount call for a bottle of champagne, even though he was in no mood to celebrate. He would have preferred something more substantial, but when

Raleigh lifted his glass, Gray joined him, swallowing the bubbly liquid with a grimace.

"I understand that congratulations are in order," the viscount said, lounging back in his seat. Gray was not fooled by the careless pose; he was well aware of Raleigh's studied gaze. "Did you bring her with you to London?"

The question both surprised and annoyed Gray. "Of course I brought her," he said. "Did you think I would leave her buried in the country?"

Raleigh shrugged and took a sip of champagne, eyeing him over the rim of his glass. "I don't know what to think of a man who's dallying at his club a day after his wedding."

Instead of facing down his friend, Gray let his gaze slide away, for Raleigh's perception had surprised him more than once. He did not care to admit why he was here, or how the need for Kate drove him, consuming him. He had thought to vanquish it in her bed, but it had only grown stronger, until he ran from it, as he had nothing in his life before. For the first time in his assured existence, Gray felt a coward, and although he did not like the sensation, he refused to be dependent upon anyone for anything, including Kate.

"Where is she, then?"

Raleigh's soft question brought Gray from his sober thoughts, and he shot the viscount a sharp look. "At the town house. In bed."

"Alone?" Raleigh asked, with a casual flicker of interest.

Gray tensed, straining to keep himself seated,

when he wanted to lunge for Raleigh's throat. "Alone."

Raleigh shrugged again, as if unaware of the dangerous ground he was treading. "But for how much longer, I wonder," he mused, swirling his champagne. "A beautiful woman like that let loose in London, and ton marriages being what they are..." With a sardonic look, he let his words trail off, allowing Gray's imagination free rein.

Yes, he knew damn well that most lords and ladies changed lovers as often as they bathed, but he had never intended his own union to be like that. He planned to be faithful, and expected the same of his wife, and he did not care to be likened to those he held in contempt. "Do not compare anything I do with that of my contemporaries, lest I take insult," Gray warned. "If I wanted that sort of arrangement, I never would have chosen Kate."

"Really?" Raleigh invested the single word with a world of skepticism. "Then I suggest you do not leave the lady alone very often, or you will have to wade through a crowd simply to get to your rooms. As soon as the male population of London discovers she is available, they will stumble all over each other wanting to be the first to have Wroth's wife and cuckold the great marquis."

Gray's fingers tightened around his glass.

"Of course, that is not to say that they won't want her for her beauty. She is lovely. Refreshing. Untouched, so to speak. Yes, she will be a prize, not only for the first, but to the very last of the lovers she will take."

The crystal snapped in Gray's hand. "There will be no lovers," he said through gritted teeth. He dropped the pieces of glass to the floor and wiped his hand with a handkerchief. A cut on his palm oozed blood, and he wrapped it.

"Lud, you've hurt yourself. Demmed shoddy cups!" Raleigh said, calling for a servant. "Now, where were we? Ah, yes! But the only couples I know who confine their favors to each other are those bound not just by vows, but by love." Raleigh paused to beard him with a knowing gaze that mocked his fierce one. "Do you love her, Wroth?"

Gray did not deign to answer, for Raleigh had gone beyond the bounds of their friendship. Rarely was he questioned, and, certainly, never taunted. No one dared. His immediate inclination was to punch the affected little twit in his handsome face. Instead, he simply turned and walked away, a restlessness driving him away from Raleigh, away from the tables, away from White's.

Kate. Kate. Kate. Like some primitive music, it thrummed through his blood in time with his heart, and the significance of that particular rhythm, he refused to question.

Kate was still awake when she heard Gray enter his room, his movements loud in the stillness. Although she turned away from the sounds, she could imagine him tossing his coat upon a chair, tugging at his neckcloth, removing his shirt… The vast room suddenly seemed close and hot, and Kate threw off the blanket she had been clutching tightly. Gradually, quiet descended once more, but it brought her no relief. Was he in bed? Was he naked? Kate rolled over, the soft feather mattress acquiring lumps as she fought off visions of Gray without his clothes. Unfortunately, she remembered his body all too well, and conjured it up easily in her mind, golden with candlelight, dark and enticing.

Rattle. Kate stiffened as the handle of the door between their rooms turned. Thump. It caught upon the chair she had anchored there. Although she had constructed the makeshift lock in an attempt to keep him out, she had never really planned for him to discover it. She had thought he would stay out carousing with his London friends until the wee hours, when he would fall into bed alone. Had he not objected to her presence there?

Yet, here he was, home early and trying to reach her. Would he take the hint and give up? Not likely, for Gray never allowed his plans to be thwarted. The ensuing silence was rather eerie, and Kate held her breath. She stared at the other entrance off the narrow hall, wondering if he would come through it, or return to the entertainments awaiting him in town. And she did not know which resolution to hope for as she waited.

*Crash!* Kate flinched, her attention diverted back to the door to the adjoining room as the chair she had wedged beneath its handle flew into the air and the door itself banged violently against the wall. In the aftermath stood Gray, a tall, dark figure filling the threshold with a vague menace that made her shiver.

"Are you trying to keep me out, poppet?" The

low velvet purr of his voice, so at odds with his recent violence, reminded her just how dangerous he was, but Kate would not quail before him. She sat up straight, the massive headboard behind her, and lifted her chin.

"You complained of my presence in your bed this morning."

"Did I? How gauche of me," Gray replied, stepping into the room. He wore a long robe of dark silk that moved when he walked, falling in soft folds over his hard body, and Kate swallowed at his approach. He stopped beside her, the sight of him, shadowy in the dying firelight, making her throat go dry.

"In the future, you will sleep with me. Always," he said, in a harsh tone that intimated a deeper meaning. "Now, be a good wife and help me out of this." It was a challenge. Kate knew that as she held his eyes in the dimness, but the great Wroth had capitulated. What more could she want?

The misery of London and a house full of strangers faded under the heat of his gaze, and Kate slowly rose to her knees before him. Her fingers trembled as she untied the knot at his waist and the robe fell free to reveal his broad chest, its dusting of hair leading down to his erection. Reaching up, she slid the silk from his shoulders and let it fall down his body in a sensuous glide. Then she pressed kisses to his chest, ran her palms across the crisp curls and touched him as freely as she had always wanted to do. Leaning forward, she licked his nipple and nibbled at the hard muscles that covered his ribs.

"Hmm. Biting me again, are you?" he said, reminding her of their original encounter in the study below. How could he speak? How could he think? Kate wondered, for her own mind was dazed. Her limbs were like jelly, yet he stood before her, controlled and steady. Obviously, she would have to change her tactics. Trailing her kisses downward, Kate dipped her tongue into his navel and touched him.

She knew a brief sense of triumph at the swift intake of his breath, but her explorations only fanned her own desires. The heat was suddenly unbearable, and she threw back her head, better to take in air as her hands moved over him. He must have sensed her distress, because she felt him lift the hem of her nightgown and draw it up slowly, cooling her flaming skin. Then, tossing the garment aside, he pushed her back upon the bed and moved over her.

"Don't lock me out, Kate. Don't ever lock me out." The words, uttered in a hoarse whisper, were both a warning and a plea. But before she could answer, Gray took her face in his hands and drew her mouth up to his.

It seemed to Kate that he kissed each inch of her: her eyelids, behind her ear, the pulse that throbbed at her wrist, the arch of her foot, her ankle and the soft spot behind her knee. His lips were everywhere, moist and hot, firing her passions, but when they touched that most intimate of places between her legs, Kate murmured a protest. He ignored it, holding her fast while his tongue claimed mastery over her senses.

And soon she was grasping the sheets in a tortured grip, lifting herself to him, knowing even as she cried out his name that she would never deny him.

# Chapter Sixteen

Gray was as good as his word. He escorted her everywhere, showing her parts of the great city that she had never seen, the elegant entertainments and exotic sights reserved for those with money to spend. Although Kate vaguely remembered visits from her childhood, not since tragedy struck Hargate had she stepped into this glittering world, and never as a marchioness. She was both enthralled and dismayed by her views of London—and the way London viewed her.

People stared. It was to be expected, Kate told herself. Gray was a well-known figure, and anyone seen with him would be noted with interest. However, the gaping that she faced on the streets soon gave way to more pointed attention, until Kate felt like one of the animals in the Tower menagerie.

Ladies whispered behind their fans of the marquis's sudden marriage and her suitability as his wife, while men speculated on her charms in an outrageous manner. Although Gray had put about the story of their long engagement, the gossips were not satisfied with such a tame explanation of the nuptials. They talked of her father's mésalliance, her parents' deaths, and once or twice Jasper's name was mentioned in the dark tones befitting a black sheep.

Even ensconced in a private box at the theater, Kate saw them pointing to her rudely from other seats. It bothered her, for she was not used to being on display. Gray, too arrogant to take notice, ignored it all, and she tried to match his aloof attitude, for such tactlessness deserved no respect.

She was becoming more adept at the charade, Kate thought, smiling grimly as she let the maid clasp an expensive ruby-and-diamond necklace around her neck. Waving the girl away, she rose to stand before the mirror in a last-minute check of her appearance. The woman who looked back at her little resembled the boyish waif who had lived at Hargate. In truth, she appeared no different from the other females of Gray's circle, but the transformation gave Kate no comfort.

It sat uneasily upon her, this notion that she had become nothing more than an elegant ornament for Gray. She wanted more, and, despite her apparent success in society, the challenge that had brought her here was still unresolved.

True, she no longer harbored fears about fitting in with the majority of boors and tart-tongued females who made up the ton. Gray was right; she had only to wear the right clothes and keep her wits about her. But what of the real dare that had kept her at her husband's side? Her efforts to win his affections had come to naught, so far. Although Gray came to her bed every night and did not argue about the sleeping arrangements, he still seemed distanced from her in a way she had not thought possible until she saw how other men treated their spouses.

It had not taken her long to discover that wealthy, titled married couples rarely were seen in public together. More often than not, they went their separate ways, sometimes each with a lover or lovers. The so-called gentlemen kept mistresses and dallied with other men's wives, while the women bore children of uncertain parentage.

Unfamiliar with such behavior, Kate was appalled—and terrified. Although Gray had stayed near to her these past few days, did a careless regard for his vows represent her future? She shuddered. Now, more than ever, she wanted to capture her husband's heart, but each day they spent in town seemed to take her farther away from the handsome rogue who had teased her from his sickbed. He was an attentive companion, his conversation interesting, and yet, he never got too close, in word or deed.

And Kate did not know how to reach him.

The sinking feeling that perhaps she never would made her draw in a ragged breath. Gray was living up to his reputation: arrogant, composed, mayhap ruthless, with a penchant for controlling people, including her. Rumor claimed he had but one passion: gaming. Perhaps he had no room for another.

With one last look at the mirror that gave her no answer, Kate donned her own mantle of disdain and went down to meet him. Although they had been to various entertainments, tonight she was to have her first official introduction to society, at a small rout held by the Coxburys.

Despite her best efforts, her heart still raced at the sight of him waiting for her, attired in a black coat and pantaloons that clung snugly to his muscled frame. Kate wondered how he could possibly look so cool encased in so much, when she felt warm in her thin gown. "I would think you would wilt from the heat in those clothes," she said, taking his arm as she surveyed him.

He glanced at her sharply and then let out a low, startled laugh. "They are rather confining, and my shoulder itches," he confided.

His wound. Kate's smile faded at the reminder. "We do not have to go. We can stay here and be comfortable," she said, her face flushing at the thought of removing some of his excess garments. "I could bathe your...shoulder," she added a bit breathlessly.

Beneath her hand, she could feel his arm tense, but he turned his head away. "Quite a temptation, I must admit," he said evenly. "But I have promised the Coxburys to show you off, and I shall. Really, Kate, you are not intimidated by these idiots, are you?"

She stiffened. It was a rebuff—a smooth one, but a reproof nonetheless—and she was surprised by how much it hurt. Didn't he want her? Had he ever truly wanted her? All the old doubts resurged, along with new ones fostered by the style of life she had observed in London. She faltered, using the misstep to pull her arm from his. He did not reclaim it as they made their way to the carriage, and Kate tugged her shawl closer, suddenly cold, despite the heat.

Her chill lasted until they reached their destination, an elegant home filled with so many people that Kate found it stifling. The hostess, Lady Coxbury, swept her away for a flurry of introductions, and she had but a brief last glimpse of Gray before he disappeared into the crowd. Suffering under the avid stares and sharp eyes of several matrons and their daughters while Lady Coxbury prattled on beside her, Kate felt abandoned.

Where was Gray? Had he left her apurpose? Her worries about his behavior grew. Was he ogling someone else's wife? Even as she nodded to the ladies, Kate looked for him, but there were too many people, too many rooms, too many servants weaving in and out.

"Lady Wroth!" The male voice made her turn, and Kate recognized Gray's friend Raleigh, who had come to call not long after their arrival. Despite his dandyish ways, Kate liked the viscount, and she smiled in greeting. "Excuse us, won't you, ladies?" he asked, and, without waiting for an answer, drew her away from the sour-faced women.

"Splendid to find you here!" Raleigh said with a sincerity that reached his eyes. "You don't mind me dragging you away from that lot, do you?" he asked, grinning shamelessly. Kate shook her head ruefully. "Just as I thought. Wretched creatures, all of them. Shall we take in some fresh air?"

With a nod, Kate took his arm and let him lead her outside. The night breeze was a welcome relief after the crush inside, and she left Raleigh's side to rest her arms upon the decorative railing.

"I have been told repeatedly that no one who is anyone is in London during the summer months," Kate said, breathing deeply. "Then who," she said, tilting her head toward the doors whence they had come, "are they?"

Raleigh laughed. "You are delightful, though I suspected as much! But they are all no ones, a houseful of nobodies, stuffed with their own consequence." He leaned back against the brick of the house and lifted his quizzing glass to study her further.

"That is quite an annoying habit you know," Kate said softly, over her shoulder.

"Eh? Beg your pardon!" he exclaimed, letting loose a startled laugh. "Lud, but you are an unusual gel. Wonder if you are real. Should I pinch myself? Or you?"

"Neither, if you please," Kate said, smiling in spite of herself.

"Demmed if I could have believed it, but you're a match for him. They're saying you are as cool as he is, a perfect companion for the great Wroth!"

"That's not all they're saying," Kate noted, her amusement fading.

The viscount laughed again. "But all the rest's a hum, and we both know it."

"Do we?" Kate stared out at the silent gardens, her thoughts upon the man whose motives for marrying her had never seemed clear enough to her.

"Lud, yes. Must say I never thought to see Wroth

fall so hard. He's a decent fellow, but more than once I've wondered if ice water flowed in his veins. Nice to know that he's human, too."

Was he? Kate wasn't so sure. Nor could she easily swallow Raleigh's claim that he had fallen hard, for Gray did not have the look of a man who felt anything, least of all bruised. There were things she could have said, but for all his amiability, Raleigh was a man, and she did not feel comfortable discussing such things with him. Slowly, she straightened.

"There now. I feel much better for the fresh air. Thank you, Raleigh," she said.

"Dash it all, I've said something wrong, haven't I?" he said, looking stricken. "My sister complains I'm a jaw-me-dead."

Kate smiled. "No, you are just as you should be, and I'm glad you rescued me from those high sticklers."

He did not look mollified. "Bah! You are worlds above most of them, so don't give 'em another thought," His boyish face turned somber. "I just... You've got a difficult time of it, and I would be a friend, if I could."

"You are a friend," Kate assured him, reaching out to pat his arm.

He glanced away and then back at her, his features more serious than she had ever seen them. "Dash it all, but I want to tell you that you're what he needs, though he may not realize it yet. He's a stubborn one, used to having his own way since he got out of leading strings."

"I know," Kate said. Although touched by Raleigh's efforts to put her marriage right, she was not ready to argue its state with him. Taking his arm, she let him lead her back into the house, but her husband was still nowhere in sight, and when another gentleman hailed the viscount, she let him go, stifling the feeling of abandonment that assailed her, along with a healthy irritation with Gray.

Once, she had been afraid of fitting into this world; now she wondered why she had even cared. Outwardly, she was at one with these people; inwardly, she would never be. And where had her elegant clothes and manners gotten her? They had not won her husband's affection, no matter what Raleigh said.

Lost in her thoughts, Kate did not at first notice the two women whispering behind their fans as they stared at her, but once aware of their scrutiny, she slipped away. Perhaps she could duck into one of the other rooms and sit down for a bit. She had just rounded a reasonably quiet corner when she heard her name mentioned, and although she knew that she would probably hear no good, she halted her steps.

"God, yes," said a portly gentleman with thinning hair. "Only Wroth would go looking for a country gel and end up with a beautiful heiress besides!"

"I had heard he was in the market for a wife, but why a provincial?"

"Had a brief interest in Lady Wycliffe during her season, as I recall, though I never pictured Wroth as the sort to embrace a vicar in the family." He laughed loudly, and Kate stepped back.

"A fresh-faced virgin to set up his nursery. Bet she'll be fat with the heir before long."

Kate could listen no more, her heart sinking even lower as she turned away. Was she to be nothing but a brood mare? A graceless green girl who filled Wroth's requirements for a mother-to-be? She frowned as another question pushed aside all the others. Who was Lady Wycliffe?

Fighting a surprising stab of jealousy, Kate did not see Lady Coxbury bearing down on her until it was too late. Swallowing a resigned sigh, she allowed the matron to present two gentlemen who immediately began spewing compliments at her head and fawning over her hand in a ridiculous manner. They were not like Raleigh, for their eyes held no sincerity, only a lascivious hunger that told her just what type of friendship they were interested in pursuing.

Where was Gray? How could he leave her to the attentions of wretches such as these? Kate looked around the room, wondering if he was paying court to some other woman, a sophisticated sort who was too exciting to be relegated to a life in his nursery. Had the future she envisioned already arrived?

Gray wandered restlessly through the Coxburys' lavish home, telling himself that he did not need to keep Kate within view. Already there was talk of how the great Wroth danced attendance upon his wife, and although Gray had never been one to heed rumors, these came too close to his own concerns for comfort.

Naturally, he had stayed by Kate's side since their

arrival in London, for had he not promised to show her the sights? And if he had delayed their attendance at the inevitable balls and soirees, it was because he wanted to wait until the gossip about his sudden marriage died down a bit.

It had nothing to do with Raleigh's sly predictions.

Gray stalked the length of the card room, but the play held no interest for him. His thoughts kept returning to Kate, feeding his annoyance. Could he not leave her even for a few minutes? He had always scoffed at those men who annually made cakes of themselves over the season's reigning beauties, but this evening he felt like one of them, chafing at the minutes he spent in any other company than Kate's.

It was absurd. Ridiculous. Mortifying. Unconscionable. And he would not have it!

"La, Wroth, you look like a thundercloud! Whatever is the matter? That new wife of yours causing you trouble already?" An aging dowager eyed him with some amusement, and Gray realized that his hands were balled into fists. Deliberately, he relaxed his fingers and fixed her with a contemptuous glare that sent her hiding behind her fan. Stifling the unruly urge to knock her on her fat behind, he stalked away, toward where he had given Kate over to Lady Coxbury. Although he had been momentarily diverted, his initial problem remained.

This need for Kate was eating him up inside.

No matter how he might refuse it or refute it, Gray knew he wanted her: her body, her scent, her soft voice, her quiet strength, her quick wit. Her elegance went bone-deep, and had nothing to do with her attire; it was a grace of spirit.

She had become his addiction—the more he fed upon her, the hungrier he grew. So he fought his desire, unwilling to give up the control he had wielded all his life. It was a trial such as he had never known. He could not avoid her, for he had promised to show her London, and he was not keen on leaving her to her own devices after his talk with Raleigh. So he suffered Kate's tempting him all day, and he held firm, though he wanted her anywhere and everywhere: in the library, across the breakfast table and off the darkened paths of Vauxhall. So far, he had given in only at night, rationalizing that any newly wedded man would not deny himself the pleasure of his marriage bed.

*Pleasure.* A feeble word to describe what he felt when he was inside her. Gray shuddered at the memory of ecstasy such as he had never before imagined. His blood quickened in response, and he silently cursed his own lack of restraint.

But it went deeper than sex.

Gray knew that was only a part of his growing obsession. Like the primitive he feared he had become, he coveted every last inch of her, every whisper of her breath, every glance from those amazing eyes. And the milieu in which he had once moved so easily now seemed like a trap, designed to keep her from him.

Snatching up a glass from a passing servant, he took a gulp. Champagne again! The frothy liquid did little to assuage his appetites. Nodding coolly to a baron who tried to snare him in conversation, Gray went on, his gaze traveling ahead, searching, despite his best intentions, for his wife. And when he found her, he halted abruptly, his heart thundering a protest.

Raleigh was right.

Too damn right. Gray could have choked the man then and there as he faced the truth of the viscount's predictions, for Kate was no longer under the relative protection of Lady Coxbury. No, indeed. The little poppet was at the center of a small group of rakes, every one of them eyeing her low-cut gown as a starving man would a beef roast.

He should have known. Kate was a beautiful woman, and, as his wife, she would draw more than her share of attention. Perhaps it was her many charms that drew them, or, as Raleigh had suggested, the challenge of bedding a famous man's spouse. Whatever the lure, they surrounded her, leering at her in a manner that set Gray's teeth on edge.

He shouldn't care. Throughout the crowded rooms were many husbands whose wives were flirting with other men. He had never marked it before, and should not now, for it meant nothing. Worldly-wise since childhood, Gray did not blink at even the most outrageous behavior, yet his gnawing need for Kate made the sight of her with other men intolerable.

Drawing in a deep breath, Gary told himself that she was handling her admirers with her usual aplomb. In fact, her manner was noticeably cooler than could be said of any of the other women, half of whom were falling out of their gowns in their eagerness to be noticed. Not Kate. Still, it bothered him to watch her turning toward them, listening to them, gifting them with a smile... His fingers closed around the empty glass he still clutched tightly.

"I see your wife has made some conquests already."

Gray did not turn at the sound of Raleigh's amused tone, his attention riveted on one particularly bold fellow, who leaned close to whisper in Kate's ear. Was his breath touching her? Gray's hand tightened.

"Let me take that," Raleigh said, prying his fingers loose from the crystal. "Can't go around breaking these, Wroth. It's a waste of perfectly good glassware, you know."

Gray hardly heard the viscount. He was intent upon the man who stood too near to his wife. Gray had met him before, a disreputable character always chasing after the newest bit of muslin. Larkin was his name, but Gray could think of other, more appropriate epithets.

While he watched, Kate inched away, but Larkin followed. When he reached over to lightly touch the bare skin of her shoulder, Gray's banked rage ignited. Throwing off Raleigh's restraining hold, he stepped forward, ignoring Kate's startled expression to put himself between her and Larkin.

"Don't touch my wife," he warned softly.

"I beg your pardon, Wroth. I didn't realize you were so possessive," the man answered, smiling slyly.

Gray fought down the primitive urge to beat the fellow to a pulp, though his hands itched to strike. "Touch her again and I'll kill you."

He heard the gasps of the onlookers, but paid them no heed as he bowed slightly to Kate. "Shall we go?"

At her curt nod, he took her arm and strode through the gaping crowd, ignoring the expressions of shocked amazement that met his abrupt departure. Neither did he acknowledge a farewell from Raleigh, who stood staring thoughtfully after them.

He was too angry to notice. Another man had felt the smooth satin of his wife's skin, and his newly awakened barbaric streak was crying for murder. He could do it, too. A duel would do no damage to his reputation; he was too powerful.

He should have called out the bastard.

Thrusting Kate into the coach, Gray took a seat across from her, to avoid the temptation of sitting too close. It did little good, because he still wanted her, now more than ever.

The ceaseless need grated in him, feeding his ire, and he wanted to lash out at something to protest his helplessness. He glanced over at the subject of his obsession. She looked out the darkened window with perfect poise, and he longed to shatter that composure, to make her into the same helpless slave to passion that he had become. Damn it, didn't she feel it, too? Muttering a curse, he fixed her with a glare that denied his longing.     "I do not want my wife's name bandied about. Whether you desired it or not, you have a position to uphold," he snapped.

Her bright eyes met his fearlessly, as always. "Whatever are you talking about?"

"I'm talking about letting other men fondle you

in public!'' Ignoring her outraged gasp, Gray went on, desiring only to punish her for his own lack of constraint. "I won't have it. Nor will I have a breath of scandal attached to your name. The rogues who flatter and fawn over you do so because you are my wife. To them you are nothing but a trophy to be won and flaunted for your name. Do you understand?''

The brief flicker of pain that passed across her face pricked him, and Gray looked away, unwilling to see the results of his own handiwork. He blew out a long, low breath that bespoke his rapidly falling opinion of himself.

"Yes, I understand my role perfectly, but what of you, Gray? Do you intend to honor the vows you forced me to take back at Hargate?''

Gray's gaze swiveled back to her, annoyed at her insinuation. "Do you doubt my word, poppet?''

"No, but this world is vastly different from my own, and I have discovered that in it few men are faithful. Will you follow the fashion and take someone else's wife to your bed?''

The question was absurd. Every drop of blood in his body burned for her and only her, but Gray would not submit meekly to her power over him. "You wound me, Kate, when you cast me in with the rest of the rabble,'' he said coolly. "I have never had any desire to be fashionable.''

She lifted her chin in that show of strength he had come to know so well. "What of a mistress, then? Will you have one? The dowagers whisper of men's needs, as if such behavior is inevitable.''

*Needs.* The word touched a nerve, and Gray drew in a harsh, angry breath, unwilling to admit where his own weakness lay. "Are you afraid you cannot satisfy me, poppet?" he drawled.

The mocking question hit its mark, for he could see her flush, even in the dimness of the coach. And although Gray knew he was being unreasonable, he continued, driven to get a little of his own back, however he could. "I have no mistress," he said baldly. "Nor is my life ordered by the whims of my cock."

Once his claim would have been the truth, for nothing but his powerful intellect had ever ruled him—until he met Kate. She had made a liar of him, but she did not know it. He saw her flinch at the taunt, so he went on, heedless of reality and disregarding her sensibilities, like a man possessed.

"Let us be clear on something, poppet. I don't *need* anything." The vehement denial gave him perverse pleasure, as if just repeating the falsehood would lend it substance. Perhaps if he convinced her of his invincibility, he would regain it. Fixing her with a fierce and certain gaze, the kind that had shattered his opponents and reaffirmed his power, Gray spoke the lie that kept her from binding him to her.

"I have *never* needed anything. Or anyone."

# Chapter Seventeen

Kate feigned a smile as she watched the dancing. A small gathering, Gray had promised, but after admonishing her to behave, he had left her, once more, to her own devices. No doubt he would soon be back, glaring at her as if he rued her very existence.

Surreptitiously, Kate lifted a hand and pressed her fingers into throbbing temples. Her head ached from the effort to try to understand her husband. Although he stayed close to her most of the day, he acted as though he begrudged her presence. Yet, whenever he let her out of his sight, he returned surlier than ever.

If it were not for his attentions in bed, Kate would have denounced the marriage as a complete failure. Yet after what she had heard at the Coxburys', she was not sure whether to read too much into those cherished moments. What she perceived as heart-rending lovemaking might only be a means to an heir for Gray.

He had made it perfectly clear during that dreadful trip home last night that he did not need her. Did he suspect her efforts to win him? Kate shuddered in humiliation. Why else would he make such a point of denying any feelings for her in that hateful tone, accompanied by that wretched fierce look of his?

It was daunting, even for an optimist like herself. As much as Kate hoped for the best, she had begun to wonder if Gray would ever care for her. Indeed, since the wedding, he seemed to be growing more moody and cold, and each day in London became more discouraging than the last.

She was miserable. And lonely. For Hargate and Cyclops and Lucy and Tom, who, although in London, was never to be seen. One day she had wandered to the stables in search of him, but a startled groom had looked so shocked at her query that she returned to the house. The next morning she had sought out Meg, only to be shooed from the kitchen as it was not a proper place for a marchioness.

She even missed Gray. Only at night did Kate catch glimpses of the man she had once known. Always arrogant, he was now positively contemptuous, and Kate didn't know how long she could bear up under the weight of it. She was not a quitter, but even the best players knew when to cut their losses—a small tidbit Gray had taught her when discussing his love of gambling. Her mouth tightened at the memory of his face when had he spoken of it, reminding her of her own inability to stir him.

Now she was jealous of a deck of cards.

Pinching the bridge of her nose, Kate released a weary sigh. Then she blinked, suddenly conscious of eyes upon her. She had become accustomed to curious stares, but this was different. She shivered as the back of her neck tingled oddly. Who was watching her?

Looking around the room, she saw the usual clusters of dowagers and daughters and dandies. Her gaze flitted past each, until coming to rest on a blond woman standing close by, who returned her notice. Instead of hiding her interest, the woman approached in a friendly fashion that told Kate she could not have been responsible for that odd sensation of wariness.

"I hope you will forgive my forwardness, but I so wanted to meet you, Lady Wroth, and when I saw you alone, I thought I might introduce myself." The lovely blonde wore a cautious expression, for this just wasn't done, but Kate found her candor refreshing.

"By all means," she said, with a nod.

She was rewarded with a dazzling smile. "Oh, thank heavens you don't stand on ceremony, though I suspected that Wroth's wife would not!" she added, her eyes sparkling. "I know we are going to be great friends, so I would have you call me Charlotte. My husband is the earl of Wycliffe."

Lady Wycliffe.

Kate couldn't help her swift reaction of dismay. The woman was beautiful—tall and voluptuous, with a mass of golden hair that fell in tiny ringlets about her face. In short, she was everything Kate was not, and Kate felt her lack sharply.

"You are Lady Wroth, aren't you?" the woman asked, her smile fading under Kate's tight-lipped scrutiny. Her clear green gaze faltered, and Kate immediately felt guilty, for she saw nothing of the calculating glint she had witnessed so often since her arrival in London.

"Yes, but please call me Kate," she managed to murmur.

The words brightened Charlotte's face like sunshine, and she leaned close. "It's a love match, isn't it?" she asked in a conspiratorial whisper.

The question so startled Kate that she didn't even think to prevaricate. "Hardly!" she protested.

Charlotte's eyes clouded in confusion, and then she turned slightly to look across the room, and Kate found herself following the path of the other woman's gaze. It led to Gray.

He was standing, casually elegant, among several men, taller than all the others, and more handsome, more self-assured, more *everything*. Kate couldn't help the little catch in her heartbeat at the sight of him. Drawing in a fortifying breath, she glanced away, trying to shore up her defenses with a cool demeanor.

"I understand that you preceded me in my husband's affections," she said softly.

It was Charlotte's turn to gape. She gave Kate a startled glance and then laughed aloud—a delightful, infectious sound. "Hardly!" she echoed. "Wroth is much too fierce for me! He was very kind, but I must admit I doubted whether he had any feelings at all. I am happy to see now that they are firmly engaged."

It took Kate a moment to understand what the woman was saying, but before she could deny that any such thing was true, Charlotte went on. "I vow I never thought to see the great Wroth so taken, especially after he teased my husband unmercifully for falling in love with me. I am glad to see him get his comeuppance.''

Kate wanted to protest. Gray no more loved her than he did Cyclops. But Charlotte was whispering like a giddy girl. "See how his eyes follow you around the room,'' she said, nodding toward where Gray stood among the men. "He has not given any-one else the full force of his attention since you walked in. I marked it myself, and knew then that he had met his downfall.''

Kate glanced over at her husband, but she could not tell whether Gray was watching her or Charlotte. And the stubborn set of his lips as he did so could hardly be construed as a sign of devotion.

"La, it is all of a piece!'' Charlotte exclaimed with a happy smile. "I had heard that you were his equal, but some people are so cruel that I was not sure whether that was a compliment or a detraction. Now I see that you are perfectly matched. How wonderful! Wait until I tell Max!'' she said, lifting her hand to wave at a man engaged in conversation with a tur-baned dowager.

Watching Charlotte, Kate had to admit that she could not imagine the hard-hearted Gray with such a lively creature, and any lingering suspicions about the woman's motives disappeared when Lord Wyc-liffe arrived at his wife's side. Max, as she so care-lessly called the earl, was nearly as tall and hand-some and elegant as Gray, but he did not share the marquis's coldness or his blatant arrogance. And he bestowed an affectionate grin upon his wife that made Kate envious.

Theirs was definitely a love match.

"Max, this is Kate, Wroth's wife! Isn't she lovely?"

"A veritable goddess, as Raleigh would say," Max said, bending low over her hand and winking conspiratorially at her.

"And it is a love match!" Charlotte whispered breathlessly.

Kate's disclaimer died on her lips under the force of Max's sudden, intense gaze.

"Really?" he said a bit archly. "I believe I will have to go congratulate Wroth at once on this happy turn of events!" He leaned close to his wife. "We are to be at your aunt's in exactly one hour."

"Yes, Max," Charlotte said.

"No dawdling."

"No, Max," Charlotte said, her eyes twinkling. They looked at each other with such affection that Kate felt heartsick. Her alternately cold and hot relationship with Gray seemed a sad mockery of what this couple shared, and all her hopeless efforts would never win her its equal. She glanced away, unable to watch what she would never have.

"He likes to be punctual," Charlotte explained with an indulgent smile as her husband left her side. "I am afraid we are not in London for long, for I hate to leave my son, but say you will join us at our house in Sussex before the summer is over."

"I cannot answer for my husband," Kate said

tightly. Some of her misery must have shown on her face, because Charlotte blinked in confusion.

"What is it?"

Kate shook her head. "Nothing. You have been very kind, and I wish you well."

"But we will see each other again soon," Charlotte said, brightening. "I shall inform Wroth myself!"

Kate forced herself to assent, but she had a sinking feeling that she would never visit the Wycliffe home or see Charlotte again. Indeed, just as the lovely blonde was making her exit, Kate caught a glimpse of Gray's face across the room, and it boded ill for anything except continued failure.

Perhaps it was time for her to give up.

Gray stalked into the town house, oblivious of the fact that his wife had to hurry to keep pace with him. Ignoring the butler's greeting, he strode toward the stairs without even waiting for her to join him. They were in the habit of going straight up to their rooms upon their return from the evening's engagements, for Gray was usually on the verge of bursting the fall of his trousers.

Not tonight. Even though he dismissed his valet as usual, Gray did not feel the throbbing need that had been plaguing him nightly when he entered his room. He was too angry. Throwing off his coat, he tossed it against the wall and cursed under his breath. *That idiot Wycliffe!* How dare he! Gray couldn't remember the last time anyone had taunted him, but Wycliffe... Although Gray wanted to smash a fist into the earl's smug expression, he had shrugged off the sly insinuations that he was as infatuated with Kate as Wycliffe was with Charlotte.

Lies! Gray would never be guilty of the sort of fawning devotion that characterized the Wycliffe union. Nor would Kate ever behave in such a nauseating fashion, thank God! And yet, Wycliffe's knowing smile had touched that nerve, that *fear* of his own weakness, that made Gray frantic and furious. Tugging at his neckcloth, he walked into Kate's adjoining room, scaring her mouse of a maid into flight. She was seated at her mirrored table, calmly removing her jewelry, but, for once, Gray barely noticed the way the candlelight gleamed on her satiny hair and her bare shoulders.

"Did you see that pompous ass Wycliffe?" he growled, throwing the white linen to the floor in a heap.

"Yes, I met him," Kate answered softly. "His wife is lovely."

"Charlotte? God knows what she sees in him! The man is an idiot!"

Kate stiffened, but Gray ignored it, too intent upon that upstart Wycliffe to do anything except stalk the length of the room in outrage. "You should have heard him prattling on about true love, like some romantic schoolgirl. It's enough to make a grown man puke!"

"They do seem to be very much in love," Kate said softly.

"Love? What an absurd label for something as simple as shared interests and intellects! They have companionship. Nothing more,'' Gray snapped, denying his own suspicions that the Wycliffes possessed some secret he had once yearned for himself.

''Perhaps you are simply piqued because Charlotte chose another man.''

It took a moment for Kate's words to penetrate his rage. *''What?''* Gray nearly shouted, whirling toward her.

She turned to face him, her beautiful eyes clear and direct, as always. ''Rumor has it that you were enamored of her.''

*''Charlotte?''* Gray asked, contemptuously. ''I found her witty and refreshing, but I would hardly call that *enamored!''* It was difficult to believe now that he had once thought the vicar's daughter would make a suitable wife, and that he had searched for a bride with whom he could share a similar friendship. For once in his life, Gray's finely laid plans had gone awry, for he felt none of those things for the woman he had wed.

He stared at Kate in shock as the realization hit him. She was intelligent, yes, and beautiful and elegant and honest and all the things he had wanted, but in no way did his vision of a companionable relationship resemble the mindless, driving need he felt for her. He must have stood there gaping while the full force of his miscalculation hit home, for she pursed her lips in a parody of his own famous disdain.

''Oh, that's right. You don't believe in love. But do you know something, Gray? Just because you don't give it your lordly approval, that doesn't mean that it doesn't exist. Theirs is obviously a love match, and I must say I think it better to marry for affection than simply to acquire a broodmare!''

Gray's mouth twitched. What the devil was she talking about now? *"A broodmare?"*

"Oh, please," she said, waving a delicate hand as if annoyed with him. "I've heard that's what you were looking for in a wife, a simple country girl to provide you an heir, and little else."

*"What?"* In his outrage, Gray forgot that the desire to set up a nursery had started him thinking about marriage. It was all so far removed from the situation in which he now found himself that he could only view her accusation as ludicrous.

"Isn't that why you come to me every night after scowling at me all day, to get me with child?"

Although there had been a time when Gray would not have blinked at such a motive, Kate's cold-blooded description of what passed between them made him turn stone-still. He came to her because he had to, because he could not deny himself, because this slender girl had reduced his powerful will to nothing.

"Is that what you think?"

She met his fierce gaze unflinchingly. "I don't know what to think, Gray. Tell me."

*No.* He refused to be a witless lapdog like Wycliffe! He was a man in control of himself, his life, his emotions, and he would not lay himself bare for anyone. Not even Kate. Without another word, Gray turned on his heel and walked away from her, and he kept on walking until he was in his own room. Alone.

Then Gray closed the door firmly on his tempting wife and weakening, insubstantial nonsense like love.

Although she wasn't hungry, Kate hurried toward the dining hall, in the hope that she might find Gray still lingering over breakfast. She had tossed and turned in the wee hours, only to fall asleep sometime after dawn. Now it was afternoon, and despite some genuine rest, Kate was tired and heavy at heart.

For the first time since their wedding, Gray had not come to her bed, and she felt the lack sorely. Not only had she missed the soaring pleasure he gave her and the brief, exquisite sensation of closeness they shared, but she had been unable to close her eyes without his warmth cradling her afterward.

Worst of all, this change in Gray's routine chilled her. Perhaps she should not have forced the issue last night, but he was the one who had begun the argument, by denigrating the most tender of feelings. It was as if he had taken her love and thrown it back in her face out of some unreasonable spite.

And yet…when she had accused him of treating her as a broodmare, Kate could have sworn that denial flickered in his face. In fact, for a moment, she had thought she glimpsed something so profound that it took her breath away, but then it had been gone, replaced by his usual cool disdain. And then he had been gone, as if to prove that he had no use for her whatsoever.

Kate drew in a shaky breath, trying to gather her

resources as she stepped into the dining hall, but it was unnecessary. A swift glance told her that the long table was empty. Gray was not there. She told herself it was late and he might be waiting for her in the drawing room, so when a maid came in with a fresh pot of tea, Kate forced a smile. "Thank you. Can you tell me where His Lordship is this morning?"

"Yes, my lady. He said to tell you that he's gone to his club. Left nearly an hour ago, he did."

Swallowing the disappointment that stabbed through her, Kate merely nodded. Then she walked to the sideboard and began to fill her plate from the various dishes spread before her. Not until she heard the girl's footsteps disappear through the rooms did she slump down in a chair, alone, staring down the length of gleaming mahogany.

Kate sat there a long time, ignoring the food she once would have feasted upon as she contemplated her failed marriage. Lost in her maudlin thoughts, she did not stir until the sound of a voice jarred her from them.

"My lady." Kate straightened immediately at the words, surprised to find one of the footmen at her elbow. He held out a small silver platter with a folded piece of foolscap on it. "This just came for you."

A letter? From Lucy? Kate snatched up the treasure and thanked the man, dismissing him with a nod. When he had discreetly left her alone once more, she eagerly opened the missive, for Kate never would have expected her flighty sister to take the time to write.

She hadn't. Kate stilled, her breath catching in her throat when she realized that the note was not from Lucy. Indeed, it was not signed at all, and the contents made the reason for that lack very clear. Still, Kate forced herself to read the message through completely before letting it drop from her cold fingers.

It was blackmail, plain and simple.

The author was threatening to ruin her by revealing certain information about her and her sister, including the details of Lucy's hasty engagement. And the cost of silence was to be two hundred pounds.

To Kate, who had been scrimping by on next to nothing for years, the sum was a fortune. For one panicked moment, she felt like laughing at such an amount, but she had only to look around her at the luxuriously appointed town house to know just where the villain expected her to get his blood money. To Gray it would be little.

A hysterical giggle rose again to her lips, bitten off only by a ruthless struggle. Obviously, the blackmailer did not know everything about her, or he would have discovered that her marriage was a mockery. What would further gossip matter? Gray was more likely to weather it than to give her two hundred pounds without question.

Nor would she ask him for it, Kate thought, with determination. He had wed her out of his own honor, and she had brought him nothing but trouble. The laugh that had threatened escaped her, transformed into a sob by the knowledge. Her mission to make him love her had failed abysmally, and now he would be forced to suffer even more indignities because of her. Because of this, Kate thought bitterly, staring at the hated missive.

Who could do such a thing? Kate shied at the question, and yet she knew that London was full of evil men, some of them passing themselves off as gentlemen. Her breath caught again. Perhaps even Uncle Jasper was responsible! Having gone through her own fortune, he might now hope to bleed her husband dry, as well.

Kate's mouth tightened. He would not succeed.

It was time to cut her losses and go home. Perhaps Gray could get an annulment. The thought sent a bright shaft of pain darting through her, but Kate knew it was better to make a clean break than to prolong the misery that engulfed them both. She could not let him go on paying for the folly of their union. Nor could she continue her struggle against his indifference. Already he seemed to harbor a resentment that would only lead to more bitterness, and Kate could not bear to watch as he slowly ground her heart into dust.

Glancing down at the letter, she made a mental note of the time for the proposed meeting. Then she rose and tossed it into the fireplace. Transfixed, she watched as the flames licked at the paper and flared brightly, consuming both the note and all the hopes she had once held for her marriage.

Kate wasn't sure what she had expected—a big man, burly and muscular or lean and wiry, perhaps with beady little eyes. Although unfamiliar with the denizens of London's seamier side, she had seen the ruffians who weaved through the crowds picking pockets, and she pictured the man she was going to meet as cut from the same cloth. Rougher, perhaps, and definitely a creature of some size. A bully. Even Jasper himself, whom she had never met, must surely look the part of a villain.

But when Kate reached the secluded part of Hyde Park where she was to meet her blackmailer, such a character was nowhere to be seen. She walked around the area twice before finally coming to a halt and squinting into the distance. She did not care to be kept waiting, especially when she had come, as instructed, without even a maid to attend her.

And then she felt it, the nagging, tingly feeling that she had known before, signaling that she was being watched. Kate turned, scanning her surroundings, but not a soul was in sight. Was he hiding behind some bush, ready to pounce upon her? Kate drew in a sharp breath, suddenly aware of just how vulnerable she was, even in such a public place.

"Hello! Lady Wroth!" Starting at the sound of a voice piercing the silence, Kate whirled around, but again saw no one. Unless... Her eyes narrowed when she glimpsed a female form perched upon a stone bench off the footpath that had led her to this clearing. Blinking, Kate watched the woman hail her, and frowned. She knew that face from somewhere.

Mrs. Parker! Kate let out an impatient breath. The last thing she needed was to be drawn into a witless conversation with the snide widow when she had

pressing business at hand. What if the wretched creature scared away the blackmailer? Kate did not intend to stay in London any longer than it took her to
confront the man. She did not want to wait for some
new meeting.

"Oh, Lady Wroth!" Unfortunately, Kate could
hardly cut the woman dead, so she forced a smile to
her lips and waved before moving away. And then,
very slowly, like someone waking from a dream,
Kate turned back toward the figure seated on the
bench as if seeing her for the first time.

She sat there alone. No maid or companion attended her in this secluded spot, a definite breach of
the strict rules that covered town behavior. Nor did
she seem dismayed by Kate's lack of company. The
realization made Kate dizzy, and she swayed a moment before regaining her composure—and her wits.
Straightening, she lifted her chin and walked toward
her rendezvous.

Kate had come to confront the villain, to find out
if it was, indeed, Jasper who threatened her so foully,
and to discover the extent of his knowledge. As painful as it would be to have her past made public, Kate
was concerned only about the shooting, for the news
that she had put a bullet in her future husband would
go beyond scandal. Still, she had steeled herself to
face it, and, if need be, her uncle, but the discovery
that it was only a spiteful widow who menaced her
made Kate furious. Approaching the bench, she stood
as tall as she could before the seated woman.

"Ah, I see you've deduced the significance of my

presence here. Clever little minx!" Mrs. Parker said, fanning herself.

"You sent me the note."

"Quite so. Have you brought along sufficient funds to quiet my sadly wagging tongue?" she asked slyly, eyeing Kate's slim reticule skeptically.

"No."

The fan snapped closed abruptly. "Perhaps you do not take me seriously, but I warn you that I intend business!" Mrs. Parker said. Pausing, she leaned back, giving Kate a calculated look. "Or do you hope to find out just how much I know?" When Kate said nothing, she smiled wickedly. "Oh, I do know a lot, more than you would ever like to be made public."

"Such as?" Kate asked.

Mrs. Parker laughed, unfurling her fan again, like a coquette. "The whole sordid business, you and your sister, reduced to mere servants, living alone! Shocking!" she said, her lips curling in amusement. "And your sister's marriage. Such a mésalliance! But I'm sure she was desperate. How desperate was she?" The horrid woman leaned forward, an eager light in her dark eyes.

"There was gossip, horrifying things that I hate to repeat, but as her sister, I'm sure you know of it— rumors that she was pledged to Wroth, that she met with him secretly at his hunting box, that they were *lovers*, and yet, suddenly, you are married to him, while she is stuck with a farm boy. Tsk, tsk, aren't you the greedy girl, to steal your sister's beau? I quite like that, you know!'' she said, reaching out to tap Kate's arm with her fan.

She settled back with a brittle smile of avarice on her face. ''But business before pleasure, I am afraid. And as much as I admire you, I cannot forget what I know without some sort of compensation. I am in need of some funds, Lady, and what is a few pounds between friends?''

Although Kate had schooled herself not to react, she could not help flinching at the insinuation that Gray had been Lucy's lover. That was a misconception that she had not foreseen.

Mrs. Parker, anticipating success, pressed her suit. ''Just imagine the damage to your reputation, should this get out. Why, you would be a social pariah! And your husband, the great Wroth, brought low by scandal! I'm sure you want to prevent that, at any cost,'' Mrs. Parker said, leaning back and smiling slyly at her impending victory.

Kate's swift surge of panic was halted by the memory of one of Gray's arrogant claims. He had said that nothing short of murder could affect his power. Well, his assertion would soon be put to the test, Kate thought grimly.

Fixing the woman with a contemptuous stare much like one of her husband's, Kate did not waver. ''No,'' she said. ''No blood money. Say what you must. I have nothing for you.'' Turning on her heel, she walked away, ignoring Mrs. Parker's screeches of protest.

Her business in London was concluded.

## Chapter Eighteen

She was gone. After Gray tore through the town house like a madman, thinking the worst—that she had been abducted, or was out proving Raleigh right with some scoundrel—Badcock had told him. Apparently the rest of his useless staff quaked in terror at the thought of admitting that his wife had left him, returning to her childhood home in one of his own coaches.

It had come back—without her, of course. Gray had nearly dismissed the driver on the spot, but he knew that the poor man could hardly have gainsaid the marchioness. And a determined Kate would have found a way, if not in his private vehicle, then on the mail or the common stage. Gray shuddered to think of such dangers.

And what of her now? How safe was she, at a house that had been closed, without even that old fool Tom to keep watch over her? Damn. The girl he had thought so sensible had proved herself to be a reckless fool. He ought to ride over there and bring her back. Bodily.

But he was too angry at her defection. What more did she want from him? he thought, tensing at the question. He had married her, had given his name, his title, his wealth and his attention, while she... She had destroyed a self-control he had honed to razor-sharpness over the years, and had turned him into a bloody slave to his own body. Wasn't that enough? What else could he possible give her, some sappy declaration of love? His very soul?

Gray's hand tightened painfully on the glass of brandy Badcock had brought him, but he did not loosen his grip. Instead, he tossed the damn thing into the fireplace, watching with satisfaction as it shattered to pieces upon the grate. So much for Wycliffe's fantastical notions of romantic love! His wife had left him, and he would be damned if he was going to chase after her like some whipped dog.

He had work to do. Ostensibly, he had come to town in order to conduct unfinished business. Instead, he had danced attendance upon his wife. No more. He needed updates on several enterprises, including the mysterious whereabouts of one Jasper Gillray. Gray's lips curved grimly, for he was eager to take out his ill humor on someone as deserving as Kate's uncle.

His smile faded. As for Kate...he didn't need her. He didn't need anyone. And now was his chance to prove it! It was time to break clean of his obsession and show his wife that he was master of all he surveyed, including himself.

To hell with her, Gray thought rebelliously, but he felt no triumph, only a dark emptiness that yawned before him like the pit itself, waiting to drag him down.

Kate walked slowly through Hargate's silent rooms, reaching out to touch a familiar object or view an ancestral portrait, but even her former house could not lift her spirits. The joyous sense of homecoming she had expected to feel had never materialized, not when she sighted the building or when she sent the coachman back to London and stood alone in the foyer. And not now, when her footsteps echoed loudly as she made her way to the kitchen.

Hargate had never seemed so big and empty before, Kate thought, even when there had been only Lucy and Tom to join her in an illusion of family. Perhaps that was the difference: As long as you were surrounded by people you cared about, the size of your residence or your purse did not matter. Blinking rapidly, Kate shied away from such thoughts, for they led in a dangerous direction. Back to Gray. And she was better off alone than clinging to that particular illusion.

A sound outside made her crack open the kitchen door, and she had to step back as an orange blur swept past her ankles. Cyclops! Kate reached down to pick up the feline and hold it close. "Have you been catching mice and staying fat, my friend?" she asked. She sank down, hugging the cat close until somehow her face was buried in its fur and the tears she had fought for so long escaped in great, endless gulps.

* * *

Twilight was settling around the house when Kate finished washing the dishes, one plate for her, one plate for Cyclops. Having been fed, the cat moved to its favorite spot by the hearth, and Kate gazed at it wistfully. Her old room would seem cold and lonely tonight, her bed huge and empty. Swallowing hard, she turned her attention elsewhere.

Tomorrow she would send word to Lucy that she was home, and then the place wouldn't seem so desolate, at least until Lucy married. As if her thoughts had conjured up her sister, Kate heard the sound of horses outside and hurried to the window. A small carriage was drawing up to the stables, but it could not be Lucy, for she recognized that crest all too well as the Wroth coat of arms. Had Gray come after her?

Kate's heart thudded wildly as she tried to come to grips with the prospect of facing her husband. Excitement, anger, despair and love all fought for supremacy as she flew to the door. In truth, she did not know what to feel, for she had never expected him to follow her.

And he hadn't.

Kate swallowed a hard lump of disappointment at the sight of Tom leaving the stables alone. Of course Gray would not charge to Hargate to retrieve her. No doubt he was relieved to have her out of his life once more. And that, she told herself firmly, was just what they both wanted. Pushing all thoughts of her husband aside, she forced a smile of greeting to her lips.

"Tom! What are you doing here?"

"You don't think I'd let you stay here all by yourself, do you?" he asked. His gruff question touched her, and Kate blinked. Although she took greedy delight in his small show of affection, she did not want to be a burden to anyone.

"Oh, Tom, you don't have to stay here," she protested.

"I do, and if you think I don't, you're a fool, Katie. You're a marchioness now. You can't live like a tenant farmer!"

Kate's smile of welcome faded. "I can live wherever and however I wish!"

"Not now that you're married!"

"Well, perhaps I'll get an annulment," she declared.

The coachman swore low and long. "Are you daft? You love the man, Katie. Anyone can see that, and he loves you, too." Before she could deny it, Tom went on, his voice rising fiercely. "You should have seen him, Katie. Why, even I felt sorry for the fellow when he came home to find you gone. He acted like a crazy man until Badcock finally got up the nerve to tell him the truth."

"The marriage was a mistake," Kate said stiffly.

Tom stared at her for a long moment and then shook his head. "Gad, you're as pigheaded as he is. A perfect match, I'd say," he added. With a snort of disgust, he stalked past her into the house.

It took two days for Lucy to come out to the house, two long days in which Kate rebelliously stamped around the grounds dressed in old trousers, while she and Tom remained at loggerheads. The peace she had hoped to find at Hargate eluded her, for the makeshift family she had once known was splintered apart.

Frantically Kate sought to repair it. She was just about to send another note round to the squire's when Lucy finally arrived in the Wortley carriage, escorted by Mr. Rutledge. Dressed in a bright, showy gown, and preening under her betrothed's attentions, Lucy sailed into her old home like a regal visitor.

Her greeting was less than enthusiastic. Suffering Kate's brief hug, she glanced about the silent foyer with a frown, as if to decry the absence of servants to attend her arrival. "Archibold, will you please wait for me in the garden? I wish to speak with my sister privately in the drawing room."

Impatient with such formalities, Kate pursed her lips, but followed her sister along the gallery. Lucy fanned herself rapidly as she stepped into the drawing room. "My, it is warm. I don't suppose you have anything cool to drink, some lemonade perhaps?"

Kate laughed humorlessly. Although the pantry was not as bare as it once had been, there were no lemons to be had at Hargate. Lucy, it appeared, had become accustomed to better fare at the squire's laden table. And, from her languid movements, Kate deduced that she was no longer used to doing for herself, either.

"Some water then, please. My condition demands cool liquids and rest, Katie," she said, piling the cushions behind her as she sank onto a sofa.

Unprepared to wait upon her sister, but seeing no other choice, Kate nodded curtly. She could hardly ask Tom, who spent most of his time in the stables, so she trudged off to the kitchen herself, suppressing a growing nostalgia for Gray's multitude of servants.

When she returned, glass in hand, Lucy looked at it and pouted. "Have you no ice?"

Kate bit back a sharp retort and smiled instead. "I did not wish to go out to the icehouse."

"At the squire's, there always seems to be plenty at hand. I vow, it's the only thing that keeps me from becoming queasy. They have quite spoiled me there, you know. I shall be sorry to leave the bosom of my dear husband-to-be's family after we are wed."

Kate refrained from pointing out that Lucy's uncle-to-be had once practically stolen the Chester heirlooms from them with his greedy bargaining, for she was determined not to quarrel with her sister. "I regret that you will miss some things available at the squire's, but I will be so glad to have you here with me, Lucy," Kate said, with a rather desperate sincerity.

Lucy's frown turned to dismay. "Here? With you? Whatever do you mean?"

Kate blinked. What else could she mean? "Now that I am back, there is no need for you to stay with the Wortleys."

"You surely cannot mean to remain here like… this?" Lucy asked, in horrified accents. "Without any staff?"

"It is no different than before," Kate said, refusing to allude to her new name or her absent husband.

"It most certainly is!" Lucy protested, throwing up her hands. "I don't understand you, Katie. The squire says that Wroth is one of the richest men in the whole country. You can have anything you want, after years of skimping and scraping by, and you give it all up to come back here to nothing! I've never understood you, but this...this is beyond folly."

Unwilling to talk about Gray, Kate turned the conversation back to Lucy. "You belong at Hargate," she said firmly, fixing her sister with a look that brooked no argument. For a long moment, their gazes remained locked, and then Lucy rose to her feet.

"All right, you win, as usual! I'll stay here, but I won't lift a finger to help out, and as soon as Archibold and I are married, I'm leaving!" With a whirl of shiny new skirts, she turned to go after Archibold, but paused on the threshold to toss one last barb at her sister.

"Enjoy your suffering, Katie!"

Gray was suffering. Leaning his head back, he released a long, guttural sigh. He had never thought it would be this difficult to survive without her, but like an opium addict deprived of his pipe, he struggled through each day. Each hour. He had hoped to regain his sanity and his control; now he wondered if he could ever go back to the man he had been before Kate entered his life.

She had changed him irrevocably.

And not for the better, he thought grimly. Yet, even as he scorned his own weakness, he was beginning to wonder if it was such a big price to pay for Kate, for her company, her warmth, her passion. He missed her, the dark satin of her hair, her amazing amethyst eyes, her mouth, her taste, the look on her face when she cried out his name...

Damn, he was mooning over her like some love-sick boy! Gray slammed his fist down on the surface of the desk, as if the act of violence could marshal his wits. He needed them today. He had kept Kate's defection quiet, for he wanted no further speculation about his abrupt, tumultuous marriage, but something must have gotten out, because he had received a cryptic note from a certain Mrs. Parker requesting a private audience with him—concerning Kate.

And he would be damned if he would let a missing wife make him vulnerable to anything or anyone. Drawing himself up to his usual, imposing height, Gray banished all traces of weariness and longing as the door to his study opened to reveal his butler.

"Mrs. Parker is here to see you, my lord," the man said, frowning slightly in disapproval. The servants had become devoted to Kate during her brief residence, and Gray had been receiving black looks from nearly every member of his household since her departure. He began to wonder if peace, or some slight semblance of it, would ever reign in his life again. Fixing the impertinent man with a fierce glare, Gray nodded, bowing slightly to the woman who stepped into the room.

"I appreciate you seeing me under such unortho-dox circumstances," Mrs. Parker said, taking a seat and fanning herself gently as the butler withdrew. "I'm sure you think it unusual of me to come here like this, but I had an errand of most pressing con-cern."

Gray thought it highly unusual for a woman, even a widow, to visit him, but nothing connected with Kate surprised him any longer. "You have something to share concerning my wife?" Gray prompted.

"In a way, yes," she said, smiling slyly above her fan.

"What sort of way?" Gray asked. Unmoved by her arch glance, Gray lifted a brow in question.

"Well, if you wish to be blunt, I can be," Mrs. Parker said, dropping her efforts at flirtation. "The truth of the matter is that I am privy to certain information about the marchioness that I'm sure you do not wish to be made public."

Anger, swift and sure, made him fist his hand at his side, but he hid it, leaning casually on the edge of the desk. He was accustomed to dealing with attacks on himself, but Kate was another matter entirely. "Such as?" he asked evenly.

"My, you are a cool one!" Mrs. Parker replied, her eyes sharp under partially lowered lashes. She leaned forward, unable to conceal her avarice. "I know plenty, but I'm not fool enough to share it without the promise that I will be adequately compensated for my trouble."

Gray laughed, startling her, and she drew back, as well she should. He fixed her with a fierce glare. "You won't get a farthing from me, and if you think to wag your tongue, let me give you fair warning. You will only ruin yourself." Reaching behind him, Gray opened a drawer and dropped a handful of papers on the desk.

"My vowels!" Mrs. Parker shrieked as soon as

she recognized the evidence of her debts. "How did you get them?"

"Do you think you are the first person to try to deal ignobly with me, madam?" Gray asked, lifting a brow in contempt. "If so, I would advise you to think again. I have bested the worst, and your feeble attempts at petty thievery hardly merit my attention. Be glad I don't have you thrown in gaol."

He stood, slanting a glance over her arrogantly. "Another warning, madam—do not trifle with me or mine again. Nor do I want to find out that you have bothered my wife with your noxious tricks."

The flicker of fear in her eyes sent unease stealing along Gray's spine, and he knew the truth before he even spoke. "You've already talked to her," he said softly.

The accusation struck home, for Mrs. Parker quaked in her seat, no longer the bold blackmailer. She must have glimpsed his rage, for she cringed, as if fearful he might strike her. He was tempted, fueled by a primitive urge to wreak vengeance upon any who would harm Kate. He was restrained only by his formidable will, and the dawning realization that this wretched creature might be responsible for Kate's flight.

Gray stilled. Was this why she had left him, to shield him from gossip? Struggling against the powerful emotions that surged through him, Gray walked to the door and threw it open. He would try to decipher his wife's strange motivations later; now, he would rid himself of her tormentor.

"Get out," he snapped at the wide-eyed woman.

"And if you breathe one word about my wife, I'll see you reduced to a Spitalfields beggar, whoring for your dinner."

Kate silently washed her breakfast plate. The pleasure she had taken in cooking for Tom and Lucy had faded, like everything else from her past. Seething with resentment, Lucy spent as little time at Hargate as possible, while Tom no longer appreciated her efforts, giving her black looks and championing Gray over the breakfast table.

"You've a new life now, Katie. It's time you left the old one behind. Your father is dead, and there will be no new earl unless you produce one!" he had said, pushing aside his cup.

Kate had flushed and glared at his bold speech. Afraid to consider the possibility of a child, she had shooed him from her kitchen, preferring to do the dishes herself to listening to his harping. He had no idea what stood between herself and Gray. No one did! No one knew how she cried herself to sleep every night, yearning for him to come after her. But he did not, and he never would; he simply didn't care enough about her.

While she cared too much to be contented with less.

Pride made Kate swallow and blink away her misery. Relegating her tears to the quiet darkness, she concentrated on the tasks that would keep her busy this afternoon. She had just decided on doing some gardening when she heard the sound of a coach outside. Rushing to the window, she looked out to see the squire's carriage. Not Gray. Never Gray. It was Lucy, but today was Sunday. Surely her pampered sister would spend the afternoon with the Wortleys and their requisite number of servants. And wasn't it early yet for church to let out?

Wiping her hands, Kate hurried toward the foyer. No doubt Lucy was too good these days to come in by the servant's entrance, she thought wryly. Sure enough, Kate reached the front doors just as Lucy burst in, Rutledge and another man following close behind. Dressed as she was in trousers, Kate was unprepared for other company, but she abandoned all hope of fleeing upstairs when Lucy threw herself into her arms.

"Oh, Kate, it is a catastrophe! And it is all Wroth's fault, lifting my hopes only to dash them so cruelly," she cried, sobbing against Kate's shoulder.

"What is it? What happened?" Kate looked frantically at Rutledge, who shook his head helplessly.

"I'll tell you what's what, young gent!" The other man swaggered forward, and Kate eyed him with curiosity. He was short and wiry, and although he was dressed like a gentleman, his clothes were ill-fitting and not of the finest quality. His hair was thin and greasy, his eyes were dark and beady, and, in fact, he fitted Kate's vision of a blackmailer far better than Mrs. Parker.

Lucy lifted her head long enough to wail loudly. "He objected to the banns!"

"What?" Lucy began crying once more, and Kate glared at the interloper. "Just who do you think you are, sir?"

"I'm Brown. Mr. Brown to you, and I've been sent by the man what runs this household. He's her guardian, he is, and she has no right to be married without his consent."

*Uncle Jasper.* Kate's heart sank. What were they to do now? Although her thoughts were in a turmoil, she lifted her chin. "And how do we know you are who you say? Have you a letter of introduction?"

Brown laughed; it was an ugly, deadly sound. "No, I don't have a letter, and I don't need one, either. Now, where's the sister? I've got some business with her, too," he said, with an evil leer.

Kate eyed him coldly. "I am she," she said, in imitation of Gray's most arrogant tone.

The fellow gaped at her, his mouth falling open. Then he shook his head. "Naw. Don't gammon me. I'm looking for one of the earl's daughters, not some doxy in boy's clothes."

For once, Kate regretted her ragged attire. As she had learned in London, appearance was everything. Nevertheless, she gave him an imperious stare. "Believe what you will. You are no longer welcome here."

"I told you Kate would make you go away, you wretched man!" Lucy said, lifting her head long enough to scowl at Brown.

His small eyes narrowing, he looked from Lucy to Kate and back again. "Kate, you say?" He smiled as he gave her a bold perusal. "Well, well. So you are her!"

The commotion drew Tom, who chose that moment to march into the room. "Who's this, Katie?" he asked, hitching up his trousers.

"He claims to have been sent by our guardian," Kate said, forcing herself to speak evenly.

"I have no business with you, old man," Brown said, dismissing Tom with a glance. "I'm just here to make sure these two behave themselves until Jasper arrives." He grinned blackly. "Meaning no weddings for the gels."

"Too late," Kate said coolly. "I already have married, and my husband, the marquis of Wroth, will not take kindly to interference of any sort." Deliberately, she kept the threat vague, for what sort of husband would allow her to remain here, virtually alone? Suddenly, her retreat to Hargate seemed unwise and childish.

The little man barked out a laugh. "Well, then, you'll just have to get an annulment, won't you?"

Although Kate had contemplated just such a course, when voiced aloud the suggestion made her flinch. It was too final. Too permanent. Too painful. With an insight born of panic, Kate realized that whether Gray loved her or not, she could not give him up, now or ever. The discovery gave her strength, and she smiled in amusement. "You cannot touch Wroth. He's one of the most powerful men in the country."

"Don't threaten me," Brown warned, stepping forward.

Kate stayed her ground as Tom moved in front of her. "Get away from Lady Wroth, you brute, or I'll call the magistrate and have you hauled away. You are not wanted here.''

Brown's face twisted into an obscene grimace. ''No, you're the one that's not wanted here. These fine ladies don't own this house and neither do you, so get out. You're fired!''

Tom would have lunged at the man, but Kate grabbed hold of his arm, restraining him. Although short, Brown had the look of a mean fighter, and he might be armed. She did not want Tom hurt, and he could do little if Jasper arrived to lay claim to Hargate. There was only one person who could help them now. Leaning close, she whispered in the coachman's ear.

''Go get Wroth.''

Giving her an odd look, Tom reluctantly turned away, muttering dire warnings should anything happen to the ladies. Brown just laughed, sending Lucy into fresh tears, while Rutledge wrung his hands helplessly. Kate eyed him over her sister's head. Although she knew her sister's lover to be a coward, still she did not think he would let anything happen to her. Unless Jasper arrived. What could the boy do then?

Suppressing a shiver, Kate knew that their only hope lay with Gray. But would he care enough to come to the aid of a wife who had run away from him?

## Chapter Nineteen

Tom left his heaving horse with a startled groom and charged into the town house. As much as he had hated to leave the girls with none but that cowardly Rutledge to protect them, he knew Kate was right. Better that he bring back Wroth.

The marquis would deal with Jasper and the little bully quickly enough, Tom thought, his original opinion of Wroth having undergone quite a change. His grudging respect had grown into full-fledged admiration since the marquis married Katie. Now, if only the two of them would let down their stubborn guards long enough to admit they loved each other!

Tom shook his head. Life was too short to spend it moping and pining when a person could have a warm body to hold close at night. Why, hadn't he been thinking of popping the question to Meg? And he would, too, just as soon as this business with Katie and Wroth and that blasted Jasper was settled.

"Where's Wroth?" he shouted to the kitchen staff.

"Not here, I don't think," Meg said, wiping her hands on her apron. "What is it?"

"Trouble!" Tom said, racing into the main rooms without pausing to explain. He found the marquis's stiff-necked butler polishing silver in the dining hall.

"Here, now, you! What do you think you're doing?" the man asked, aghast at Tom's rough appearance.

"I'm looking for Wroth."

"Well, he isn't here. Now, be off with you."

But a number of servants, headed by the formidable Meg, had gathered behind Tom. "Tom, is that you? What's this about trouble?" asked Wroth's valet.

"I must find His Lordship, and quickly. Katie's in danger!"

Several gasps rose from the crowd. "Where is he, Collier?" the valet asked the butler.

The old gent looked flustered. "I don't know. Perhaps at one of his clubs! He didn't say, just took off riding after breakfast. You know how he's been...lately," the man finished lamely.

The valet turned toward several of the footmen who surrounded Tom. "Johnny, take Jem with you and check the clubs."

"I'll have a look round the park!" another volunteered. Soon, they were all rushing off to find the marquis, but Tom felt no measure of relief. Once the man was found, he would still have to make the trip to Hargate, and Tom didn't like the idea of leaving the girls with that bully of Jasper's any longer than necessary.

"Mind, we don't have much time!" he shouted

after the departing servants, unable to repress a shiver of dread at the delay.

An hour later, Tom was feeling no better. After the last of the footmen returned empty-handed, he called a meeting in the kitchen, where it seemed every member of the marquis's large staff was talking at once.

"Hush, now, so you can hear me!" Tom shouted, and the group quieted obediently. They were obviously used to taking orders, Tom thought grimly. Now, if he could just convince them to follow his own.

"Most of you know me as Tom from the stables. I came aboard with the marchioness. As you know, there's been a bit of a tiff between the lord and his lady." He held up a hand to forestall any gossip. "That's neither here nor there, except that Katie, being a stubborn sort, took off for home by herself. Now she's there alone, and some bullyboy sent by her uncle Jasper is there, threatening her and her sister."

Noise erupted again as everyone broke into speech, and Tom lifted a hand for silence once more. "She told me to hurry here and bring back His Lordship, but I can't do that when no one can find him. That's the situation right now, as I see it. Now, I'll turn this meeting over to my associate, Sadcock."

"Badcock," the valet said. He gave Tom a wilting look before turning toward the assembled staff. "Does anyone have any other ideas about His Lordship's whereabouts?"

One of the maids blushed furiously, but spoke up. "What of that secretary of his, the fellow with the glasses?"

"Good thinking, Lizzy! Bob, run round to the man's house, will you?" the valet said, and one of the footmen hurried out the door. "Anyone else?"

Another footman stood. "Begging your pardon, Mr. Badcock, but he could be anywhere—visiting his friends, or gambling in some hell we've never even heard of."

There was a rumble of agreement. "Well, then, since the marchioness is in danger, and His Lordship isn't here, I suggest we go to Hargate ourselves," the valet said, startling everyone but Tom, who grinned from ear to ear as he watched the butler's mouth pop open. "This bully claims he's in the employ of Her Ladyship's uncle. Well, we're in the employ of one of the most important men in England, and I say we go and show him what's what!"

A rousing cheer met his words, and while the servants all began talking, Wroth's valet moved through the crowd, picking the largest, most imposing of the footmen to join him.

"But...but...this is unheard-of!" the butler protested as they headed toward the door.

"I'm coming, too!" Meg shouted. Grabbing up a fat rolling pin, she slapped it against her palm, and the butler backed away quickly.

"You are all mad!" he protested.

"No, we're going to rescue Her Ladyship," Meg said.

"On whose authority?" the butler called after them.

"On my authority!" the valet shouted over his shoulder.

The sound of another cheer followed them out the door, and Tom grinned. "You know, I never much liked you, Limpdick, but you're all right." He slapped the man on the shoulder heartily.

"Badcock," the valet said dryly. And then they were on their way.

Gray listened absently as Daniel Wells reported on his vast number of businesses and investments. Although Wells called himself a secretary, he was more of an overseer. He left the handling of correspondence and accounts to lesser employees, but looked after everything, keeping a vigilant eye on all of Gray's holdings and making sure that all ran smoothly.

He was invaluable, and Gray had been especially grateful for his assistance in the past month. During his absence from London and even after his return, Gray's mind had been elsewhere, yet he had known that nothing would go seriously wrong while Wells was in charge.

And so Gray nodded briefly, gave his approval when required, his disagreement when he felt it necessary, and let his thoughts wander back to Kate. His interview with Mrs. Parker yesterday weighed heavily on his mind, reminding him vividly of his wife's vulnerability. Despite her boy's clothes—and her marksmanship, Gray thought, flexing his shoulder slightly—Kate was not invincible. And suddenly he was very aware of the fact that she was at Hargate, essentially alone.

At first, anger at her defection had kept him from sending anyone after her. She knew what condition her former home was in, and if she was determined to play the peasant, Gray had been inclined to let her. If she would rather muck about like a tenant farmer than live with him as a pampered marchioness, then he wished her happiness in her choice!

Gray had hoped that she would have enough wits to realize her precarious situation, but now he wondered why he had ever thought her sensible. Of course, that idiot coachman had run to join her, but Gray knew just how little help Tom would be, and if she preferred Tom's presence to her husband's, she was welcome to it!

Gray frowned, shifting in his seat, as all his outrage at her perfidy returned. Although he ought to be glad that she was no longer at hand to drive him to distraction, he felt betrayed, as if a valued friend had quit his company. As if his parents had abandoned him once more.

Damn! Where had that thought come from? His parents had not been responsible for their own deaths, nor had he wasted a lot of time grieving their absence. He had been too busy taking the reins of the enormous fortune left in his charge. And anyway, the situation with Kate was not at all similar, for her loyalty, always very much in doubt, had been tested and found wanting.

Or had it? His interview with Mrs. Parker shed a

new light upon the situation, forcing him to wonder if the woman's threats had put Kate to flight. Certainly, the poppet's pride would not let her ask him for the blackmail money, nor would she even come to him for advice, Gray suspected. Perhaps Raleigh was right, and they were too much alike, too stubborn and willful, to make the compromises that their intimacy demanded. Frowning at the thought, Gray only gradually became aware of Wells's scrutiny. He stilled, eyeing his secretary sharply.

"What?"

Wells shook his head. "It's just that I've never seen you so distracted. Are you feeling all right?"

No. He felt lousy—angry, betrayed, worried, and a host of other useless, annoying emotions he was unaccustomed to embracing. "I'm fine," he said, lifting a brow.

Wells knew better than to pursue the matter. He shrugged. "Well, I expect that you will want to pay attention to this last bit of news."

"Yes?" Gray asked, tensing in spite of himself.

"Jasper Gillray is on the move," Wells said, and Gray's casual attention became sharp and focused. "Perhaps he got word that one of his charges had married, or that banns were being called for the other's nuptials. Or maybe he wearied of his self-imposed exile. Whatever his motive, he has returned to England, and is heading this way."

"Or north of London, to Hargate," Gray mused.

"Perhaps. Our sources could not get near enough to discover his plans. He has a small cortege they have been unable to penetrate, but they will keep as close as they can.''

Nodding, Gray leaned back and put a finger to his lips. Of course, there was nothing particularly alarming about Jasper's approach. He might simply be on his way to his solicitors in order to squeeze more money out of the Courtland estate. Yet, if he had gotten wind of the weddings, he might be inclined to protest the imminent loss of his livelihood.

Gray straightened. Perhaps he ought to send someone to retrieve Kate, and Lucy, too, but if he knew his wife, she was liable to shoot anyone who interfered with her plans. Gray frowned. Damn. He supposed he would have to go himself.

The idea should have been objectionable. Instead, it managed to set his blood racing. Suddenly, the very thought of seeing Kate again was enough to nearly send him from his chair. Leaning back deliberately, Gray pushed aside such thoughts to concentrate on Jasper. If the bastard did show up, it would be a perfect opportunity for him to release some of his growing frustration—by beating Kate's uncle to a pulp.

A knock on the door brought Gray out of his grim musings. He was not accustomed to interruptions, and he glanced at Wells in question. The secretary shrugged as he answered the summons, only to stand aside as one of Gray's own footmen rushed in, breathless.

''My lord, you must go at once!'' the young man exclaimed.

*What the devil?* Gray straightened. ''Where?''

"It's Her Ladyship, my lord! She's being held against her will!"

At the sight of Hargate's chimneys, Gray slowed his horse and guided it off the road into the meadow. Although nothing looked amiss from here, he wanted to be prepared for anything. He had made enough mistakes already where Kate was concerned, not the least of which was leaving her here alone and unprotected.

He should have sent a full staff to run the house, and men to guard it. Hell, he should have been there, keeping her safe, instead of concentrating on himself. As he had so often during the seemingly endless ride, Gray blamed himself, a novel exercise. Although he took full responsibility for his staff and his businesses, rarely had there been any problems in his smoothly run life—until Kate.

Now every moment was a struggle of some sort, against himself, against temptation, against the fear that threatened to consume him. If anything happened to her... Gray sucked in a breath, unable to complete the thought, as he crested the hill and saw the Courtland home lying silent and peaceful before him.

By the time he reached the stables, Gray had begun to wonder if his footman's frantic summons had been a mistake, a hysterical reaction to something that idiot Tom had said. He frowned as an ugly suspicion took root. He would not put it past the coachman to have contrived some ruse to bring him running up here to Kate's side. Damn. If that was the case, he would head straight back to London, for he refused to play the fool—even for Kate!

Scowling, Gray led his mount into the back of the building, only to halt in surprise. The formerly empty stalls were lined with horses. His horses. Stepping forward slowly, Gray also recognized his coach, and a landau that he had driven more than once. *What the devil?* Annoyed, he marched to the house, determined to find out how and when half of his London stables had arrived at Hargate without his knowledge.

The noise hit him as soon as Gray opened the door, such a din as he had never heard during his residency. It was the sound of many voices raised in argument, and he followed it down the gallery to the drawing room. There, he stopped in the doorway, stunned by the sight that met his eyes.

His coachman, his valet, half a dozen of his footmen and even his cook, brandishing a rolling pin as if it were a weapon, were gathered with Lucy and Rutledge, around some central figure Gray could not quite make out. How his servants had come to be at Hargate he had no idea, and what they were doing here he would not even have hazarded to guess.

Choosing the one he hoped would give him the least convoluted explanation, he stepped forward. "Badcock," he said, his voice unintentionally soft with menace. "What is the meaning of this?"

His valet whirled immediately, revealing a small pistol tucked into his waistband that made him look like some sort of debonair pirate, or an exalted footpad, Gray was not sure which.

"My lord!" Badcock shouted. At his words,

everyone began talking at once, moving toward Gray
like a swarm of loudly buzzing bees and abandoning
their previous quarry. Gray knew that because in
their wake he saw a single gentleman seated in a
medallion-backed chair in the center of the room,
with hands and feet bound to the piece of furniture.

Gray refused to be startled. Telling himself that
nothing at all could surprise him anymore, he walked
toward the fellow, who was trussed up like a
scrawny, ill-dressed chicken. As far as Gray could
see, the man did not look big enough to threaten
Kate, let alone the dozen denizens of the room. "And
who," he asked, lifting a brow, "is this?"

"My name's Brown, and I'm glad to see someone
with sense in this bedlam! Get me out of here!"

"He's a wretched creature! A devil!" Lucy's wail
rose above the other voices, loud and piercing, making Gray realize just how little he had missed Kate's
sister.

"Badcock," Gray said, his tone brooking no resistance.

Instantly, the valet was at his side, babbling excitedly. "We couldn't find you, my lord, so we were
forced to take matters into our own hands!"

"And what matters might these be?" Gray asked,
fixing Badcock with a stare that made the valet
squirm.

"Why, this, this ruffian, my lord! He endangered
the marchioness!"

As if on cue, the crowd ebbed and parted around
him to reveal Kate, who stepped into the room, as
regal and graceful as any queen. She was dressed in

a simple gown of pale striped silk that made her skin appear all the more flawless, her hair as dark as a midnight sky, her eyes as beautiful and mysterious as twilight.

Gray's breath caught and held. He had not expected the jolt of awareness that rushed through him, or the certain feeling that he was home at last. He stood unmoving, drinking in the sight of her, until he realized that the previously lively occupants of the room had all fallen silent, watching the interchange with great interest. Straightening, Gray pushed aside his stark, bitter yearnings with disgust. Not only had Kate robbed him of his own dignity, but she'd turned his household into a bunch of raving lunatics, too.

"Well?" The word came out rougher than he had intended, and Gray felt, rather than saw, her recoil before she regained her composure.

"Mr. Brown claims to have been sent by my uncle Jasper."

"That I have, lady, and when he arrives, you'll pay for your little prank!"

Gray turned slowly, fixing the little man with a curious stare. "I beg your pardon?"

"See? He's a fiend!" Lucy cried, taking the opportunity to faint into Rutledge's waiting arms. The little drama made Meg drop her rolling pin to rush to the girl's side, and Gray was forced to draw in a deep, calming breath. He still had no coherent explanation for the chaotic scene before him or the presence of the beady-eyed Brown. And the quiet that had reigned abruptly disappeared, replaced by escalating noise behind him. Ignoring it for the moment, Gray studied the man, whose speech and clothes marked him as less than quality. What was Brown's relationship with Jasper? And why would he call an employer by his first name?

"When Jasper arrives—" the man began.

Gray cut him off with a sharp glare. "And just when is Jasper to arrive?"

As if in answer, he heard an angry rumble from Tom, and then Badcock's more reasonable tone. "I believe he just did," the valet said.

Gray turned to face Kate's infamous uncle, eager for some kind of resolution at last, hopefully one that involved Jasper's blood. He assessed his nemesis carefully. Dressed in the bright colors and high collar of a dandy, he was of medium height, his hair a shade darker than Lucy's. His body was not fat, but had the slightly fleshy look of one who had reveled in too many dissipations. While Gray watched intently, Jasper blinked, as if bewildered by the confusion. He scanned the room, his gaze coming to rest briefly upon Gray, who thought he saw a flicker of recognition in the dark eyes before they moved on.

"No one answered the door, so I let myself in. Kate? Lucy? Where are my lovely nieces?" he asked.

"Jasper! Make them loose me!" Brown cried.

Ignoring his man's plea, Jasper stepped toward Gray. "Wroth, isn't it? I believe I have seen you in town." At Gray's nod, he smiled. "My heartiest congratulations, my lord! I only recently learned of your marriage to my niece, and I couldn't be happier, to be aligned with such an exalted personage! Dearest

Kate deserves the best! Where is my darling girl?" he asked.

"I am not your darling, by any means," Kate said coolly, and Gray had to admire her aplomb. He couldn't help feeling a swift surge of pride.

"What is it, Kate? Don't you know me?" Jasper asked, crestfallen.

"You must pardon my wife for her less-than-enthusiastic welcome. This man came to the house earlier today, claiming to be your representative and threatening her and her sister," Gray said.

"Indeed," Kate added, lifting her chin in a pose Gray well recognized. "He objected to the banns for Lucy's nuptials, and told me that I would be forced to get an annulment."

Gray stiffened, his attention swerving back to Brown. Annulment? All his anger over his obsession with his wife fled at the thought of losing her forever. It was one thing to live apart, quite another to give her up. He couldn't. He wouldn't. Then Gray's heart skipped a beat as his gaze swung back to her. Surely, she would not condone such a suggestion?

Weakness. As soon as he recognized it, Gray stamped on it savagely. Right now, he needed all his wits to handle Uncle Jasper and his henchman. He would deal with Kate later.

As if her accusation had finally sunk in, Jasper gave a horrified gasp and whirled upon Brown. "What lies are you spouting now?" he asked the man, who gaped stupidly. "This fellow worked for me at one time, but I dismissed him after I caught him thieving from me!"

Brown sputtered a protest from his chair, but Jasper ignored it. "Indeed, that is one of the reasons I am here, for I discovered he was taking the money I entrusted to him to send to my precious girls—stealing it to pay his gambling debts!" Jasper said, waving his hand with a flourish. Turning to Brown, he said, "Now answer truthfully, and it will go easier on you. You are no longer in my employ, are you?"

The man stared at Jasper for a long moment before hanging his head. "No, sir," he muttered.

"There, you see? There is no reason for alarm," Jasper said. "The culprit has been apprehended, and now I would but make amends for his dastardly deeds."

Gray studied Jasper carefully. "I'm afraid you have a little bit more explaining to do concerning your management of the Courtland estate, Mr. Gillray."

Jasper looked nonplussed. "Why, whatever do you mean, my lord?"

"Perhaps we should adjourn to the study to discuss this in private."

"Why, by all means, but if you are going to talk of finances, I must plead ignorance," Jasper said, shaking his head with a rueful smile. "I'm afraid all that business is handled by my solicitor. Why don't we just go on to London, so that you can ask him directly? If there has been some misunderstanding, I would like it taken care of, so that I can come back and relax for a nice long visit with my girls."

Gray hesitated. He had just arrived, as had Jasper. As much as he would like to see the situation resolved as soon as possible, he saw no reason to rush off at once, when they could stay here for the night.... The very thought fired Gray's blood, and he looked to his wife, eager for a reconciliation. When she refused to meet his gaze, turning toward Jasper instead, he felt as if she had dashed him with cold water.

"I think that would be a fine idea, Uncle. I'm certain that you two can come to some agreement. You see, I'm afraid we haven't the staff here to entertain guests, anyway, so better that you find accommodations in London," Kate said. She glanced toward Gray then, her gaze cool and remote, and he stiffened, while Jasper looked around the room with a puzzled expression. Although fewer than the usual complement, the servants who crowded the drawing room must have seemed sufficient.

"Very well," Gray said. Masking his anger with contempt, he dismissed her with a glance. "You may stay with me in London, Mr. Gillray."

"Oh, you are too gracious by half, my lord," Jasper exclaimed with a delighted smile. "I appreciate your generous offer, but I believe the Chester town house is still available, is it not?" he asked Kate.

"I wouldn't know," she replied.

"Oh, dear. I should never have left the country! Obviously, my solicitor has not handled things properly in my absence. Let us go to his office at once to straighten things out! I swear I will not be able to sleep a wink until all is well again."

"Very well," Gray said. "Shall I follow you?" He had no intention of letting the elusive Jasper disappear once more. Of course, it was possible that Kate's uncle was speaking the truth, for even the smartest of men were duped by schemers and sharpers. If so, Gray was willing to accept an arrangement for repayment to the estate. If not, then he looked forward to getting his hands on the duplicitous bastard.

Evidently having no inkling of Gray's thoughts, Jasper smiled. "Why, yes! That would be delightful! And, girls, I do promise to come for a nice long visit once everything is settled." He winked at Lucy. "And I wouldn't miss your wedding for anything, my dear."

"Badcock, see that all is readied for our departure," Gray said.

"Yes, sir," the valet replied with a frown of disapproval. "And what of this fellow?" he asked, pointing at Brown.

"Have one of the footmen take him to the magistrate, and then return here. We'll send a replacement tomorrow." Although Gray hated to make any of the servants stay when they were unprepared to do so, he was not willing to leave Hargate unattended again. Tomorrow he would arrange for a proper staff. In the meantime, the footman, along with the two men Wells had sent after him, would have to suffice. At least the place wouldn't be unprotected. As for Kate...

Gray's jaw tightened. He would deal with her later. By supreme force of will, he bowed first to Lucy and then in the general direction of his wife. "Good day, ladies," he said coolly.

Striding from the room, Gray realized that on the surface, at least, it appeared as though he had the polite marriage that he had once desired. But the knowledge gave him no pleasure, and behind that civil facade, the primitive that Kate had awakened surged to life, roaring his displeasure at their separation. By enormous strength of will he reined in that savage side of himself and promised that soon there would be a reckoning with his wife.

## Chapter Twenty

Gray nodded to the unsmiling butler as he entered Lady Lynford's elegant home. He had been here many times before, but tonight he resented the social commitment. He was tired, physically weary from racing around the countryside, and emotionally spent, besides.

By the time they had reached London, the sun had been setting, and he had agreed to meet Jasper and his questionable solicitor for supper. After changing into evening clothes, Gray had returned, hoping to gain some answers, only to face interminable hours alone with Jasper. The solicitor, already out for the evening, had been impossible to reach, but Jasper had left a message. They would make arrangements for tomorrow, Kate's uncle promised.

Meanwhile, Gray was forced to dine and make conversation with a man he was beginning to believe was a complete imbecile. Although he was accustomed to dealing with persons of inferior intellect, Gray's patience had been worn thin by the long day, and he found himself more than eager for an excuse to quit Jasper's company for the night.

And so he found himself at the Lynford house, though he could hardly call the society much of an improvement. Straightening, Gray wrestled his inner turmoil to a dull roar as he walked through the crowd. His old restlessness seemed to have returned, stronger than ever, only now his vague longing had a focus: Kate. Frowning, Gray made his way to the card room, where he stood surveying the play with little interest. Although he could find better games at a club or one of many gambling dens he had frequented in the past, his old passion no longer tempted him.

He had a new passion.

The reminder weighed heavily upon him. He stalked out the French doors into the garden at the back of the house, but there was no escape from the woman who had invaded his life. She was in his thoughts constantly, in his blood, in his heart... Rebelling at the notion, Gray told himself that Kate was on his mind because of what lay unresolved between them. He needed to find out why she had left him, why she had denied him today, how she felt about him...

Folding his arms across the stone balustrade, Gray gazed out into the night, suddenly aware of his own solitary existence, his own mortality. His separation from Kate did nothing to ease his obsession with her. It only added a new sensation: a dull ache that told him he missed her with every breath he drew, every beat of his heart.

"Wroth?"

Gray pushed aside the maudlin thoughts at the sound of his name, but he made no move to greet the woman who spoke. Most females knew better than to approach him, and his lack of answer ought to send this one scurrying away.

"Where's Kate?"

Momentarily surprised, Gray lifted a brow and turned. It was Charlotte, looking a bit overblown in a fancy silver gown. Briefly, Gray wondered what he had ever seen in her, for her wild hair bore no resemblance to Kate's smooth curls and her excessive contours were a far cry from Kate's slender shape.

God, he missed her. His fingers balled into a fist. "Gone home," he said tightly.

"Why? It's obvious that she loves you."

The words sent a thrill shooting through Gray, and he stiffened, denying their power over him. If Kate felt anything at all for him, then why had she left? He had been a good husband, kind, attentive, generous with his purse and in his lovemaking. And all the while struggling against his attraction to her, calling it base and primitive, ashamed of his weakness... He sucked in a harsh breath. "You know what ton marriages are like," he said tightly.

"Stop it," Charlotte said, with surprising vehemence.

Too tired to glare at her, Gray simply stared out into the darkness. "Damn it, Charlotte, not everyone subscribes to the ridiculous fancies of that idiot you married! My wife and I have a civil arrangement."

"The great Wroth would hardly settle for that,"

Charlotte said chidingly. "Love, genuine passion, or whatever you want to call it, is worth more than a hundred light flirtations, a million polite contracts."

When Gray said nothing, she drew out her fan and leaned back to study him. "You are known for your honesty. Let me ask you this, and answer quickly—would you rather be married to me?"

Gray blinked at her in surprise, stunned by the question. Once, he would have thought her a suitable wife, but now... His heart started racing frantically at the thought of trading Kate for anyone else.

"I thought not," Charlotte said, smiling and tapping his arm with her fan.

"But it's not easy to have more than the standard agreement. For grand passion, you must give something of yourself. You cannot have it both ways, Wroth," she said softly. "Either you have an empty marriage, like most of these wretched creatures, or you risk yourself on something better, finer, richer. You are obviously a man of fierce passions. Why would you accept anything less?"

*Because it's a sign of weakness,* Gray thought bitterly. But was it? Perhaps weakness lay in following the simple course, the one set by other men who felt nothing for their wives or the mistresses paraded before them. Suddenly, Gray wondered if Wycliffe was not to be admired for his bravery. He had the courage to care.

As if anticipating his capitulation, Charlotte leaned close. "Go to your wife," she whispered over her fan. "Go to her and tell her what's in your heart."

* * *

Kate tossed and turned in her lonely bed, as she had ever since her arrival at Hargate. But this evening was worse. Tonight she was acutely aware that she could be lying beside her husband. Gray. His image filled her mind, and she shut her eyes tightly, forcing away the vision of him sleek and golden in the moonlight, loving her with his body, if not with his heart.

Just seeing him today had shattered all her fine vows to forget him, and Kate began to wonder if she was running from the one good thing that had ever happened to her. Plumping the pillow violently, she paused to consider that Lucy might be right. Was she so accustomed to suffering that she could take no pleasure in happiness? Had Gray been insupportable, or had she searched for a reason to hide from the strongest feelings she had ever known?

Flopping over in the suddenly still and eerie silence, Kate felt the hairs on the back of her neck rise as they so often had in London, and her eyes flew open wide, searching the darkness. She let out a shaky sigh. No one was watching her here. She was alone, but for Lucy in the next room.

And then she heard it. The quiet glide of the handle that gave entry to her room. Shooting upright, she clutched the blanket to her breast as the door swung wide to reveal the shadowy figure of a man.

"Well, well, if it isn't the high-and-mighty Lady Wroth." Kate stared, unable to believe her ears, for the voice was that of the man who had bullied her all afternoon. But hadn't Brown been turned over to the magistrate?

"What are you doing here?" she asked, lifting her chin.

"I'm holding a gun on you, my lady." The scrawny fellow taunted, and Kate sucked in a breath as moonlight glinted off the metal in his hand. "And none of your ragged band of rescuers are going to save you, either. Now, didn't I tell you that you'd pay for tying me up? Well, now's the time. Get up!"

"Let me dress, at least," Kate said as steadily as she could, while her thoughts raced ahead. Was he alone? How had he escaped? And where were Tom, the footman, and the two men Gray had left to protect them?

"No! You just get up as you are and get your fancy self downstairs. Jasper's waiting."

Jasper! Kate's heart thudded wildly as she rose to her feet. This was no petty revenge from a thieving bully. This was more, much more, for Gray had left with her uncle in good faith. *Gray!* Kate stumbled as fear suddenly swamped her. What if Jasper had done something to Gray?

She would kill him.

Determination steadied her, driving away the panic and the fright and clearing her head. As she reached for her robe, Kate slid the pistol she kept beneath the bed into a pocket, glad for the voluminous velvet garment she would once have scorned, for its thick folds hid the weapon cradled in her palm. Stepping into her slippers, she straightened, head held high.

It was up to her.

Silently, she led the way downstairs, Brown following close behind. The large windows flanking the entrance sent shafts of moonlight across the foyer, where Jasper stood, his hand resting on Lucy's shoulder. She was seated in a small straight chair to which her hands and feet were bound, as Brown had been earlier. Kate gasped in outrage.

"Ah, there you are, Kate, darling. We thought we had better take care of dear Lucy first, just in case we had difficulty persuading the headstrong elder sister to cooperate, eh, Brown?" Jasper asked, while his cohort chuckled appreciatively.

"And I must say, it was nice of you to keep the house so deserted. My confederates had the situation neatly in hand in but a few minutes. Really, Kate, a house this size should have a proper staff, don't you think? But I must admit, I am impressed that you hung on to anything. Did your dear papa have some private funds hidden away here that kept you going?"

When Kate did not answer, he merely shook his head. "Ah, well, it is of no consequence now. I still have the bulk of your fortune, and the land. The house will, unfortunately, have to be burned down in order to make the deaths of you and your sister appear to be a tragic accident."

At his words, Lucy moaned softly, apparently too frightened to engage in her usual histrionics. Although Kate ached to comfort her sister, she did not want to be bound, as well. She had to maneuver herself into a better position, for she would have only one chance to shoot her uncle, and then she would still have to contend with Brown. Stepping away from the little man, she eyed Jasper coolly.

"Surely you do not intend to set fire to Hargate?"

"Oh, but I do, Kate darling. You see, I simply cannot afford to lose all that lovely money. This way, Lucy dies, unmarried, so I retain her share, and as for you..."

"But I'm already wed," Kate said. "What about Wroth?" She held her breath, unable to bear the thought that Jasper had already killed her husband. Her mind, cleared of its usual clutter, focused on Gray with startling clarity. All the disagreements between them now seemed petty and absurd, as nothing compared to what she felt for him, and Kate realized that she wanted him always, whether he loved her or not.

Jasper shrugged. "Naturally, I would have liked to include Wroth in our little conflagration, but he is a bit too clever to fall into such a simple trap. However, since he is as rich as a nabob, I doubt he will begrudge me your trifling estate."

Kate released a ragged sigh of relief into the stillness, cut off when she saw movement in the shadows.

"You are wrong. I begrudge you anything, you bastard."

Gray! Kate's joy at the sound of her husband's voice was tempered by fear for his safety. Was he alone? Armed? Jasper was a desperate man with no conscience, capable of anything, and as if to prove it, he smirked in greeting. "Welcome to our little party, my lord. You're just in time to die."

"I think not," Gray said, with his usual cool confidence, and Kate saw the moonlight glint off a weapon, pointed straight at her uncle's chest.

Jasper sucked in a swift breath, but made no move. "It appears that we have a stalemate, my lord. You may shoot me, but then what of your wife? Brown here will take delight in killing her, I'm sure."

"Oh, no, he won't," Kate said, and before Brown could turn toward her, she pulled out her gun and fired. The explosion rocked her, and she blinked, opening her eyes to the sight of Gray knocking out Jasper with a fierce blow to the face.

"Gray, there may be others outside!" she warned, afraid that the noise would draw them.

"No, I came upon them when I arrived," he said, stepping gingerly toward where Brown lay prone on the tiles. Kate had no idea how Gray had subdued the others, nor did she care. He was alive! Her hands began to shake as he stood looking down at the bully. Then Gray lifted his head, his mouth twisted into a shaky grin.

"I see your aim has improved," he said.

Gray made his way upstairs, his weariness overtaken by an unusual excitement, a mingling of both anticipation and wariness at the prospect of facing his wife.

They had not had a moment alone since the shooting. He had been busy meeting with the magistrate, arranging for Jasper's imprisonment and the removal of Brown's body, and taking care of other details that could not be left to his newly revived men. Kate, meanwhile, had been brewing tea and tending to a distraught Lucy, whose condition had made the night's events even more harrowing for her.

Not for Kate. She had braved it all with her usual strength and spirit.

Gray sucked in a breath as he remembered the sight of his wife, facing her uncle and his henchman. For the first time in his life, Gray had known real fear, watching from the shadows as she stood her ground, knowing that any moment they might hurt her, that he might be too late.

It had been a nightmare, but at least he had been here. If not for Charlotte... Gray vowed to send Wycliffe's wife a belated, yet very expensive, gift for her baby. If she had not challenged him, he might not have ridden back to Kate, heedless of the hour, only to find Hargate under siege and his guards knocked senseless.

The denouement had come quickly, thanks to Kate's quick thinking and marksmanship, but whenever he thought of her risking herself for him, Gray felt nauseous and dizzy. He drew in a shaky breath, his emotions running primitive and strong. And now he must find his true courage, the kind necessary for him to lay his soul bare to another.

Silently he moved to the bedroom door and turned the handle, unwilling to disturb Kate, if she slept. It was near dawn already, and she deserved to rest. Slipping inside, he shut the door quietly and leaned against it, only to see her rise from the bed. She was awake, waiting for him, and Gray expelled a ragged burst of air at the knowledge.

"Kate."

She came to him, a shadowy vision in a lacy white gown, and all thoughts of speech fled as desire struck him more powerfully than ever. It had been so long. Too damned long. He reached for her, his hand winding into her soft curls, his mouth closing over hers.

"Kate, Kate, my God, Kate." He was babbling, and she was making soothing noises as she pushed the coat from his shoulders and dragged his shirt over his head. He let her, reveling in her touch, in her sweet, minty fragrance, in Kate. She kissed his chest, running her tongue over his nipples and whispering breathlessly.

"You are so beautiful. I've missed you so. Gray, oh, Gray!" She made a little sound in her throat as her hand moved down to the front of his breeches. He jerked at her touch, his head falling back against the wood. And then her fingers were on his buttons, fumbling as she loosened the fall and he sprang out into her palm. She stroked him, gently at first, then harder.

"Yes," he whispered, incapable of anything articulate. To his utter astonishment, she lowered her head, kissing his erection, swirling her tongue around it, licking the hard length of him, and for the first time in his life, Gray indulged in pure sensation. Burying his hands in her dark, silky curls, he guided her into the rhythm, groaning beneath her inexperienced but enthusiastic ministrations. Resting his head against the door, he closed his eyes and gave himself up to her.

Nothing existed but Kate: her mouth, her heat, her moist tongue. He bucked against her, forcing out a warning with his last vestiges of control. "You had better stop now, poppet," he whispered. But she didn't.

And then all he knew was release, endless, welcoming and wonderful, beyond anything he had ever known. He leaned back against the door, dragging in breaths, unable to move as his body basked in complete and utter repletion. And when he finally was able to open his eyes, Kate was there, smiling up at him and licking her lips devilishly.

Taking her hand, Gray drew her to her feet and said the first thing that came into his head. "I love you."

She blinked. "What?" she whispered.

He took her face in his hands and stared into her twilight eyes, seeing there the nebulous something he had been searching for for so long and fighting against ever since he first glimpsed it. "I love you. And if you want to stay at Hargate, I will, too."

She blinked again, as if in disbelief. "That is not necessary. I'll go with you. Wherever you are, that is where my heart is." Her composure faltered then, and she put her arms around him and laid her cheek against his chest, hugging him as if never to let him go.

"You won't run away anymore?" Gray asked. Although his tone teased, he needed that reassurance, just as he needed Kate.

She lifted her head and looked at him with the direct gaze that he so admired. "I'm through running away, if you are."

"I am," Gray answered. He was done with running and hiding from his own feelings and struggling against his primitive urges. It seemed he had been fighting temptation ever since he met Kate, but no longer. In one swift movement, he swung her into his arms and carried her to the bed, where he planned to keep her until they both were weak and limp and sated, no matter how long—or how often—it took. Gray grinned as he lowered himself beside her. "Promise me one thing," he said.

"Hmm?"

"No more pistols."

\* \* \* \* \*

# HE SAID ♥ SHE SAID

Explore the mystery of male/female communication in this extraordinary new book from two of your favorite Harlequin authors.

Jasmine Cresswell and Margaret St. George bring you the exciting story of two romantic adversaries—each from their own point of view!

DEV'S STORY. CATHY'S STORY.
As he sees it. As she sees it.
Both sides of the story!

The heat is definitely on, and these two can't stay out of the kitchen!

Don't miss **HE SAID, SHE SAID.**
Available in July wherever Harlequin books are sold.

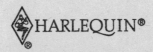

## HARLEQUIN®

# Let's Celebrate!

# LOVE & LAUGHTER™

## invites you to
## the party of the season!

Grab your popcorn and be prepared to laugh
as we celebrate with **LOVE & LAUGHTER**.

Harlequin's newest series is going Hollywood!

Let us make you laugh with three months of terrific
books, authors and romance, plus a chance to win a
FREE 15-copy video collection of the best romantic
comedies ever made.

For more details look in the back pages of any
Love & Laughter title, from July to September,
at your favorite retail outlet.

### *Don't forget the popcorn!*

Available wherever
Harlequin books are sold.

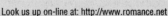
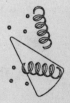

HARLEQUIN®

Look us up on-line at: http://www.romance.net

LLCELEB

# HARLEQUIN WOMEN KNOW ROMANCE WHEN THEY SEE IT.

And they'll see it on **ROMANCE CLASSICS**, the new 24-hour TV channel devoted to romantic movies and original programs like the special **Harlequin® Showcase of Authors & Stories.**

The **Harlequin® Showcase of Authors & Stories** introduces you to many of your favorite romance authors in a program developed exclusively for Harlequin® readers.

Watch for the **Harlequin® Showcase of Authors & Stories** series beginning in the summer of 1997.

*If you're not receiving ROMANCE CLASSICS, call your local cable operator or satellite provider and ask for it today!*

*Escape to the network of your dreams.*

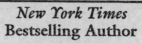